Home for a Spell

Berkley Prime Crime titles by Madelyn Alt

THE TROUBLE WITH MAGIC
A CHARMED DEATH
HEX MARKS THE SPOT
NO REST FOR THE WICCAN
WHERE THERE'S A WITCH
A WITCH IN TIME
HOME FOR A SPELL

Home for a Spell

Madelyn Alt

BERKLEY PRIME CRIME, NEW YORK

THE BERKLEY PUBLISHING GROUP
Published by the Penguin Group
Penguin Group (USA) Inc.
375 Hudson Street, New York, New York 10014, USA
Penguin Group (Canada), 90 Eglinton Avenue East, Suite 700, Toronto, Ontario M4P 2Y3, Canada
(a division of Pearson Penguin Canada Inc.)
Penguin Books Ltd., 80 Strand, London WC2R 0RL, England
Penguin Group Ireland, 25 St. Stephen's Green, Dublin 2, Ireland (a division of Penguin Books Ltd.)
Penguin Group (Australia), 250 Camberwell Road, Camberwell, Victoria 3124, Australia
(a division of Pearson Australia Group Pty. Ltd.)
Penguin Books India Pvt. Ltd., 11 Community Centre, Panchsheel Park, New Delhi—110 017, India
Penguin Group (NZ), 67 Apollo Drive, Rosedale, North Shore 0632, New Zealand
(a division of Pearson New Zealand Ltd.)
Penguin Books (South Africa) (Pty.) Ltd., 24 Sturdee Avenue, Rosebank, Johannesburg 2196,
South Africa

Penguin Books Ltd., Registered Offices: 80 Strand, London WC2R 0RL, England

This book is an original publication of The Berkley Publishing Group.

FIRST EDITION: January 2011

Library of Congress Cataloging-in-Publication Data

Alt, Madelyn.
    Home for a spell / Madelyn Alt. — 1st ed.
        p. cm.
    ISBN 978-0-425-23867-7
    1. Witches—Fiction. 2. City and town life—Indiana—Fiction. 3. Murder—Investigation—
Fiction. I. Title.
    PS3601.L75H66 2011
    813'.6—dc22   2010033625

PRINTED IN THE UNITED STATES OF AMERICA

10   9   8   7   6   5   4   3   2   1

For Josh and Rose, whose dedication has now paid off.
As if we ever thought otherwise!
Congratulations, dearhearts!

And for Matt and Lindsey. You know why.

Out flew the web and floated wide;
the mirror crack'd from side to side;
"The curse is come upon me,"
Cried the Lady of Shalott.

—ALFRED, LORD TENNYSON

Home for a Spell

Chapter 1

To the world at large, I am Margaret Mary-Catherine O'Neill. A good Irish name for a good Catholic girl, strong, sturdy, steadfast, true to the religion that was bestowed upon me at the moment of my birth.

Most of the time, though, I'm just Maggie, a somewhat neurotic, normal, everyday kind of girl, living large in a small, conservative Midwestern town.

Notice, I did not say *normal* town.

Because my beloved hometown of Stony Mill, Indiana, is as far from normal as you can get these days. But hey, so long as we keep pretending that everything's still hunkydory around these parts, pilgrim, none of that should matter. It's appearances that make you or break you.

Right?

But it is hard to gloss over murder. Especially when month after month the body count kept rising. Unrelated, all of them, but still sordid. This town evidently carried a lot of secrets.

Always with the secrets.

There was more to the sense of something being very wrong in town—like all the paranormal stuff that didn't even register on most people's radar. But as an empath—a person of heightened sensitivities, both intuitive and physical—I was especially atune to extrasensory signals. Had I really been oblivious to it prior to meeting my boss, mentor, and good friend Felicity Dow, aka Liss, owner of the superfab boutique Enchantments? In the last not-quite-a-year, with the help of Liss and the N.I.G.H.T.S., the ghost-hunting group of friends I had hooked up with in my pursuit of understanding the supernatural events that had been haunting our town, I had made a kind of uneasy peace with the forces that seemed to run as a dark undercurrent through neighborhoods and residents alike. Why it was happening, well, I couldn't pretend to have an answer to that, but perhaps with enough study, understanding would follow.

At least I had some truly great friends to walk the path toward understanding with me . . . including my lovely new boyfriend, Marcus Quinn. Marcus, whose dark and dangerous good looks had once unnerved me as much as they attracted me, even as I tried to deny said attraction. Marcus, whose inner beauty far outshone his outer deliciousness. Was it true love? Meant to be? Were we MFEO? I think we are all looking forward to finding the answer to those scintillating questions.

Stay tuned . . .

I am Maggie O'Neill, empath, intuitive, and sometimes witchy nice girl, and this is my story.

Life . . . happens.

The worn bumper sticker on the aging, oversized sedan taking up the lane in front of us—us meaning Marcus and me—caught my eye as we made our way across Stony Mill proper bright and early that Monday morning as we moved into September. *Boy howdy*, I thought as my mouth formed a wry grimace. *Did it ever*. Case in point being the solid lump of a cast that had been my boon companion for the last four weeks. All seven hundred and fifty pounds of it. Seriously. What did they put in these things?

Life had happened to me when I stepped down wrong on a step at Stony Mill General while visiting my little sister Melanie on the maternity ward and—painfully—broke my ankle. Life had then happened to Mel herself when her perfect world shattered into a million jagged little pieces around her when her husband of six years abruptly shocked us all by leaving her and their family, now four daughters strong as of the birth of the twins. None of us, not even Mel herself, had seen that coming. To be honest, life seemed to keep happening around all of us in Stony Mill an awful lot lately. Or should I say, death? Murder, to be more to the point. The multiple murders that the town had endured in previous months had certainly been a shock to the town's nervous system. Once a quiet, unassuming town of friends and neighbors who knew one another's comings and goings (not to mention the goings and comings), Stony Mill was changing before our very eyes. Whether it was fate, karma, unerringly bad timing, or just plain, dumb luck, for this town life and death seemed incontrovertibly tied.

That morning Marcus and I were on our way to the X-ray lab at that self-same hospital for follow-up shots of my ankle, and I was sitting on the edge of the bench seat of his old pickup truck with anticipation. Dr. Dan Tucker had written up the orders for the follow-ups. When he'd been reminded that I had lost my family practitioner last December under less-than-auspicious circumstances and hadn't yet felt the need to find a new one, he'd volunteered to keep an eye on my ankle situation throughout my healing process. Such were the perks of having a doctor in the "family." Besides, he kind of owed me for having hijacked my thirtieth birthday party in order to propose to the love of his life and future wife, my longtime bestie, Steff. At least that's what Steff insisted. And who was I to complain if Dan didn't seem to mind?

We pulled into the circular drop-off zone at the front of the hospital, and Marcus set the emergency brake before coming around the truck to help, but I was too quick for him. I slid from the seat and down onto both feet, including the Casted Glory, which didn't go beneath his notice.

"Hey," he protested, "you're supposed to wait for me, Miss Independent."

I made a face at him. "I'm fine. Look. See? I can stand." I mimed a little tap dance, quickly smothering a wince when the foot-in-place movements brought a small jab of pain.

Not quick enough. My lovely honey of a man's dark eyebrows raised, and he took my hand and placed it on his arm. Pointedly. "*You* push things too fast."

"Fuss, fuss."

"Someone has to look out for you."

I smiled to myself, recognizing the stubborn angle of his jaw. Protective. But not overbearing. "Well, then, how about you hand me my crutches so we can get this over with?"

If he knew I had been practicing putting weight on my casted foot, testing out a few steps here and there with my arms outstretched for the next handhold like a toddler taking her first tottering wobbles, he might be a little less forgiving of me pushing myself. But what he didn't know wouldn't hurt him. To appease him, I dutifully took the crutches in hand and let him guide me through the rotating door and down the hall to the X-ray department.

The X-ray process was over within minutes (one of the benefits of living in a small town, I suppose—there is rarely a line of any length unless it's at the Friday night game at the high school) . . . which was a good thing, since Minnie—my foundling feline and the best friend a girl could have—was waiting for us in the shade with the windows down. I left my phone number at Enchantments—Indiana's finest mystical antique shop, where I could often be found tending counter—and my personal cell number with the woman in blue scrubs behind the desk, and moments later we were out the door and on our way.

"Think we can spare a few minutes before I take you in?" Marcus asked as he got into the truck beside me as I gently stroked Minnie's silky black fur through the mesh opening of her soft-sided carrier. She was still dozing. Kitty bliss. "I need to drop something off with Uncle Lou, and this is right on the way. And since I have rehearsal later with the guys and they'll kill me if I cancel on them again, this is probably my only chance today."

I winced, this time from guilt, not pain, and for once his gaze was still on the road ahead and he missed it. He had cancelled on his band's rehearsals at least twice that I knew of in the last two weeks alone. I also knew it was because of me. He'd gone out of his way to make sure I knew that, at least on those occasions, his presence wasn't required . . . but a part of me still wondered. Worried. We'd only been seeing each other for five or six weeks, and he'd already been required to go above and beyond. Nothing like throwing a guy into the deep end right off the bat. "Sure," I told him, hoping my voice wasn't as weak as it sounded. "Stop away. We're making good time."

"Great, I'll give him a call."

Uncle Lou would be Louis Tabor, a history teacher at

Stony Mill High. Lou was a lifelong Stony Mill resident and also happened to be the stepdad to one Tara Murphy, Marcus's cousin, a high school senior who now spent many of her afternoons working part time at the store and adding color and mischief to our days. Unlike Tara, Lou was just your regular guy leading a regular life. I had often wondered if he knew he had two witches in the family, or if he knew, if it even mattered? One thing was for certain: he and Marcus were very close. In many ways, Marcus seemed to look up to him as the father he had never known.

Our timing was perfect. Lou had a free hour between second and fourth periods. He told Marcus he'd meet us in the teachers' parking lot behind the C-shaped high school building. He was waiting for us, there in the streaming sunshine, when Marcus pulled right up into the vacant Visiting Administrator's spot without pause for thought or concern. I shook my head and grinned. Once a rebel, always a rebel.

Lou held up a welcoming hand. He was a big man, every bit as tall as Marcus, though he probably outweighed him by a good thirty to forty pounds, most of which was held for safekeeping around his middle and barrel chest. Still, he cut a handsome figure, complete with the same dark, softly curling hair and piercing blue eyes, though his were a darker shade than Marcus's azure. "The Irish in us," he said the one time I'd mentioned it. "Black Irish." Whatever it was, it was an attractive look, at any age.

Marcus hopped out of the truck, and I rolled down my window. "Hello there, Mr. Tabor. Nice to see you again."

"Lou, remember? Only my students call me Mr. Tabor. And that's only because the school board frowns on more familiar forms of address. It's nice to see you, too. How's that ankle doing?"

"Fine. Great." I put on my brightest, most confident smile. "I'm getting this thing off in a week or two."

"And I'm sure you're champing at the bit," he said, laughing.

"Champing?" Marcus snorted. "I think that bit has been clean chewed through. Days ago."

I pretended to pout, crossing my arms. "You try lugging this thing around every day for a month and see how you like it, big guy."

"She's getting testy, too," Marcus added with a twinkle.

Lou nodded sagely. "Keeping you on your toes, I'll bet." He winked at me, then leaned forward and in a conspiratorial whisper said, "Someone's got to do it, eh?"

"Hey, now. Whose side are you on?" Marcus asked over his shoulder with mock indignation as he lifted a piece of black casing out from behind the driver's seat. "I have half a mind to take this back with me."

Lou lifted his hands in surrender. "Now, now. No need to get hasty there."

Marcus handed over the black metal box. "One better-than-new, completely up-to-date, revved-up and tricked-out computer, sir, as per the request. Whoever this was for should be pretty happy. There's enough space and speed in this to run a small space station. Okay, well, maybe that's an exaggeration, but still. I take it the guy plays a lot of video games?"

"Video games, videos, photo galleries. You know how it goes these days. All those things take up memory and speed."

Marcus nodded in agreement. "Software, too. The whole computer industry is in cahoots. They want you to feel like you need a new computer every year, just to keep up."

"You got that right." Uncle Lou scratched his head, and a sheepish expression came over his face. "Er . . . come to think

of it, my home computer is a little sad. Maybe I should have
you do the same for me."

"See? What'd I tell you? They got to you, big guy."

Lou laughed. "I guess they did at that. Maybe that can
be your next project—when you get a little free time," he
amended with a sidelong glance in my direction.

Urg. Again with the guilt.

"I've been doing a little project work with photos and
video myself lately—and don't tell your aunt, that's to be kept
under your hat—and my hard drive is really complaining,"
he continued. "It was fine before electronic mail and digital
photographs and all the other bells and whistles I can't seem
to do without these days."

"You mean, back in the stone ages, when photo sharing
meant sending them along with the family Christmas card?"

Lou's right eyebrow slid up, just the way Marcus's did
when he was playing things cool. "Hardee-harr-harr. Keep it
up and I'll send your girl here a copy of you in your Christmas sweatshirt, circa 1992."

Marcus laughed. "No need for threats. I'll do it, I'll do it."

"Thought you might see it my way. Oh, before I forget, you
brought the old parts with you?"

"Got 'em right here." Marcus handed over a zipped gallon-
sized plastic freezer bag. "If you think your guy might change
his mind, I've got a friend who could repurpose them—he
does it for the county to help out people with needs that otherwise couldn't afford it, and—"

"I'll mention it to him, but my lodge brother was pretty
specific about wanting 'em back. Listen, I've got to get back to
my classroom. I'll catch up with you later about this stuff"—
Lou held up the baggie—"after I talk to him and collect your
fee. For all I know he's just concerned about personal security."

With identity fraud being one of the fastest growing

crimes in the world, it certainly seemed a valid concern to me. And not just identity fraud. Consumer shadowing was happening every day, too. Viruses, spyware, malware. And that was only the beginning. Just the other day a story had hit the news about a school corporation using the webcams in the students' school-supplied laptops to spy upon them outside of school hours. Big Brother is watching . . . and evidently, personal privacy doesn't seem to matter in the least.

Lou's friend was right to be cautious, in my humble opinion. Better to be safe than sorry.

"I'd insist on wiping it myself before just handing it over, but whatever he decides is fine by me. It was just an idea." Marcus got in the truck and started the old engine with a rumble and a powerful surge as he toed the accelerator to keep the pistons churning. He gave the dashboard an affectionate pat.

"Oh, hey. I almost forgot," Lou said as an afterthought. "You ready for next week?"

Marcus cleared his throat, but it was the hesitation that made me pause. "I, uh . . . well, I meant to talk to you about that." His gaze flashed in my direction and then back. "I, uh, think I'm going to have to postpone that. Just for a little while," he said when Lou's brows knitted together slightly. "I've waited this long. A little longer won't hurt matters."

"But you've already paid for your cl—"

"I've done a little checking. I can defer. Extenuating circumstances. It's okay, Uncle Lou. It's a few months, not forever."

Wasn't it the thought that counted?

"Okay. Well. You know what's best, I guess." A pause and then, "I just thought, with everything arranged and all, that—" He bit the words off suddenly. "Well, anyway. Will we see you two at Sunday lunch next weekend? Your Aunt Molly's talking about doing it up right. And with your mom in Wisconsin for the last couple of months, she thought you might enjoy a little togetherness with the family."

"Sure, sounds great."

"Yeah? Maggie, you okay with that?"

"Great," I echoed warmly, not about to let my questioning nature get in the way of a home-cooked meal surrounded by good people. Good people who didn't put me on the hot seat with regards to my job, my finances, my relationships, my attitude, or my lack of interest in getting on with it and getting married and popping out grandchildren. Like my own family. Well, like my mother, to be more precise. "With any luck I'll have this thing off me by then, and you can finally teach me how to do the limbo properly."

Lou laughed. "I'll look forward to it."

He let us go then, with a wave and a blinding smile that stripped years from his face.

Marcus looked over at me when we were on our way. "Limbo, huh? I don't think you're going to be dancing anytime soon, sweetness. Not for a while anyway."

We would see about that. I didn't know when I'd hear the verdict from Dr. Dan on my healing progress, but I had high hopes for that very afternoon.

"So," I began, gazing over at him curiously, "what was all that about?"

"All that?"

His attempt at nonchalance did not fool me. "Yes, all that. With Uncle Lou. About next week."

"Oh. That."

"What was next week?"

"Nothing for you to worry about, Maggie. Honestly. I've got it covered."

Something wasn't sitting right with me. He was keeping something from me for sure. But why? "Uncle Lou mentioned you having paid for something," I persisted. "If you've already paid up for whatever it is, there's no sense in putting it off. You should get what you paid for."

If a man could squirm without actually, in fact, moving a muscle, Marcus would be doing just that at that very moment.

A sudden suspicion struck. "It was because of me, wasn't it?"

He reached for his sunglasses from the visor clip and slipped them on. "What gives you that idea?"

It totally was. My heart sank. My stomach joined it.

He glanced over at me. "Oh, don't look like that, Maggie. Look, it's no big deal. I'll start taking classes next semester. Like I said, I already looked into a deferral, and I think it's the way to g—"

"Classes? Marcus, no! You can't be thinking of putting that off. You've been planning this for months!" Marcus had been planning to return to college with an eye toward completing a teaching degree, an idea Lou had suggested originally but that Marcus had latched on to with an enthusiasm that made it seem especially meant to be. How on earth had I managed to forget about that? Why hadn't it occurred to me to ask? Was I so wrapped up in my own egocentric world that I couldn't see beyond my personal problems? Please tell me I hadn't gotten that narcissistic.

"It's no big deal—"

"No big deal? Of course it's a big deal. It's important to you." I couldn't be the reason he put off going back for his degree. I just couldn't. Miserable, I wracked my brain. I had to think of a way to make him see reason. "You have to go. If you don't, I won't be able to live with myself."

"Maggie—"

"I'm serious. Because what if something happens before the winter semester starts? Would you put it off then, too? People who put things off are just asking for something to happen, Marcus. And the universe is tricky that way. And if you didn't go back, it would be all my fault." I was on a roll. I barely noticed when he pulled the truck over to the curb and let it idle in neutral while he turned toward me.

"You're being unreasonable."

"No, I'm not. I'm telling you I don't want that guilt to be on my head, hovering over me, waiting for something to go wrong."

He sat there with his brows furrowed and a small, bemused smile tugging at the corner of his mouth. "You're kind of a glass-half-empty person, aren't you. Always waiting for the other shoe to drop."

I couldn't exactly disagree with him, at least not about that, so I didn't say anything.

"Well, you don't have to be." He reached out and tugged at my fingers. "Nothing is going to happen." When I opened my mouth to disagree, he shook his head. "Nothing. Look, the world isn't a perfect place. Things happen—"

Yeah. Life. And worse.

"—but I prefer to think of them as challenges, not roadblocks. Just things that need to be worked around. That's what our Guides are for. Ask and you shall receive. There is a way. A solution will come. You just have to be patient, have faith. Trust your Guides."

I would have said more, but something wasn't letting me. It might have been the voice of Grandma C quavering in my ear in a surprisingly authoritative tone. Considering the fact that she is, you know, dead. Deceased. No longer of this earthly domain. Moved on to bigger and better time zones in the sky.

You gotta trust somebody sometime, Margaret Mary-Catherine O'Neill. And since you won't put your trust in God or his host of saints and angels, you might as well put your trust in me. You know I would never steer you wrong.

In my ear. Damn and double damn. I wished the voice would go back to being thought based. Somehow when it was within my head, it was a whole lot easier to imagine that it was probably just the voice of my conscience manifesting with my grandmother's voice. Now I wasn't so sure it *was* just my imagination. But if not that, what was it?

"All right," I relented, trying for a smile. "I'll try."

"That's my girl."

Trying. What exactly did that mean?

I pondered that for the rest of the morning and into the afternoon while I puttered and clunked about at Enchantments. For a chronic worrier-slash-thinker-slash-overanalyzer like me, trying is exactly what trying proved to be. How was I supposed to just let him put everything aside for me and not wonder on a daily basis whether or not he was wishing he had just gone ahead with his plans? What if something happened to prevent him from going back after the fall semester? What if something happened to prevent him from going back at all? Wouldn't he always wonder if he should have?

Must. Stop. Thinking.

From a shelf just overhead, Minnie made her agreement known with a soft murmur of a meow. I reached up absent-mindedly and scratched her behind the ears, knowing she was right.

Maybe I was overthinking it. All of it. Maybe all I needed to do was to just cross my fingers and hope for the best as far as healing my ankle was concerned. Because if it was all good with my ankle, that meant life as Marcus had previously known it could get back on track.

Liss sensed my preoccupation and left me alone for the most part. It was for the better. Not even the scents of spiced pear tea and caramel apple cinnamon buns could lure me out of my guilt-induced preoccupation. I clumped around gloomily here and there on my crutches, halfheartedly dabbing at imagined specks of dust with a microfiber cloth even though I had just done the same spot hours before. Liss just watched me from over her half-moon glasses, quiet sympathy shining in her eyes, but like the wise woman she was, she kept her opinions to herself.

The shelves done, I moved on with a restless sigh to our sales counter and surrounding area. Not that it really needed it.

Respite came briefly when the phone rang just before one that afternoon. Liss had been walking past me with a pencil tucked behind her ear and a fresh cup of tea held aloft in one hand. She reached around behind me before I could even respond to the tweedling jangle of the phone.

"Enchantments Antiques and Fine Gifts, Felicity Dow speaking. How can I be of service?" It was her usual greeting, nothing out of the ordinary. I went back to flicking my cloth unenthusiastically at the cash register. "Oh, hello, Dr. Tucker. So good to hear from you, as always. And how is that lovely fiancée of yours? How wonderful for you both. And when will that be? So soon. Well, we'll miss you, of course, but of course we wish only the best for you both. You will know the best path for you both. Precisely that. Oh, good heavens, listen to me. Yes, of course, she's right here." She listened another moment, then laughed. "Yes, as a matter of fact, she is behaving herself today. I know. Yes, it is rather a rare occurrence." Ignoring my tongue poking out at her, she handed the phone over to me with a wink.

I cleared my throat officiously. "Dr. Dan."

"Miss O'Neill," he said with an equal amount of tongue-in-cheek formality.

My heart was beating an anticipatory tempo for the words I had been waiting for. Something along the lines of, *Your bones look great. Fabulous! How do you do it?*

"Sooo," I said, "don't keep me in suspense! How did the X-rays look?"

Chapter 2

There was a pause on the other end of the line. That should have been my first indication that what was coming would not be to my liking. "To be honest, Maggie"—and there it was, that was my second—"things aren't quite where I would like to see them."

Hm. Not quite the enthusiastic response I was looking for. "Oh?" My fingers tightened around the phone.

"No. Actually, I'm a little surprised. For a young woman of your age and health, by now I would expect to see the bony bridge of hard callus starting to form. We may want to consider leaving the cast on longer"—I groaned, so his voice grew louder to press the issue—"than previously anticipated. I know that's not what you wanted to hear, but . . . honestly, it's better to take your time with this, Maggie. Don't rush things. Why don't we give it another four weeks and then take some more pictures."

"Four weeks! But—"

"The additional time is not out of the realm of normalcy for healing a broken bone. The time frame you were first given was a guideline more than a rule, so we'll give it a few more weeks and then see where to go from there. You're still taking the antibiotic?"

"Just finished up," I said, trying not to sigh my disappointment too loudly.

"And the pain meds?"

"Don't need 'em. I didn't like how they made me feel, so after the first few days, I just stopped." A pause, then quickly, "That's okay, isn't it?"

"Oh, yeah. More than okay. Most people take them to the end of the 'script without listening to the true needs of their bodies. All rightee, so, let's go four weeks out, and then I'll write up an order for another set of X-rays. Sound good?"

"When you say 'Sound good?' how literal do you want my response to be?"

I could almost see the smile on the other end. "Well, at least you haven't lost your sense of humor."

"Don't be too sure about that," I sniffed. "This is not the sound of a happy woman."

"Better to heal in leisure now than repent in leisure later."

"Now we're mixing metaphors *and* proverbs?"

Dan laughed. "I'm a doctor, not a wordsmith. Four weeks, Maggie, then we'll talk. Give that ankle as much rest as possible. Stay off of it, I mean it"—I blushed a little at that; good thing he couldn't see me—"and call me if you have any problems. Otherwise, I'm sure I'll see you around here and there with Steff."

I set the cordless phone back on its charging base, unable to hide my disgust and dissent toward the prospect of another four weeks in the company of the incredibly weighty, incredibly yellow (*what was I thinking?*), incredibly glitter-fied, sparkle-fied, painfully *ugh*-ly Casted Wonder currently taking up real estate in the far southeasterly portions of my anatomy. I knew I should be more grateful to Dan for doing all of this gratis for me—and honestly I was, incredibly so—but disappointment was a sour medicine to swallow. So much for my hope that everything could magically be back to normal, thereby allowing Marcus to magically get on with his nonmagickal plans.

I couldn't bear to tell Marcus yet. I knew what he'd say. That it was no big deal. That it was a good thing he was postponing going back to school. That it was the only logical decision.

"Bad news?"

I glanced up into Liss's soft, empathetic gaze. "Very bad."

She waited for me to go on. That was the best thing about being so close to Liss. She was the kind of friend who was always there for you, ready and waiting to lend a sympathetic ear, a font of both earthly and unearthly wisdom at her beck and call. While Steff was my go-to girl whenever I wanted to rant and rave and needed my best girlfriend to have my back and even to head up my posse if necessary, it was Liss I went to when I needed solace and solutions. With both of them in my corner, I couldn't go wrong.

"My ankle's not healing. At least," I amended when I saw the concern leap to her eyes, "it's not making improvements with the speed Dan might expect or hope to see. I have to wear the cast for four more weeks."

Her posture relaxed by the end of my short explanation. "Well. That isn't the best news, but not so terrible, in the long run. I shouldn't worry about it if I were you, ducks."

"But . . ." To my horror, I found myself unable to speak. My lip quivered. I bit it to nip that nonsense in the bud.

Liss took a seat at the counter. "There's something more to this story, I take it?" she suggested quietly.

Still no voice. I nodded.

Liss waited, but when it became apparent that I wasn't quite functional yet, she leaned forward and whispered, "You know, it is much easier if I don't have to guess each and every admission along the way, darling. Is it to do with your ankle?"

I shook my head.

"Very well. Marcus?"

I hesitated.

"Aha. Marcus, it is. Well, then, out with it, love. You'll feel better. Shall I make you a cup of tea?"

I shook my head.

Liss waited, watching me as she sipped from her own cup, the quintessential personification of patience.

I took a deep breath. All of a sudden I found my voice, and it all came flooding out in a torrent, all of my newfound fears that I was holding Marcus back, that he was putting off his life because of me. There I was, staying with him at his house, intruding on his solitude, eating his food, sleeping in his bed, and he hadn't asked for a dime from me. He drove me everywhere I needed to go, without a single complaint, rearranging his own schedule in order to do it. And yes, he had canceled out on at least two band rehearsals that I knew of. "So now, not only do I feel like I am I mooching off of him and taking advantage of his kindness, but he is also being forced to make choices that go against everything he wants, and I just know he will resent me for this," I vented. "And I can't say that I blame him. I mean, the whole situation is all about me and nothing about him, and now—*now!*—he is putting off going back to school, too? When he's been talking about going back and getting his degree for months? Please tell me you see why I have a problem with all this."

Liss had listened to my emotional explosion without a word. Now she cut to the chase with the unerring precision of someone who has had much practice. "Maggie, has Marcus ever indicated to you that he doesn't want to do all of these things for you?"

I blinked as the interruption caught me off guard. "Well, no . . ."

"Then what makes you think that this isn't exactly what he wants and intends to do?"

I shook my head, unable to conceive of that, as I went through the motions of making myself the cup of tea I had just told her I didn't want. "He may want this right now . . . but what about later on? No, I have to come up with something to take the pressure off him. Something that will give him the freedom to keep moving along with his plans. Going back for his degree is so important. I don't want to be the one to take that away." A thought struck me just then about something she'd said to Danny before handing the receiver over to me, and I paused in midstream as I poured the hot water over the loose leaves in the tea strainer. "What was Danny telling you?"

"I'm sorry, dear, what was that?"

"When you said 'We'll miss you,'" I reminded her. "Why will we miss him, where is he going?"

"Oh, didn't Dr. Tucker tell you? Evidently, once the dear doctor's residency is completed, he anticipates having to move to another city in order to start his practice. I imagine that's fairly standard for young doctors and their families these days. Perhaps he'll head toward New England. I understand his people are there . . ."

In my mind, I'd been expecting news of a trip. A business conference, maybe, or even a spicy, sexy vacay to Aruba. I had *not* been expecting *that*. "Move? To another city?" My face fell. *Oh, but that would mean . . .* "That can't be right. Steff would have told me." Wouldn't she? Maybe she did. I started to rack my brain for any hints, anything that might have been said that I hadn't picked up on, but I was at a loss.

"Oh dear. Perhaps I shouldn't have said anything. I just assumed . . ."

At her crestfallen look, I rushed to reassure her. "No, it's okay. Really."

"No, I shouldn't have said anything."

I shrugged, miserable. "You couldn't have known that I didn't know. It only made sense." Because Steff was my best friend. Why wouldn't she have told me that she was going to be leaving me behind? Panic started to set in as I tried to remember when, specifically, Danny's residency was officially over. Was it November? December? That was right around the corner. The first sunny days of September were already upon us. The next couple of months were bound to be a whirlwind for Steff, preparations for leaving, tying up loose ends.

I just hated the thought that I was another of those loose ends.

"Perhaps I shall just have to cast about the universe and call up some angels for you," Liss mused, probably to distract me, "to summon a viable solution to your current problem. Not the ankle, though," she said when she saw the sudden flare of hope in my eyes. "I've found it's best to allow that sort of thing to heal with time."

It didn't appear I had any choice in the matter.

Heartsick, I found myself dialing Steff's number when Liss

took Minnie along with her to the office in back for some product surfing—aka scouting the web for new suppliers with a witchy background. Etsy had become her favorite source of the moment—boatload upon boatload of supremely talented artisans and crafters, the likes of which would never see the inside of a department store. All the better for boutiques like Enchantments and its dedicated clientele.

Steff's number rang once, twice. "Hiya, chickie!" Her voice chirped in my ear, sweet and bright.

"How could you?" I wailed without preamble.

And because she was my lifelong BFF, no explanation was needed. She knew instantly what I was talking about. "Who told you?" she asked, then without waiting, continued, "Because if it was Danny, I'm going to kill him. I specifically told him that I have to be the one to break it to you. Aw, honey, I'm sorry. I wanted to tell you. I did. But I wanted to tell you my way. You know. Ease you into it."

Damn. That made me sound like I was, um, needy. "It's not that you're going so much"—okay, that was a lie, but she didn't need to know that—"it's more that I found out elsewhere. And no, it wasn't Danny. Danny didn't say a word to me." I might be sad and pathetic, but that didn't mean I was willing to rat Danny out. Besides, technically speaking, it was true.

"So. Yeah. We're going to be moving. Wow, huh? And I have no idea where yet. And I'm a little freaked out about it. Say something, Mags?" she begged. "I need to know you're going to be okay with this. *We'll* be okay, won't we?"

And that's what did it. Her hopeful plea snapped me out of my sinkhole of self-pity faster than a thousand feel-good affirmations meant to bolster and uplift a sagging emotional state. "Well, of course we'll be okay. I haven't been your best friend for nineteen and a half years to lose you over something like this, silly. That's what instant messaging is for, right? Have webcam, will chat?"

The relief in her voice was instantaneous and huge. "Oh. Honey. I'm so glad you understand. I'm going crazy trying to think about all the things that need to happen in the next three months!" Three. That was a relief; she must mean December. "I've got an ongoing list started in my phone, and it is getting longer and longer. And Danny's crazy busy. I need you in my corner to keep my spirits up on those days when it feels like nothing is going right."

"I'll help with whatever I can. I would say 'running errands and such,' but, well, I'm not doing much running these days. And it doesn't look like I will be for at least another four weeks." I told her about Danny's findings on the X-rays.

"I know you don't want to hear this right now," Steff said, "but it really is better to be safe than sorry."

"I know, I know. I think I've gotten over the disappointment"—albeit barely—"but what I'm really worried about is how all of this affects Marcus. Steff, he's put his whole life on hold for me, and I just found out he's even putting off returning to college, and—"

"You're feeling guilty for putting him in that position to begin with, and worried that he'll hold you responsible if something goes wrong."

"Exactly."

Steff took a deep breath, then let it out slowly. "I see your point actually."

"So I'm right to worry?"

"I didn't say that," she said. "I only said I see your point, and . . . I might feel the same way, were I in your position."

Great. You know, sometimes solidarity wasn't all it was cracked up to be. "What do you think I should do?"

The two of us were silent, contemplating the possibilities. Conjuring possibilities. Any possibilities.

Any at all.

"Well," Steff said with a little hesitation in her voice, "there is always your mom and dad as a last resort?"

Eek. Banish the thought! My mother would love only too much to have me come crawling back home after turning my nose up at the offer a month ago. "Could we save that option for the last possible of all possible fallback plans?"

And because she was my best friend, I didn't even have to explain. "Forget I mentioned it."

Any possibilities at all . . .

Another thought struck me, just then. "You're not going to be living upstairs anymore."

"Oh." Steff's voice was extra quiet. "No, I'm not."

This was, truly, the end of an epoch.

And then, contemplatively, "You're not going to be living upstairs anymore . . ."

"Yes, we've already established that, Mags."

"No," I said, getting excited, "what I mean is . . . this is the end of an era."

"That's right. Just poke that arrow in farther and turn it a little harder to the left there. Sheesh."

I laughed. "No, what I mean is, maybe, just maybe, it's time for me to embrace change. Not fight it."

"Do explain."

"Well. Instead of looking at this as a problem, maybe I should be looking at it as a good time to make some other changes in my life as well. Like . . . maybe moving into a new apartment. One that isn't in a basement. Maybe you moving out is actually a cosmic sign that I need to pay attention to."

"I . . . well, I guess you could look at it that way, sure."

"I mean it," I said, seriously warming up to the idea. "It's not like I have a lease to worry about, since our landlord is old school. Maybe I should be looking at this as the opportunity it is to get out there and look. Think about it. A different apartment, one without stairs, would mean I could at least take care of myself for the most part. Without a keeper. Well, except for getting back and forth to work. That might take a little thinking." Hm. "And maybe this is just the kick start I need. I mean, looking back at my life, it's only in the last year that I've been digging myself out of the rut that was my life. Maybe this is meant to be. Fate. Kismet."

Steff laughed. "Well, I'll let you get back to that, Kismet Girl. I'm actually supposed to be getting ready for work, so I'll talk to you *lataaaah*."

Kismet Girl. I liked that. Kind of like Wonder Woman, except without the unforgiving costume.

Energized into action by the possibilities I sensed opening up in front of me, the first thing I did upon hanging up was clump around the counter to where my laptop was resting, opened and logged in, next to the cash register. The two customers who had been milling around had just left without a purchase, so I was free and clear until the brass bells on the front door rang again to alert me to our next customer of the day. I pulled up the local Craigslist site to search for all apartment rentals. The list was, I must say, a disappointment. Granted, Stony Mill was a small town and limited in rental properties, but I had been hopeful to find more than the paltry few entries the search pulled up. None of which suited my needs. Darn. I even searched on homes for rent, knowing before the search yielded results that the two homes that appeared in ad form would be priced way out of my league. Nothing. Nothing affordable, that is. And then, just in case someone had gone old school, I dug yesterday's newspaper classified section out of the recycling bin and spread it out wide to catch the light. It was the same as the Craigslist offerings. So unless I wanted to rent a space at the local Jellystone campground and pitch a tent, there just didn't seem to be anything out there for me.

Double darn.

Maybe tonight's newspaper would be better. Or maybe I'd take Liss's way out of things and try a simple Finding and Summoning Spell. Put the energies of the universe at work for me.

Sighing in momentary defeat, I went back to the laptop and pulled up my email account, looking for distraction. And there, between the advertisements from my favorite retail establishments, churchy forwards from my mom's ladies' auxiliary group (*gosh, I wonder how they got my email address; it's a mystery . . .*), a joke video featuring two dancing squirrels who may or may not have been putting the moves on, and a couple of rogue emails hawking a certain little blue pill that had somehow made it through my spam filter, there was an email from Uncle Lou, sent just this morning. Curious, I clicked on it.

Maggie,

Just a quick note. I sent a text to Marcus, but my phone has been on the fritz lately and I'm not sure it went through. My darling wife has reminded me that dinner will be Saturday, not Sunday. I think I told you the wrong day. See you Saturday instead? Molly makes a mean apple pie, and I was hoping to get Marcus to take a peek at my computer. After the whopper he put together for my lodge brother, it was a kick in the pants to get the ball rolling to upgrade my own monstrosity. Molly even gave the okay. I'm delivering it after school and have no doubt in my mind my guy'll be pleased.

I'll call Marcus later, but if you see or talk to him, give him the news if you would.

Thanks,
Lou

I replied back to say of course I would let Marcus know . . . and as an afterthought asked whether by some odd chance Lou or Molly might know of any ground-level apartments or single-story homes for rent in the area. To spark his interest, I explained that I wasn't comfortable with Marcus putting off his return to school for the semester because of me because I felt it was really important to him, and that perhaps if I could secure housing that was both affordable and workable around my broken ankle, then maybe I could convince him to keep on target with his plans. I wasn't expecting much, but I figured, what the heck as I fired it off.

I certainly wasn't expecting a reply less than ten minutes later.

As a matter of fact, I might just know of something for you. The lodge brother I mentioned is actually the general manager of an (admittedly older, if that kind of thing bothers you) apartment complex. He had mentioned at the last meeting that they were nearly finished remodeling and were ready to start placing tenants again. A couple of the newer teachers here at the high school have already leaped at the chance and are happily in residence. How'z about if

I place a call and ask him whether he'd have anything that
might work for you? If so, I have to go over there this afternoon to drop off the refurbed hard drive. I'd be happy to
drive you.

Could that be right? Why wouldn't the rentals have been
listed in the newspaper? I could scarcely believe my luck.
Instead of responding by email, I texted back quickly, just in
case he had logged off, that it sounded great and I would be
waiting to hear. "Liss?" I called out.

She appeared suddenly, pulling aside the deep purple velvet curtain that separated the storefront from the office in
back. "You rang, ducks?"

"Would you mind if I left early to see an apartment this
afternoon? I could come back afterward to make up my
time."

"*Pshh,*" she said with a wave of her hand. "Of course I
don't mind, and there's no need to make up any time. After
all the extra hours you've put in this year? I'm fully aware
that I am lucky to have you, and I am not one to look my
good fortune in the eye. Did you find something, then?"

"I'm not sure. I hope so." If I had, it would certainly be a
definitive example of kismet. One for the books, even. I told
her about Lou's timely email. "I'm just waiting to hear back
from him—" Right on cue, my cell phone vibrated like a
hive full of distressed bees on the antique wooden countertop. "*Ooh.*" I grabbed it. The display panel on the front read
Uncle Lou. Excited, I flipped it open and lifted it to my ear.
"Hiya! So, what's the verdict? Did he have anything? No
biggie if he didn't, I'm probably getting ahead of myself
here. I know these things don't grow on trees around these
parts, and—"

"Uh, Maggie? Can I cut in here a minute? Because I have two minutes to get to my last class of the day."

Heh. Verbal incontinence again. Oops. "Sure."

"My guy—Rob Locke—he says he does have something that might work for you. Should I stop by, pick you up, let you take a look-see?"

"Yes, please," I said, trying to be concise. For his sake. "If you don't mind."

"No trouble at all. School lets out at three-oh-five. I need to take care of a couple small things, but I should be down your way before four."

"Great, see you then!" Maybe it wasn't time to back down quite yet after all.

Liss promised to cat-sit Minnie for the evening so that I didn't have to worry about dragging her around town, and it was a good thing, too, since Big Lou happened to own one of the miniature ecofriendly cars that looked like it might be comfortable for seating a hobbit. I quickly disguised the skepticism that made my brow shoot straight up as I considered whether such a miniscule vehicle could possibly have room enough for one barrel-chested Irish American, let alone one big man, one medium-sized woman, and a massively large, brilliantly yellow fiberglass cast. Adding a cat into the mix, even in a soft-sided carrier, was bound to be trouble. I gave Minnie a kiss between the ears and a back scratch, telling her I'd see her later. The twitch of her black tail as she turned and presented her behind to me before nonchalantly padding away told me just how concerned she was.

An old-fashioned kind of guy, Lou helped me into the small car—that must be where Marcus got the endearing habit—and within moments we were off, tootling across town in our goofy-looking chariot, making small talk that was just a little on the uncomfortable side of things because we had never been one-on-one together before today. It wasn't as awkward as I had feared, though. Get Lou talking on all things high school, and there was no opportunity for embarrassing silences. Quite handy, that trait.

The apartment complex proved to be in the older, southern end of town, over the Bolander bridge and south of the river. In fact, it was no more than five blocks from Marcus's little Craftsman bungalow. It was an older complex, seventies-tastic in so-called architectural style, a typical two-up, two-down with exposed central stairs and a faux brick front. Maybe the age of the building should have scared me. It didn't. For one thing, Lou had said something about the place being remodeled and ready for new tenants, so it was worth my time to take a look at it. And besides, Stony Mill didn't have a whole lot of options. Beggars could not be choosers. Unless I wanted to move out of this town and to the city, which would tack on more than an additional hour of driving time each day, plus gas and wear and tear on my old VW Bug, Christine—which wouldn't even work until this cast came off my leg anyway, which kind of made the urgency of the plan a moot point—or unless I wanted to pay a premium for the few up-to-date condos listed on Craigslist, then I would be smart to keep my worries to myself at least until I'd had a chance to see the place firsthand.

Lou toured the parking lot in front of the row of apartment buildings so that I could see the lay of the land, then pulled up into the drive along the side road, where the office shared a backyard with the first apartment.

Gentleman that he was, Lou helped me out of the car, and it was a good thing, too—sliding down off the bench seat in

Marcus's truck was different from rising from a tiny car that rode only a foot off the ground. I was grateful for the hand up.

"Why don't we head up to the office first?" he suggested.

A sign pointed the way for us. The sidewalks weren't pristine, but they weren't yet too pitted and gouged by the weather extremes that plagued Indiana from season to season. The office door had an "Open" sign stuck to the window. Lou opened the door for me, and as soon as I put one crutch over the threshold a chime sounded loudly. Surprised, I pulled my crutch back, then tentatively set it down again. *Ding-dong, ding-dong* . . .

Lou pointed to a red light inside the door frame. "Infrared scanner. Nifty. I need one of those for my dog door."

The office appeared to be empty, so Lou and I entered and stood in the center of the lobby, gazing at our surroundings. The space was fairly spartan. A single desk stood in the open room, opposed by two utilitarian chairs. Another seating area had been created by the placement of a small loveseat and cheap-looking coffee table with the requisite magazines spread over its tired surface in front of a fake fireplace to our right. The lobby also boasted a pair of windows on the opposite wall that opened onto a grassy yard behind the first of the five apartment houses. The room was rectangular, smallish, with another boxy enclosure cutting into the space, the wall of which was broken by two interior doors.

In other words, it was just your typical everyday office. Boxy, lifeless, utilitarian. I hoped it wasn't indicative of the apartments themselves.

"Hello, hello!" Lou called, not one to mince words or gestures. "Anyone home?"

My ears picked up sounds of movement, like shuffling or shifting, and then a thud and a muffled curse. I saw a shadow cross the band of faint light coming from beneath the farthest door along the inner wall. After what seemed like forever, but was probably no more than a minute or so, the door was yanked open and out came a youngish man, probably no more than thirty-five, wearing—or should I say straightening— what amounted to casual business dress of khaki pants, a cotton button-down shirt (*whoops, someone missed one; thank goodness for undershirts*) that stretched somewhat unattractively over a pudgy middle, and a tie that he was in the process of straightening. I noticed his belt was only mostly fastened, too, and I had the sneaking suspicion we had interrupted him. Um . . . how embarrassing. Leave it to me to arrive for an appointment while the man was in the bathroom.

He turned his back to us and quickly locked the door before coming toward us, holding his hand out to Lou in greeting. "Ah, Tabor," he said, "good. You made it." He gripped Lou's hand hard, his thumb pressing down on Lou's knuckle as though trying to make him cry uncle. And as I watched on, Lou seemed to return the favor. How . . . odd. Must be a guy thing. Some of them seem willing to do almost anything to be top man on the totem pole. "Is this the young lady you told me about?"

"It is indeed. Maggie O'Neill, this is Robert Locke."

"Rob, please." Locke held out his hand and smiled down at me as his somewhat buggy pale hazel eyes—which looked more gray than green or blue—roamed over me. He wore his sandy brown hair slicked back because it was growing sparse up front, but his crazy eyebrows more than made up for the loss, as did the hair sticking out around his ears. No . . . no, it didn't. Poor guy. I dropped my gaze to his hand, then took it gingerly, unable to help wondering just how much we'd rushed him. His hand was dry. I hoped that meant he hadn't skipped bathroom hygiene entirely. If there was anything more off-putting than encountering a wet grip after a person used the facilities, the thought that he hadn't washed at all was it. "A pleasure, Miss—it is Miss?—O'Neill?"

I nodded, politely extricating my hand when he didn't immediately let go. "Mr. Locke. Hello. You're the manager here?"

"General manager, chief maintenance facilitator, community planner, and chief hand-holder when any of our tenants have an issue," he returned agreeably as he used his just-freed hand to smooth down the front of his tie. Which had palm trees on it. And a bikini babe, complete with grass skirt. Classic.

Well, I didn't expect this to be the Ritz, so I couldn't expect the manager to be the Stony Mill equivalent of Carlton, sophisticated man-about-town, now, could I?

"I hear you're looking for a place," he continued. His gaze lowered, taking me in, as though assessing my viability as reliable tenant. I hoped the bedazzled cast wouldn't put him off.

I nodded. "Ground floor, hopefully." I wiggled my cast around for good measure.

"I understand completely. And I think I have one available that might interest you." He sat down and opened his desk drawer, indicating the chairs opposite with a wave of his hand. "Sit, sit."

Lou turned his attention away and wandered over to the windows, obvious in his efforts to give me some room to do my own thing. I lowered myself to a chair and perched on the edge while Locke dug around in his drawer.

"Ah, here it is," he said. He pulled out a folder and opened it, removing a couple of cheaply printed brochures and a few photos on glossy stock. "Let me just run through general items quickly, hey? We have a number of apartments that are

currently unoccupied due to our recent across-the-board renovations. The complex was purchased a year ago last fall. At the
time it was in a condition that was not conducive to renting.
The owner decided that it would make the most sense to do a
complete overhaul of the property and then begin renting out
the spaces as each separate apartment house was finished. Unfortunately, with the economy being what it is, not to mention a few personal issues on the part of the owner, it made
funding a bit difficult from time to time over the course of the
year, which stretched out renovations . . . but, I'm happy to
report we are nearing the finish line and have several apartments to begin marketing. One of which is the space I'm
going to show you today."

He spread the photos out in front of me.

"One of the upgrades to the property is something I think
you'll enjoy. A health center, complete with a weight and exercise room, properly air conditioned, of course, and a brand
new, inground pool. Now, you may not get to make use of
that this year," he said apologetically with a deferential nod
toward my cast, "but I'm sure it will be a big hit next summer once the temperatures warm up."

"I'm sure," I said agreeably. I reached out and picked up
each photo spec sheet, murmuring with approval over each
one, as expected to. It wasn't difficult, truth be told. The new
tenant community spaces really did look quite nice, and I had
to admit, the idea of having a sunny, bright, and cheery exercise room and a pool handily located too close to ignore
sounded like a really good idea. Oh, what Steff and I could
have done with a perk like that! Unfortunately, the Victorian
was all there had been when we were first looking for a place,
and there had been no reason to pull up stakes. Until now. On
the other hand, the fact that this place had been unrentable

prior to being purchased by this new property group kind of gave me pause, as did the casually mentioned mid-remodel funding issues. I'm sure he thought nothing of his comment, but it made me wonder what kind of, er, shortcuts might have been made in the reconstruction process.

"Now, you'll notice," Locke said, sliding the brochure over in front of me, "the apartment you'll be looking at is a two-bedroom, one-bath selection. Galley-style kitchen, living room, and French doors opening onto the private patio."

I cleared my throat and took a look at the brochure. The apartments pictured seemed fairly typical, though the low-quality inkjet print job used for the brochure made it hard to see the details in the photos.

"I'll just"—Lou cleared his throat and jerked his thumb toward the door—"I'll just head out to the truck and get the drive for you. My nephew delivered it just today."

"It's here?" The news seemed to reach beyond Locke's attempt at an all-business façade. Excitement burst in his eyes like surprise fireworks. His nostrils flared. Then in the next moment it was gone, hidden, as he licked his lips with a flickering dart of his tongue. "That was good timing. Excellent, excellent. Thanks, Tabor."

Lou left, and Locke turned his attention back to me, but as he went over the details, room sizes, laundry facilities, and utility arrangements, I couldn't help noticing his focus was sketchy. I caught him glancing over my shoulder toward the door at least twice. I got it. I did. A new, high-powered, superfab computer trumped renting out an apartment . . . but still.

Locke stood up and reached into the center drawer for a tray of numbered keys. "Well, let's go take a look at it, why don't we?"

I used the chair arm in conjunction with my crutches to push myself up to balance on one foot, but before I could get myself turned around, the door swung inward behind me and slammed into the wall behind it so hard that I nearly sat back down in surprise.

Chapter 3

"What the—" Locke's face reflected stunned surprise.

"This is it, Locke. This is it! You and me, we've got to have ourselves a discussion." The African American man who stalked into the office literally took my breath away. It wasn't physical beauty—his features were regular, even ordinary— and it wasn't his body, which also appeared to be ordinary beneath loose-fitting jeans and an untucked button-down shirt. It was more his energy, which swept ahead of him like an invisible corporeal presence to announce his arrival much akin to trumpeters heralding the kings of old. It came in with a hint of swagger and the kind of attitude that said he knew what he wanted and he knew that you had it, and he was now going to see about removing it from your possession, *thankyouverymuch*. "Angela has asked for your help. I've tried to be civil. We've tried doing things your way. And you . . . you refuse to cooperate."

Locking eyes with the complex manager, he moved across

the lobby as though only one thing mattered, and for him, I didn't even exist. And perhaps in that moment, I didn't. His entire outlook was pinpoint focused on the man behind the desk as he skirted me without a sideward glance or a by-your-leave. I wondered if Locke was grateful for the size of the piece of furniture. I would have been. The man didn't crack his knuckles, flex his muscles, or even cross his arms, but he didn't have to. The attitude said it all. I found myself easing away to a safer distance.

To his credit, Locke stood up straighter. He did not back down. "I thought we'd finished this conversation this morning, Mr. Hollister. I think I was clear when I explained the situation to both you and Miss Miller—"

"The situation is, the contract is a scam, and you know it, Locke."

"It's legal and binding—"

"It's a scam contract. No termination clause. It's either stay or go, but pay us our money any damn way."

"It's a standard contract," Locke said succinctly, taking the business high road. "Vetted by our attorneys. And, I assure you, it will hold up in court." His words were calm and measured. His expression was anything but.

"Standard contract? That's shit, man, and you know it." Frustration blazed in the man's dark brown eyes, and he gritted his teeth. "Look, Angela is trying to do things the right way. She's been trying to work with you. And you're doing everything in your power to shoot her down. Why can't you just put the apartment on the market? Why is that too much to ask?"

"This is not the time, and it's not the place—" Locke said with a sideways glance my way.

The guy caught the look and sneered. "Oh, you're with a

would-be tenant? Well, maybe Miss Would-Be would like to know about the problems, huh? Maybe she'd like to know about all the weird sounds we hear, and things that move around or even go missing that no one could have taken. Maybe she'd like to know that, huh?"

Whoa there. Sounds? Things going missing? Were there spirits at play here? Certainly that was common in places where remodeling chaos churned the energies that had lain dormant over time. No matter that the brochure had said, the apartments had been built in the 1970s. A building didn't have to be ancient to have spirits wandering its rooms. Heck, it didn't have to be a building at all. Lots of open land boasted spirit activity, earth energies, even nonhuman entities to be wary of. Scary, but true.

Locke shrugged away his accusations. "Buildings settle over time."

"Settling buildings don't explain missing personal items," he pointed out angrily. "It's a security risk."

Well . . . to any normal person who didn't know what odd things had been taking place in Stony Mill in the last year, yes, missing personal items might indeed indicate a safety issue, worthy of a home security system and new locks at the very least . . . but I wasn't about to enlighten him. What he didn't know, he wouldn't be watching for. And without actively watching, there was less risk of accidental awareness. Less awareness equaled a probability that he and his girlfriend would be left alone. Better he didn't know.

"Angela won't stay here. She's made up her mind. All we're asking you to do is to show the apartment. That's all we ask."

Locke sighed dramatically. "I don't have the time to market an apartment that has already been leased. I did my job with your girlfriend. Everything was aboveboard. Cut and dry. She's lived there for eight months. Why is she just now having these issues? You know what I think. I think the two of you are just trying to get out of your lease, period. Maybe you found another place, one with more room or closer to work. Ah-ah"—he held up his hand when the guy started to splutter—"I'm just saying. So you've found another place. She's just going to have to do the right thing, *what she is contractually bound to do*, and pay through the term of her lease. It's over and done with in, what, four months? It's not the end of the world."

"For Chrissakes, you're not listening. She doesn't have the money to pay for two places. She's a teacher. I don't know if you're up on all the reports about—"

"Neither of which is my problem. Now, if you'll excuse me," he said, holding out a hand and officiously gesturing me forward, "I have another apartment to show."

Glowering, Hollister stared at Locke, as if in disbelief that he would dare be so rigidly insensitive. The next few moments seemed to happen in a blur. As Locke made to move dismissively past him, Hollister's hand whipped out with the swiftness of a cobra striking and grabbed Locke's arm. Uttering a coarse word in surprise, Locke made an attempt to shrug him off, but Hollister wasn't having it. He gripped Locke's shirt and tried to yank him back around. The subsequent testosterone-charged scuffle resulted in one ripped shirt sleeve, one chair knocked over, a plant that narrowly missed the same fate, and a couple of punches that missed their marks—mostly—before Lou charged into the room and inserted his bulk between the two slighter men.

"What in Sam Hill is going on in here?" Lou bellowed, holding each off at arm's length. An impressive feat, I must say, the way the two men were surging and twisting to get back in the fray and take each other down.

I had watched the whole shebang from the sidelines (that is, the *far* end of the desk) from start to finish, half in disbelief of what I was witnessing and half in fascination. Men . . . they are a strange breed at times.

With a stern look in his eyes as a warning, Lou took immediate control of the situation. He pushed Locke back with a shove to the shoulder and said, "You. Stay put. And you," he said, taking Hollister by the shoulder, "come with me. We're going to get this sorted out."

"Like hell we are," Hollister said, scrambling for purchase on the tile floor. Lou grabbed him by the scruff of his neck and headed for the door.

"Like I said. We're going to get this sorted out. Aren't we, mister?" He nodded Hollister's head for him, bringing on a fresh string of muttered curses. "I thought so. Good man."

Hollister's heated words trailed back in before the door closed on its pneumatic hinges: "This isn't over, Locke, you hear me? If you're not going to play fair, then—"

"Keep it to yourself, mister." Lou's baritone cut him off. And then the door shut with a sybillant *snick*.

Locke straightened his shoulders and clothes the way a rooster might ruffle his feathers, and then glanced my way. The bikini-babe tie looked a little worse for the wear. "I'm very sorry you had to see that, Miss O'Neill. These things, well, do happen. It's the nature of the beast, dealing with the public. Sometimes you suffer a little collateral damage. That's a big reason why I prefer to rent to women. By and large, they make far better tenants. Unless they have big, beefy black boyfriends who think they can push and shove until they have their way. I should have called the cops, so they could slam his ass in jail with all of his gangsta buddies. That would teach him." He cleared his throat before I could even react to the not-so-subtle racial slur. "If you'll excuse me for a moment, I think a change of shirt is going to have to be in order."

Gangsta buddies of big, beefy black boyfriends. I didn't even know what to say, other than, "Wow." So not cool. It was a little discussed fact that Indiana had ties back to the very earliest days of the KKK. One would have hoped in our modern age that we had grown past such nonsense, but the reality was that some people still clung to their old prejudices about color and creed. Not to mention, the Hollister guy didn't look remotely "gangsta." No more than Marcus, Lou, or even Mr. Locke here, whom I suspected was just stuck on the color of his skin. Furthermore, the only "gangstas" to be found here in Stony Mill were pathetic wannabe-bads acting out against society by painting unrecognizable symbols on the backs of privacy fences and selling drugs to other wannabe-bads and breaking into cars and houses and somehow coming to the conclusion that the life of a petty criminal was somehow preferable. In other words, fail, big time, as far as "gangsta" goes. Thank goodness for the rest of us.

But Locke? What. A. Jackass.

Locke headed off to the nearest of the two interior doors, still gazing with annoyance down at his torn sleeve. As the light flipped on, I saw the unmistakable glint of light reflecting from a mirror, and in the corner, a toilet. I guess I had gotten it wrong earlier. To give him some privacy and keep my lunch from coming up, I crutched my way over to the windows and took a moment to try to get my bearings. To the far right of the grassy yard that lay between me and the first apartment building were a pair of small enclosures that hugged the parking lot. The latticework meshed with the plain fencing surround indicated their probable designation as Dumpster disguisers. At a right angle to the enclosers stood the first of five apartment buildings. From the windows here, I could see plainly into the windows of the apartments in most of the buildings. Well, at least the ones where the curtains weren't drawn. To the left was another building, and between me and it, the pièce de résistance: the pool. An actual, in-ground model, fitted with both deep and shallow ends and a diving board. Hallelujah and glory be. Rare around these parts. If I weren't wearing a cast, I'd get down on my hands and knees and kiss the concrete surrounding it.

"That right there is the new health center."

Locke's voice came from right behind me. Startled out of my musings, I turned my head to find him leaning close over my shoulder, his face inches from mine. I gasped and clumsily sidestepped away. "Oh my goodness. You scared me."

Amusement played in the five o'clock shadow that made his cheeks and chin look scruffy and borderline disreputable when combined with the wrinkled shirt he'd changed into and the mangled tie, which was . . . well, it was not likely to see better days once again. "Sorry about that. I thought you'd heard me come out. Shall we go look at the place, then?"

His gaze had dropped to my chest, not long, just enough to ensure that I noticed he'd looked. I lifted my shoulders slightly, just enough to take any interpreted prominent display out of the equation. "Sure."

As long as he didn't get too close again, and as long as he didn't breathe on me. The guy had some serious coffee breath going on.

He held the door for me, stumbling over a box just outside on the step. "Christ! Who put that there?"

I recognized the box Marcus had loaded into the miniscule storage area in Lou's car just that morning. "Lou. It's your computer. He must have set it down when he came in to break things up."

"Oh. Well, all right, then." In an instant annoyance transformed into excitement in his pudgy features. He even rubbed his hands together. "I can sure use that." He picked the box up and carried it almost reverently to his desk, placing it in the position of honor, smack in the center, actually running his palms over the box like a lover. Someone needed to get out more. It took him a few moments, but he finally seemed to come back to his senses. He licked his lips, looked over at me, and laughed self-consciously. "It's the little things in life."

Yeah, like a souped-up, tricked-out, uber-pumped piece of electronic wizardry.

Lou had maneuvered the Hollister dude down the sidewalk toward the cross street. I could see them there, speaking earnestly together, and, thankfully, not coming to blows or scuffling in any way. As for Locke, he lead me off in the opposite direction toward the health center. Very nice. Sunny, airy, plenty of fans, and air-conditioning. Oh, and the equipment looked decent, too. I also drooled over the pool area as we walked past. So calm, so peaceful, so blissfully blue. In my mind I was already coming up with elaborately creative ways to use the pool while still preserving the relative water-free state of my cast.

"The apartment I'm going to show you is in Building One," he told me as he lead the way up the brand-spanking-new sidewalk toward the apartments themselves, and I forced myself to leave the pool behind, both literally and figuratively, and pay attention. "It's the only ground-level apartment I have open and available for rental right now."

The architecture of the building made for a walkway

around the exterior center stairwell, so we cut through it to get to the front of the building. "The apartment upstairs was just recently taken by a teacher at the high school," he was telling me. "Young. Nice. Pretty. Just getting started in her career, I should think."

Curious, I peered at him. "Not . . . the Angela person that that man was talking about?" I could just see myself walking into a situation that would put me in contact with disgruntled neighbors.

"Angela Miller? No, she's in another of the buildings. We have a couple of young teachers here. And nurses. We're very popular with newly established ladies in both of those fields. Nice, clean apartments that are safe and well-maintained and affordable are hard to come by, and . . . well, word gets around." He was in manager mode again, using the detail as a selling point. I had to say, I much preferred it to anything more personal. And, technically speaking, he was right. Good apartments were few and far between, especially in a small-town environment.

The walkway area was clean, the external siding intact and probably not asbestos. The exposed stairs looked sturdily built and well maintained. All good.

He put the key in the dead-bolt lock and paused before turning it, his hand on the knob. He cleared his throat. "I do have to admit, for the sake of disclosure, that the apartment was tenanted for a couple of months this summer. Meaning, you are not the first tenant to have this apartment after renovations. Not that that is important in any way. The apartment has been completely cleaned and repainted, again, naturally."

The news surprised me. "I thought the apartments had been involved in renovations since the new owners bought the property," I commented.

"Yes, that's true."

"The tenants must have moved out very quickly."

He turned his back on me and turned the key in the knob. "I'm afraid I was forced to remove them."

"Remove them?"

"Yes. They violated the lease. I had no choice but to evict them. I'm afraid I can't discuss it, though. Privacy laws."

Why did I feel so certain there was more of a story behind that action? "I see."

He cleared his throat again and pushed the door open. Back in manager mode, he said, "Here's what you really want to see. Feast your eyes on the apartment itself. I think you're going to like it."

The blinds were all drawn, making it difficult to see much. But as he reached to flick on the lights, a sound came from somewhere deeper in the apartment itself, and it definitely didn't sound like your average noise caused by settling. Locke froze. I froze.

In the next moment Locke lurched into action like some landlocked sea beast, clumsily searching from room to room. *Probably just a squirrel*, I thought, oddly at ease with the notion that a squirrel could be in residence in the same apartment I was considering renting. I opened my mouth to voice my thought to Locke, but as he lunged to look beneath the sofa, he paused and cut off my first syllable with a gesture that was both a warning to keep silent and an instruction for me to stay where I was. Properly chastised, I decided to continue letting him make a fool of himself as much as he wanted to and zipped my lips as requested. Instead, I remained hovering in the doorway, propping the door open with my back as I waited.

The apartment wasn't bad, from what I could see of it. Not bad at all. Granted, the dim lighting prevented me from making out any great detail, but it seemed to be pretty nice. Nicer even than I had hoped. One open-concept and large living-slash-dining room, carpeted with what looked like Berber, with a galley kitchen and island-slash-bar lining the wall in the northeast quadrant from where I was facing, and big windows facing out on both ends of the extended space. In the kitchen I saw decent-looking cupboards and a supernice countertop that might be some sort of stone, and there were two barstools facing the island counter. Awesome.

I was considering stepping farther into the confines of the apartment and exploring while Locke did his thing. I mean, it couldn't *hurt*. Right? Especially since he was now moving down the dark hall toward the back of the apartment. I could hear the shower curtain being pulled aside, the hooks making scraping noises against the rod, and then a door. Linen closet, maybe? Oh, I hoped so. I closed my eyes and tried to feel the room, letting the sounds pull me in. The ability to remotely view an unseen target had certainly intrigued me, but it was not something that seemed to come naturally to me. Maybe starting small like this would help. I took a few deep breaths, in and out, to center myself, focusing on grounding here in this place, then allowing my inner self to drift out, to follow the manager's path. In, out, in the bathroom. In, out, down the hall.

He let out a muttered oath. I heard him ranting to himself, but it was as though his voice existed on another dimensional plane: faint, faraway, thready. What was he angry about? What was he saying? Did it even matter?

I felt an odd sensation, almost a perceivable shift of sorts, as though I had moved but my body itself had remained in place. Was it working? I tried not to let my excitement knock me out of the sensation, tried to remain centered and not try too hard with my focus. It might have worked, too, if a faint, secretive *click* hadn't sneaked its way into my conscious mind. It was the secretive sense of it that caught my attention and jarred me out of my meditative state and back into my head. I reeled my energies in and let my eyelids flutter open.

Just in time to see the closet door next to me start to open, no more than a crack of darkness around it.

Chapter 4

At first I wasn't sure that I was seeing what I thought I was seeing. My eyes opened wider, and I blinked to clear them, in case the lingering mists of third-eye vision were still affecting me. The door opened a little bit more, a fraction at a time, stopping at about an inch. I turned my head in that direction, my eyes now in hyperfocus on the thick line of black space between the door and the door frame. My heart started beating faster, tripping over itself. All of a sudden, Hollister's claims rang in my ears. Sounds. Things moving. I knew, there and then, it wasn't just settling. And I knew there was something in that closet.

But some*thing* turned out to be some*one*.

Just as I found myself turning my body on crutches in that direction and reaching for the door, I was forced to take a step backward when a small form launched from the closet and rushed headlong past me. One of my crutches went flying when the shape scrambled for forward momentum. The other crutch jammed hard into my underarm as I lost my balance and fell back against the front door.

The figure stopped on a heartbeat as the realization of what had just happened struck her. Because it was a her. The girl turned back toward me in one freeze-framed moment. Wide green eyes, peering out from beneath the low brim of a cap, locked with mine before she turned again and in the next instant was out the door, zipping away in a flash of jeans and a sassy pair of purple Chuck Ts.

By the time Locke responded to the metallic clatter of my crutch crashing against the door frame and came lumbering out from the nether regions of the apartment, the girl was long gone. I was carefully balancing myself to lean down and pick up the wayward crutch.

"What was that?" he demanded, turning his head wildly this way and that. "Oh. Your crutch."

I nodded. "Uh-huh. That, and a girl in the closet. Nice feature, I guess," I quipped, "although if your tenants are in fact mostly women, as you've said, I would think someone of the male persuasion might be a better selling point."

"A gi—" His brow rose and fell like the swell and ebb of the ocean, ending in a crescendo of aggravation that caused him to push past me, nearly knocking me off my feet again. Unlike the girl, the manager didn't stop. He continued lumbering down the interior pass-through toward the parking lot. I heard his pounding feet stop a short distance away and could picture him searching to and fro.

I straightened up again and got my crutches beneath me, moving out of the way of the door so I couldn't possibly get trampled again. Locke was gone only a short time before he came tramping back through the door with his bearlike, side-to-side shuffling gait, his breath coming in uncomfortable puffs and a gleam of perspiration on his large forehead from his short-lived exertion. I had a fleeting sense of him kicking back in a dark apartment somewhere, playing online video games in loose-fitting athletic pants and a sloppy sweatshirt, and I wondered how close it came. This was not a man you'd find working out at the health center. Most definitely not some type of sports junkie. I didn't even think he was a couch-bound quarterback.

He ran his hand back through his hair and let his breath come out at once.

"What was that all about?" I asked him.

Locke shook his head. "Teenage hijinks, I expect."

"That's kind of bold, don't you think?" I pressed. "Breaking into an empty apartment like that. What could she possibly have wanted? I didn't see any sign of forced entry when we came in—you should probably check for an unlocked window somewhere."

But no matter what I said or asked, Locke was ready to move on to other things. "I'm sure it's nothing. An annoyance, but unoccupied apartments are always at risk. It will solve itself. Let's go take a look at the other rooms, huh?"

It was his apartment complex. Or more accurately, his to manage. But as I made a walk-through of the bathroom (utilitarian, but clean and fresh), past a small bedroom-office combo, I couldn't help wondering why he didn't seem overly concerned about it as a security risk. I mean, sure, if it *was* just hijinks, I suppose the threat to a future resident was probably minimal. Maybe I was worrying about nothing. I had seen with my own eyes that it was just a girl, a teenager, with enough mascara and eyeliner surrounding her luminous green up-tilted eyes to rival Marcus's semi-goth cousin, Tara Murphy, and blond braids poking out from beneath her hat that made her look younger than she probably was.

Finally, we moved into the main bedroom, and I was

pleased to find a bit of luxury. Plush carpets and a walk-in (*be still my heart!*) closet. There was one surprising feature that claimed center stage: a huge, heavy mirror, presumably in the place where the bed would be situated. I didn't like it. It was too large, and besides, something about a mirror over the bed made me cringe. I also discovered what I could only assume was the cause of Locke's earlier outcry when he was searching the apartment: a spiderweb of cracks radiating from a center point in the glass.

"Oh, what a shame," I commented, though I didn't really mean it. "The mirror is broken. Perhaps it could just be removed." As in, hope hope, hint hint.

Locke shook his head adamantly. "No. It's a built-in. Dammit, it's the second time I've had to have it replaced, too. The owner is going to have a cow. But don't worry. I'll put it on the list of items to be repaired. It will be taken care of."

Hmm. Just my luck.

"So, Miss O'Neill," he said, making his voice light and conversational as we exited the apartment at last and he turned the key carefully in the dead-bolt lock, "now that you've seen the place, what do you think?"

Locke, evidently, was a man to cut straight to the chase. Then again, it was late in the afternoon. Maybe he just wanted to get his hands on his new computer.

"I don't think you'll find another housing complex like this," he continued in his sales pitch. "Predominantly female, which in my mind would be reassuring to the single young woman like yourself, no children under the age of eighteen, stable tenants. Good people. The rear of all the apartments face the manager's office; you can't beat security like that. You would have a neighbor just overhead. The building next door is fully occupied but for one. Buildings three and four are unoccupied, and currently under renovation. The last building, five, was the first to be renovated, and is fully tenanted. What would it take to put you in this particular apartment?"

I didn't know if I was quite ready to make a commitment. I mean, there was the issue that the Hollister guy had brought up. I decided being straightforward was the only way to go. "Well, to tell you the truth, I'm a little concerned because of what that gentleman brought up about the lease agreement not having a termination clause."

"Oh, it does have a termination clause," he assured me. "It just wasn't to Mr. Hollister's liking. You can't please everyone." He shrugged as if that proved his point.

"I would have to review the contract," I shrugged right back at him.

He laughed. "How about I let you do that, and . . . now, I'm not supposed to do this, but Lou is a lodge brother, and one of the perks of belonging to the Eternal Order of Samaritans is, we take care of our own . . . What would you say if I offered you a special deal?"

Hm. Something told me if I played this right . . . "What *sort* of special deal?"

"Normally, I'm sure you know, a lease is a lease. But, I'm prepared to offer you this: how does a short-term lease sound, just to get your feet wet? Six months, with the option to extend the preliminary low monthly rent to a term of two years."

"And how low are we talking?"

He named a figure that was, in fact, surprisingly affordable. "And, because I like Lou and he was kind enough to recommend his nephew to me for that hot new piece of equipment I have waiting for me back in my office, I am prepared to also forgo a security deposit *and* offer you two months' free rent. Beginning with October, though you could move in any time that you like, so essentially you will be receiving three-plus months' free rent. How does that grab you?"

I had to say, it was a *very* tempting offer. My rental agreement for my basement apartment allowed me to leave at will with thirty days' notice—like I reminded Steff, old school—and I was already paid up for September. Three months' worth of free rent would give me two whole months with no rent payments whatsoever. Rainy day money, anyone? Still, I hedged. "I'm not sure. I'm just not comfortable making snap decisions. Will you let me think about it?" I asked.

He looked disappointed. "Sure. But not for long. I do have other people that are interested." He took his cell phone out of his pants pocket and consulted his messages.

Of course he did. Isn't that what they all say? "I will get back to you shortly," I assured him.

"I appreciate it." He held the door to the office for me, and I swung past him, over the threshold.

Lou was there, waiting for our return. He looked up as I entered the lobby with Locke bringing up the rear. "How did it go?" He directed the query to me.

"Good," I told him. "Mr. Locke has made a very tempting offer. And, I believe he was about to get me a copy of the lease so that I can look it over." I glanced over at Locke inquiringly.

Locke nodded. Circling the desk, he pulled open the top drawer from the file cabinet behind it. He pulled a few pages, stapled together, from the nearest file and handed them across the desk to me. I accepted them and, folding them in half, tucked them into my purse.

"I'll get back to you just as soon as I can," I told him.

"I'll let you know if someone else is interested in the apartment," he replied.

I glanced over at Lou and smiled. "Ready, then?"

Lou nodded and handed me his keys. "Why don't you go on ahead? Locke and I have some business to take care of. I'll be along in a jiffy."

Said business had to do with the computer, I was positive. I knew Marcus was waiting for payment. I took the keys and gave them the privacy to complete their transaction. It was a beautiful afternoon, and I had a lot to think about. Like whether or not I could feasibly uproot myself on the spur of the moment, for instance.

I have always been a spontaneous person. My mom might say impulsive was more par for the course. But these were big changes we were talking about here, and as ready as I might have convinced myself I was to bring the sweeping winds of change into parts of my life, when actually faced with making it happen, I hesitated. Something was telling me without words that I should take a moment. A sense of uncertainty that stiffened the muscles between my shoulders and settled in the pit of my stomach. But then, if I looked back at the last year, it was easy to see that change had been a part of my life for quite some time. It had actually started occurring the moment I walked (*fell!*) through the front door of Enchantments to discover a witch in residence . . . which then led to me finding the witchy woman within myself. I had been up to the challenge then, even though at the time I would never have guessed it. Was I up to the challenge now? Could I pull up stakes in the apartment on Willow Street once and for all? Could I pull away from Marcus's temptingly sweet arms in order to give him back his autonomy?

As far as I was concerned, that might actually be the best reason.

The pool and health center might come in a strong second. Perhaps even enough to outweigh one slightly creepoid complex manager who was probably harmless, despite ringing my Early Pervy Warning System.

I shoehorned myself into Lou's little car and started it up, powering down the windows to enjoy the temperate temperatures and afternoon breezes. While the car was roomier than I'd expected, it was still a bit crowded with the bulk of my knee-high cast and with the crutches, which I had to situate just so over my shoulder in order to fit them in with the rest of me. Once in position and as comfortable as I could possibly make myself, I pulled the folded-up pieces of paper that Locke had given me out of my bag and smoothed them out over my knee to read all the jargon and legalese that made up the leasing agreement.

Locke was right—there was a termination clause. Unfortunately, it was completely one-sided, offering the option of termination only to the apartment complex at their own discretion; hence, its inclusion was not helpful to the prospective tenant in any way. And there was nothing in the lease that said anything about the actual offer he'd made me, including the monthly rent itself. All of that would need to be changed. Assuming, of course, that I was going to accept his offer. Everything else looked fairly standard. I made a few notes on the back of a receipt I found tucked into the coin pocket of my purse.

Off in the distance I saw Lou just exiting the manager's office. At the same time, a car pulled up next to me and parked. A woman stepped out, trim and cute in high heels and tights, a sober knee-length skirt that hugged her slim hips, and a structured jacket. Her hair was long and lush, bra-strap length with loose, perfect curls in a warm, glossy, honey brown. Envy struck me—the color almost matched my own, but the soft, nonfrizzy curls? Want, want, want, didn't have, didn't have, didn't have. She bent over to reach into the backseat and pulled out a saddle brown leather satchel briefcase. Stuffed full, the thing must have weighed a ton, but she pulled it out with nary an exhalation of breath. Instead, she slung it over herself in one movement, then picked up an equally loaded handbag and the usual suspects of keys, cell phone, and to-go beverage of choice, which in her case appeared to be some sort of fountain drink in a big foam cup. Given the shape of things—her killer figure—I was guessing it was diet.

It was enough to make a girl feel . . . somehow a little less than. I looked down at my perfectly acceptable wide-leg summer pants and a perfectly serviceable cami and unbuttoned cardigan, and I sighed. Serviceable and acceptable, yes. But some days, all a girl wants is to rock an awesome pair of heels and know that she owns 'em.

I sighed even more when she strode purposely to the very same apartment building I had toured earlier and began to climb the stairs, her killer calf muscles and slim legs screaming of endlessly repetitive hours on the stair-stepper machine. Of course she would live in the self-same building I was hoping to sign on to. Nothing like a daily reminder of your insecurities living over your head. I'd bet I could wear those shoes just as well, though. I wiggled my toes and flexed my foot up and down within the close-fitting confines of the cast, just to prove the point . . . and sighed when pain shot through the offending appendage.

Sigh, sigh, sigh, sigh. And sigh.

Yet another reason to bring a little bit of change into my life. Because if I was in the middle of trying to find my sea legs (without the despised cast, of course), I would be too busy to worry about anything else.

The door opened to my left, and Lou eased himself into

the small car with a grunt and a sigh. "Was that Alexandra Cooper I saw?" he asked me.

"The woman going upstairs? I don't know her, but the manager mentioned that a teacher lives upstairs. You know her?"

He nodded. "English teacher at the high school. Don't know much about her, really. She's been with us awhile. Not my department. I see her around the teacher's lounge, and of course I've seen her at all the functions—the administration likes to get us all together under one roof, no matter where we teach. Supposed to give us a feeling of comradery. Very kumbaya, doncha know."

"I see."

"She seems nice," he offered as he searched behind us, over both shoulders, before backing out of the parking space. "Quiet. Keeps to herself at the functions a little more than some of the others. An introvert, I expect. That's pretty common with the English department. They like the books and writings. But nice."

That was good to know. Nothing like having a raging lunatic living overhead, either.

"The strangest thing happened while we were touring the apartment," I mentioned offhandedly.

"Oh?"

I told him about the apartment and the sounds that we heard and how it set Locke off on a mission to inspect the entire kit and caboodle, while in the meantime I had been standing three feet from what we discovered was an actual intruder who had been hiding in the entry closet. Who, as it turned out, was probably no more than a high schooler run amok, but I couldn't blame the manager for going around like a chicken with its head cut off looking for the wielder of the hatchet.

"High schooler?" Lou frowned. "What did she look like?"

We were just passing one of the town's small community parks, where the neighborhood children could play in peace and relative safety. Nothing much to look at, just an expanse of parched grass and the requisite swing set, merry-go-round, and curly slide, rutted in the usual places by the scuffing of thousands of pairs of feet over the last half century or so. And there, sitting on the grip bars of that merry-go-round, was the girl I last saw bursting from the closet.

I nodded past Lou at the playground on the left. "She looks like that, actually."

He slowed the car to a crawl, staring in the direction I had indicated to where the girl was sitting, sheltered, in the lee of a boy's arms and legs. I got a good look at her this time. She and the boy only had eyes for each other, as wrapped up in each other emotionally as they were physically. Neither of them turned to look at us, even though we might as well have been stopped in the middle of the road, two faces gaping in their direction from within the confines of the car. It was only when a car horn sounded a quick blip from the road behind us that it spurred Lou into motion again.

Lou was nodding to himself.

"You know her?"

"Abbie Cornwall," he said by way of acknowledgment. "Tenth-grader this fall. I had her in track last year."

"And the boy?"

"Yup, he's mine from track, too. JJ Perkins. Junior. He's a good kid. They both are. I think they're each other's rocks. Rough home situation for him, and single-parent mom for her. Story of the times, I guess. Sad, but true."

I could see that. The protective posture of the boy spoke volumes of shouldering the harshness of the world away from his chosen one. "Why would she have been in that apartment?"

He shook his head, as baffled as I was. "I don't know. She's not the type of kid who would break into a place for the hell of it. Wonder if I should make mention of it to her counselor. Probably so, probably so. Head off any trouble before it can get started."

Some world-wizened folk might suspect drug use as a possible reason. Only a person with no other course of action might feel called upon to risk personal safety and freedom by doing something stupid. Like breaking into an unoccupied apartment, for instance. What on earth could that possibly gain? It's not like there was anything in there for her to steal, if that was her objective.

Of course, we were talking about a teenager here. Logic and reason didn't always apply.

"Abbie Cornwall," I mused. I saw her again, in my mind's eye, frozen in time for one split second when she paused in midflight and turned back toward me, surprise and something else in those ultra-green cat eyes. Despite the heavy rimming of smudged eyeliner, I couldn't help thinking that the something else I had seen was regret. Even apology. And then she had flown for real, out the door, up the pass-through to the parking lot, and down the street . . . straight to her boyfriend's arms. That could only mean one thing. Whatever it was that drove Abbie Cornwall, it was something that they were both in on.

Tenth grade. Hm. I wondered whether Evie or Tara, shop-girls extraordinaire and fellow N.I.G.H.T.S., knew either the girl or the boyfriend.

Perhaps I should have been wondering why I cared. Idle curiosity, I supposed.

"Mind if I stop somewhere before I take you home?"

Lou's question broke into my reverie. "Sure. Suit yourself."

"I promised Molly I'd bring home dinner since I have a

meeting tonight—that way, she and Tara get a night off cooking, too."

I smiled. "Aw, you're a peach, Uncle Lou."

"I know which side my bread's buttered on." He chuckled. "Got any suggestions?"

"How about Annie-Thing Good? Have you ever been?"

"Downtown?" he asked. "Nah, I never have. Marcus has raved about it before, and I keep meaning to, but for some reason we always seem to go to the same old tried-and-trues. Is it that good?"

"Trust me. It is outta-this-world a-*ma*-zing."

"When you put it that way, it sounds like a thing I shouldn't pass up. It'll do us good to break out of the mold. Molly's always telling me things like that. She'll be surprised I listened."

Lou was in for a treat. I remembered my first time at Annie Miller's gourmet version of a small-town café—I thought I'd died and gone to restaurant heaven. I still felt that way, every time I had one of her double-fudge caramel cheesecake brownies. Annie's place wasn't *just* a café. It was an experience.

It was also kind of out of the way, but Lou didn't seem to mind. He tooled across town, chattering away about his track team and his history classes and the silly things kids did these days. They were all subjects he was passionate about. You could tell by the light that came into his eyes.

"Do you want to stay here in the car?" Lou asked me when he pulled into a parking spot.

"I'll go in to say hello, too. It's been awhile."

I was out of the car before he could help me up, but he did get to the door before I could manage it, so I guessed it balanced out. Oriental brass bells rang in a minor key, somehow still melodic, as we ducked inside. It was a little early for the

dinner rush, but we were right on the first fringes. Good timing. Everything would be uber-fresh. My mouth was watering
already.

While Lou went to stand in what for Annie's was a rela-
tively short line, I crutched my way carefully between the
tables, bedecked as always with unapologetically casual red
and green gingham tablecloths, toward the heavily laden
dessert counter. To drool, naturally. I knew Marcus had prepared monstrously large burgers that would be ready to plop
on the grill the moment we got home, but that didn't mean
that a couple of pieces of dessert wouldn't be a really good
idea. He'd be all softened up for the discussion about the
apartment and returning to school as planned before he even
knew what hit him. I was thinking a couple of pieces of Annie's Original Sin cake might do the trick. Bittersweet dark
chocolate cake, with a chocolate mousse center, and a thick,
shiny layer of dark chocolate ganache sealing it all around?
That was enough to make anyone forget themselves.

My decision made, I hobbled over to wait with Lou. Annie
wasn't behind the counter, I noticed. Instead it was Dorothy,
her late-middle-aged Annie-labeled Counter Goddess who
looked a little like a benevolent troll at first prejudiced glance
but had the personality of an earth angel on a sugar high,
which of course made her the perfect addition to the busy
café.

"Sugar!" she cried when she caught sight of me. Her smile
hit me on high beams, and it was a doozy, packed with love
and light that a person could feel physically. "How are you?!"

I grinned back at her. "I'm just as fine today as I was yesterday, Dorothy, but then, you know that." Dorothy claimed
to be a plain woman and loved to address her customers using
her version of the endearments with which genteel Southern

ladies often addressed their loved ones . . . or anyone else who happened to come into their bubble of interest. For Dorothy that meant anything with "sugar" attached to it: sugarbabe, sugarhoney, sugarbritches, sugarplum, sugardarlin', and my personal favorite, sugarbabydoll. But, when it came out as just plain "sugar," it really packed a punch. I had it on good terms that her claim to the South was more likely just south of the Wabash River, but what she didn't know I knew would never hurt her.

"Oh, *pssh*." She waved me off with a good-natured shake of her head.

"Where's Annie?" I asked her.

"Oh, here and there, buzzin' around like usual. You know how she is. What can I get for you today? And who is this big, strappin' hunk of honeycomb?" she asked, giving Lou the appreciative once-over. I really needed to introduce Dorothy to Marian Tabor. I think they would be fast friends.

A dark red flush deepened Lou's cheeks. I laughed. "Dorothy, this is Lou Tabor, Marcus's uncle. We just stopped by to pick up some dinner for Lou's wife and daughter. Tara, from the store."

Dorothy tsked. "Taken. Pity. All the good ones are. What can I get for you?"

Having been startled out of his absorption of the menu, Lou glanced over at me. "What should I get?" he asked helplessly.

Dorothy turned her eagle eye back on him, assessing his inner nature. "You look like a ham man to me," she suggested at length. "We have a lovely ham and spinach ciabatta with Annie's special gorgonzola and brown-sugar bacon drizzle, topped of course with a side of fried red onion fire rings that are just the right mix of crunchy and chewy. Now, with that you get a side of my specialty baked beans, slow cooked with molasses, *not* barbecue sauce, mind." She glanced my way and winked. "It's a Southern thang."

"Sold," Lou blurted out. "I'll take three, please. And for dessert, I'll also take three pieces of that apple pie over there."

"Oh, honey," she said, shaking her head at his gaffe, "that's no ordinary apple pie. That, darlin', is deep-dish caramel apple pie, and it's got special powers. If you are even remotely in the doghouse, you take a piece of that pie home to your missus and you will be sittin' pretty for the rest of the week."

His eyebrows shot up. "That good, huh? Maybe I should take home a whole pie."

"Hey, while you're packaging that up, I'll take two big pieces of Original Sin," I called to her.

"Original Sin? Oh, Lordy. You're bringing out the big guns, huh?" she asked over her shoulder. "What did you *do*, sugar? Never mind, never mind. My old ears probably can't take it."

Lou was shaking his head, but I couldn't help thinking it was more to hold in his amazement. "I should have come in here eons ago," he muttered. "Original Sin. I'm definitely going to have to remember that, too."

I would have joked with him about it, but then I realized I was, er, planning on using the cake for the very same reason he was considering it, and I decided I'd do better to keep my comments to myself and not risk the karma kickback.

Dorothy was whisking about, crafting Lou's sandwiches like a pro, when Annie emerged from the swinging door to the kitchen carrying a big pot of soup. And right behind her, carrying a second steaming kettle, was the young man whom I had last seen tussling with the apartment manager, the man I knew only as Hollister.

"Maggie!" Annie said with a bright smile on her shiny-clean, freckled face as she passed by me on the other side of the counter . . . and then she paused and looked back at me oddly. I think because my mouth had fallen open. "Are you all right?"

I quickly closed my mouth when Lou nudged me. I nodded, but I was even more surprised when the young man set down the pot where she indicated, took Annie's from her and set it down as well, then leaned in and gave Annie a big, resounding smooch on the cheek. And even more surprised when she reached up and patted him on his cheek.

"You hang in there, Tyson. Everything will be fine. And tell Angela I insist that she brings you with her when she visits this weekend. I'll fix you both right up with some home cooking and a piece of special cheesecake that'll make all the troubles in the world go away."

"Thanks, Auntie," I heard him say. "I'll let her know. I'm taking her out to dinner in the city tonight to cheer her up, and then maybe a movie. I might even let her pick it."

Annie laughed. "Good idea. I'm sure the two of you will think of something. A little thinking goes a long way."

He nodded. "Understood. I won't do anything stupid, I promise. And thanks for being here for us."

"I wouldn't have it any other way," she told him.

Angela Miller. Locke had mentioned the tenant's name, but I hadn't connected her to Annie. Angela must be Annie's niece? And this Tyson Hollister guy was her boyfriend, according to Locke. This was awesome—I could have an inside view into the goings-on at the apartment complex, if I wanted one . . . and if I worked it right, the details on what *exactly* had made them want to leave in the first place. I couldn't help wondering if maybe there was more to it than even what Tyson Hollister and Rob Locke had been arguing over. Maybe I'd ask Annie for an intro . . . though with the line lengthening behind us by the minute, another time would probably be a better choice. I watched him leave, noting that he gave me and Lou a sidelong glance and a wide berth. Still, he made no trouble; his beef was not with us, and we certainly didn't have anything other than curiosity about the situation crossing our minds.

"Here you go, Maggie. Mr. Tabor," Dorothy sang out as she handed us a pair of paper sacks, bringing my attention back front and center. "Maggie, for you that's eight sixty-four, and Mr. Tabor, your total is twenty-eight-oh-eight."

"I'll get that for you, Maggie," Lou offered, handing over two twenties.

"You absolutely will not!" I protested, attempting to hand a ten to Dorothy myself.

"Sure I will," he said, with a firm nod at Dorothy. "I owe Marcus for going with me to pick up that load of donations for the school sports funding drive anyway. I could have done it by myself, but it was a whole lot easier with another set of hands and eyes and ears, and I like to pay back in kind. Take the desserts, Maggie."

Well, okay, then.

Annie was still tied up transferring the soups over from the pots to the heating bins up front. I balanced one crutch and lifted a hand to blow a kiss to her, then pantomimed *Call me!* She waved and nodded, smiling back.

And then we were on our way, leaving me to mull over the odd events of the afternoon.

Chapter 5

I had texted Marcus earlier to let him know I had found another way home and that I would meet him at his little bungalow. He was waiting for me when we arrived, coming out onto the porch to greet me with Minnie in his hands. Lou opened the old iron gate for me, and I crutch-hopped myself on through.

"Hey." His eyes locked with Lou's in both surprise and in question as he came forward. "I didn't get your text until I was already at the store to pick you up."

I bit my lip. What was it about having a secret from your partner that made things shift into weird levels of discomfort and discombobulation? "Oh, I'm sorry. This—thing—just came up this afternoon and I had to jump on it and—" I shrugged helplessly. "Thank you for picking up Minnie, though. Liss was going to kitty-sit her so that you wouldn't have to bother."

"It was no trouble. She's been keeping me company while

I got dinner started. Haven't you, Minnie?" His fingers were rubbing in firm circles under Minnie's chin. Minnie was purring her approval loudly, barely aware at that moment that I even existed.

Marcus, however, was still transferring his gaze back and forth between me and Lou, patiently waiting for an explanation. I hadn't quite come up with a way to approach him yet about the apartment, so of course the moment I was faced with explaining, my mind went blank. But like a real trooper, Lou came to the rescue. "Got your payment for you from Locke. He was very, very happy." He handed Marcus an envelope. "Said he might know some others who might be interested. Said he'd pass on your name and number. Could be good business in it for you."

"Oh, thanks, Uncle Lou. I appreciate it."

"Don't thank me yet. I still want you to take a look at what can be done to upgrade my beast of a system."

Marcus looked amused. "I didn't say anything earlier because you were in a hurry, but . . . are we talking about the same beast that you bought circa 1998?"

A sheepish grin pulled at Lou's lips. "Well . . . er, yeah."

"Hm." Marcus pretended to think. "I'm sure I can make a recommendation . . . for an entirely new system. Ah-ah," he interrupted when Lou started to protest, twitching a held-up finger back and forth, "I'll make sure it's very affordable. Besides, think of how happy Aunt Molly will be when you finally finish those video projects you've been claiming to work on for years now."

Lou sighed. "You're probably right. But ouch—my bank account."

"Sometimes," Marcus sympathized, "you just have to suck it up, man. Take one for the team. Open up your wallet and let the sun shine in."

"You know, your distorted proverbs are even more painful than the probable assault on my paycheck. Maggie, I don't know how you put up with this guy."

I let my eyes flirt with Marcus from beneath my lashes, taking him all in: from his worn but beloved chunky boots, up lean legs encased in distressed denim, and a plain old-school-style white T-shirt with navy arm and neck bands, to the braided leather wristlet with a single turquoise stone for protection and the dark curls pulled back at his nape with a strip of suede. "Oh, I don't know. Somehow, I manage."

Lou laughed. "Well, I can see when I'm not wanted. Marcus, I'll leave you two lovebirds to your dinner. And Maggie can tell you all about the apartment she just took a gander at."

Marcus's dark brows shot up as I winced. So much for my plans of feeding him chocolate to soften him up before any discussion took place. His brows were still parked midforehead when, without a single clue as to the gaffe he'd just let slip, Lou turned on his heel and waved over his shoulder to us. "Cheerio, you two! See you Saturday, if not sooner."

"*Soo,*" Marcus drawled, "what's shaking, sweetness?"

I dared to peep into his eyes, wondering why I was feeling so awkward. To hide it, I reached out and scratched Minnie behind the ears. "Oh. Nothing too much."

"Which would be why Uncle Lou out of the blue decided to come on down to the store and give you a ride home, huh?" he said gently. He opened the screen door and set Minnie down just inside with a soft pat to her rump to set her in motion. She chirped a meow in protest as her feet touched down and immediately stood up on her hind legs to peer out at us, disapproval and concern mingling on her furry face.

Not even Minnie could keep this conversation from happening. I cleared my throat. "Well . . . he *kind of* did it as a favor. To me."

"A favor for what?"

I knew I was going to have to tell him. I had been planning on it . . . but now that the time was at hand, all I wanted to do was postpone. "Maybe we should sit down."

I could feel his gaze on me, unrelenting, serious. "That bad, huh?"

His voice was so quiet, but it carried easily to my ears, even on the open air with the breezes and the voices of distant lawn mowers buzzing. "What? No! No," I hurried to say, leaning in to kiss him softly. "Gosh, it's nothing bad or anything. In fact, it could be a very good thing, I think. For both of us." I lingered there for a few extra moments while I breathed him in.

He smiled down at me, nuzzling back, already relaxing. "Why don't we sit down over here, then?" he asked, putting his arm around me to guide me over to the old-fashioned porch swing, his arm taking the place of one of my crutches. Was it a wee bit on the clumsy side? Sure. Did I prefer it over the old crutch routine? You bet your booty.

I sank into the swing while he held it steady for me, and sighed. My ankle was starting to complain about the long day, but I still had plenty of time to keep my promise to Dr. Dan a little later. Marcus sat next to me, but instead of sinking into him as I usually would, I kept my distance, leaning as far away from him as I could while still maintaining closeness.

My efforts did not go unnoticed.

"So."

"So," I said, trying to keep my voice conversational.

"You were saying."

"Yes. Yes, I was saying." I took a moment, trying to gather my thoughts.

Again, Marcus took notice. He let me stew a moment and

then finally took my hand. "You might as well just come right out and say what's on your mind, sweetness."

I nodded, knowing he was right. "Well . . . I was thinking today . . . about what we had been talking about earlier. You putting off going back to school the way you'd planned, I mean."

"And what were you thinking?"

The time had come. *Spit it out, Margaret. Keeping it all in never helped anybody. It only draws out the misery*, I heard in my head in those familiar, gratingly unyielding tones. And while I was grateful that Grandma Cora (aka the voice of my conscience) seemed to have my back, I couldn't help wishing she (it?) would pipe down and butt out. For. Just. One. Second.

But in the end, I did just what she suggested. I blurted. Actually, this was more than a blurt. This was a blurt that could rival Tara's or Evie's in tandem. This was a blurt of epic proportions.

"Well, see, I was thinking that you were making all these decisions about your future with an eye toward helping me out, but you are doing it without even asking me my opinion, and really, I don't think that's right, I mean, I think I should have some say in this, because really, it affects me, too, right, and shouldn't I feel free to give my input on things that I am involved in, because I really feel that I should, and I don't want you to put off your future, not even for a second, and especially not if your reason behind putting it off is me, taking care of me, because I can take care of myself, you know I can, and I think that's more than obvious, and my ankle is no excuse for thinking otherwise because obviously my ankle was a freak accident and freak accidents don't count for a hill of beans, in other words, at all, because, well, they just don't, and, to make this short, I don't want you to put off going back to school, I just don't, because honestly, I couldn't bear it if something happened that would make me responsible for you never getting your degree, that would be just awful, I mean, can you blame me, you have to admit, the guilt would just kill me, I'm sure you can understand why that might be, and . . . I said I was making this short, didn't I? Huh?"

Marcus took this all in like a pro, his expression slightly stunned but still standing. Er, sitting. "So I'm to understand that you don't want me to put off going back to finish my degree."

"Exactly!" I said brightly, relieved that he understood.

"And . . . *how* . . . does this involve Uncle Lou bringing you home?"

Oh. I didn't quite cover that, did I. "Well . . . I was looking at apartments. Because," I continued quickly as he opened his mouth to protest, "I just found out that Steff and Dr. Dan will quite probably be moving away before the end of the year, once his residency is done. And if she's not there, then I just don't see any sense in staying there myself. I think . . . maybe it's time for me to move on. To forge a better way. A nicer place for myself. A better life. And yes," I hurried to say, when he'd opened his mouth again, "part of it is to make sure that I can take care of myself and get around easily so that you can feel free to do what you need to do in your life without me hanging like a stone around your neck. But that's not the only thing weighing in on my decision. I want you to know that. And that's why the apartment I was looking at is on the ground floor and easily accessible for me. And, it's only a few blocks from here."

Marcus waited for several moments with his eyes on mine before he spoke at last. "Are you finished?"

I blushed, realizing he'd been waiting for me to cut in on him again. "Yes, I am. You can go ahead now."

"Thank you." He shook his head, the quirk at the corner of his mouth telling me he wasn't mad. "Maggie. You don't have to apologize or explain or feel guilty for anything. I hope you know that. I'm touched that you are worrying about me. Thinking about me, and about my future. That speaks volumes as to the kind of person that you are. Not that I didn't know that about you already. Steff will be leaving, you say?"

I nodded, but I was determined not to let the glumness I felt about losing my best friend settle in for a good, long stay. "I'll miss her," was all I would allow myself.

He didn't say anything for at least a minute, and I knew he was taking it in, all of me, feeling me out through all of his senses, and not in a physical sense. I let him, opening to it, enjoying the feeling of the energy flowing freely back and forth between us. It was so easy with Marcus. So easy to open to him without feeling naked and vulnerable. "That's not going to be easy for you, letting go. But it's her path, and you'll honor it."

"Yes. I'll honor it." I closed my eyes and breathed deeply to find my inner peace. To release any longing I had to control or manipulate the outcome. "There's always Facebook and Skype chat and texting."

"And long weekend visits."

"And holidays where we blend our families together. Someday."

"Yes. Someday."

It could be good. It would be fine. We would be fine. Distance didn't mean separation, not of heart and spirit, and that's what really mattered.

"Is this really something you've been thinking about a lot?" he asked, playing with my fingers. "This apartment thing?"

Well, I couldn't exactly say "a lot" . . . "It's something I think I'm ready to consider."

"Something that's important to you. To be on your own."

He didn't say it in an accusing way, more as though he was trying to feel things out, trying to understand. And yet I felt an overwhelming need to make sure he understood. "It's not that I don't like staying here with you," I told him, running my thumb in circles on the inner flesh of his palm. "Honest. It has been . . . wonderful. *Really* wonderful."

"But . . . ?"

"No buts. None. I just really want you to have the freedom to move within your life, Marcus. To do the things that are important. And I don't want to feel like I'm holding you back from doing those things."

He nodded sagely. "I know. You're right."

"Well, I'm glad you're seeing reason. Of course I'm—wait, what?"

"It hasn't escaped my notice that you're always underfoot. Always making me wait on you. Always wanting me to get you water . . . run your bath . . . rub your feet . . . rub your back . . . I guess I should have expected you to take advantage of me. It is so like you to be unscrupulous and devious that way. Ow!" He rubbed his shoulder where I'd smacked him.

"That's not very funny," I sniffed.

He laughed and tweaked my chin. "You do like me to rub your feet. Admit it." He reached down and pulled my legs up over his lap, bracing them there with his arms.

I blushed as he slowly slipped my only shoe, a ballet flat, off my left foot and let it fall to the painted wooden floorboards of the porch. "Well . . . maybe a little . . ."

"A little." His hand closed over my foot, putting delicious pressure on my instep with his fingertips. I gasped. "Uh-huh."

My mouth had gone dry with the jolt of pleasure that had weakened my knees. I licked my lips. "You're not playing fair."

"I'm not?" He pressed again, digging in a little deeper and adding a sinuous little glide to the movement.

This time I managed to resist the knee-buckling sensation. But only barely. "Ahem. You still haven't said what you think about the whole apartment thing."

Marcus leaned over purposely until his lips hovered just an inch from mine. "Hm. You're right."

I would not cave in, I would *not* cave in. "And, we're on your front porch."

His gaze flicked left and then right, but he didn't withdraw. "Uh-huh. We do appear to be on the porch."

"And your neighbors are out."

He squinted at me. "I'm thinking you probably have a point to all this."

"I do."

"I'm thinking you're probably going to tell me what that is."

"Marcus Quinn, you are incorrigible, did you know that?"

"I might have heard that a time or two before."

"Just once or twice?"

"That's probably not going to change, you know." He dipped in for one, quick, warm, wet kiss, and then, just as I was starting to think maybe it wasn't so urgent to address the apartment issue right at this moment after all, he pulled away abruptly and I was left blinking into space.

Once I came back into myself, I stuck my lip out in a pout. "*So* not playing fair."

"Haven't you heard? All's fair in love and war."

"And it was a man who came up with that particular sentiment," I complained.

"Uh-huh," he agreed. "One who had a very good idea just what he had to do to please his woman."

Somehow, when he put it that way, it didn't seem quite so bad. *Focus first*, I reminded myself. *Fun later*. I cleared my throat and my spinning head, all at the same time. "So, what *do* you think?"

He sighed and leaned back, reconciled to the knowledge that I wasn't going to give up. "I think you are one stubborn woman."

"About the apartment."

"I rest my case. And," he continued before I could interrupt, "if it's important to you, having this sense of freedom and independence . . . then I will support your decision."

I smiled and melted for him. He had such a lovely way of saying the simplest things. "Thank you."

"So long as you let me buy you a security system. No buts!" he said when he saw my mouth open to object. "I would have gotten one for you for your current place, but somehow you seem to have ended up at my place far more than at yours, thanks to this little lovely." He rapped with his knuckles on the cast and laughed when I made a face. "Hey, don't knock it. I'm certainly not complaining."

I sighed. "Actually, the security system would be a welcome addition. Not that there's anything to worry about. But I will say, the girl in the closet was a bit of a surprise."

"Girl—?" The look on his face was priceless. "I think this is going to take a bit of explaining."

So I did. Jumping straight past the situation between the manager and the young man whom I later discovered was in a relationship with Annie's niece, I instead told him about taking a tour of the apartment, only to be surprised out of my skin when the girl burst past me from the closet by the front door. "At least I know now that the strangeness I felt at the apartment complex had a physical cause and not a metaphysical one," I finished. "Because if given a choice in the matter, I think I'd choose physical. One that can be detected by a good security system and eliminated by either a studly boyfriend or a call to the local police department."

I knew as soon as I added the police department comment into the mix that I probably shouldn't have. Any reminders to Tom Fielding, Special Task Force Investigator with the Stony Mill PD and previous boyfriend, were not taken lightly. He and Marcus had never gotten along, for reasons I'd never been forward enough to ask about. Maybe I should have . . . but then, maybe there was nothing meaningful about it at all. Maybe it was just the downside of chemistry. Some people just rub each other the wrong way.

But if Marcus was bothered by it, he didn't let it get the better of him for long. "Why was the girl there?" he asked.

I shook my head, just as puzzled as he was. "I don't know. I only got a glimpse of her at the apartment—after she nearly knocked me over—before she ran off. Lou actually recognized her, though—she ran, but she didn't run far. We saw her when we drove past the little community park just down the street. She's on his track team. I don't think she saw him, though. She was too involved with her boyfriend to pay attention to either of us."

Marcus was still absorbing all of this. "So, this afternoon, you left work with my uncle, went to see an apartment I didn't even know you were interested in looking into, and were nearly knocked down by an intruder in said apartment who turns out to be a teenage girl that my uncle knows?"

I grinned sheepishly. "Yes, I'd say that about sums it all up."

"You lead an interesting life, Maggie O'Neill."

A year ago, I would have agreed with him. But with the

events of previous months laid out on the table, who could dispute it?

"So, this girl," he mused at length. "She broke into an empty apartment? Or is there a current tenant?"

"No current tenant. The manager said he'd had to evict the previous tenant for breaking the terms and requirements of the lease . . . or something like that."

Marcus frowned. "That doesn't sound all that great. Did he say what his reasons were? I would hate to see you give up your current apartment for a potentially unstable situation."

"He didn't go into specifics," I explained, "but at the time it didn't sound like that big a deal. Just one of those things. A product of doing business in the modern age. Whoever it was, they were the only tenant since the remodel, and it didn't sound to me as though they were there long. The place was clean. Well, all except for the big, huge mirror in the bedroom. It was broken. The manager said he'd put it on the list for replacement."

One eyebrow slid up, just a tad. "Big, huge mirror in the bedroom, huh? Um, *how* big?"

In-*corr*-igible. "Broken, big guy." And then I darted a sideways peek at him through my lashes. "But an intriguing sentiment, nevertheless."

"We could continue this conversation inside, you know," he said, sliding his hand up to cup my knee.

A knowing smile touched the outer corners of my lips. "Hmm. I suppose we *could* do that." And then, just because I was so relieved, and equally because I should have known better: "I'm so glad you didn't get the wrong idea about the apartment and my reasons behind it. You really are a good guy, you know that?"

He leaned in to kiss me. Despite what I'd said, neither one of us seemed to care at the moment that the neighbors could see. If they were watching, they should probably have the decency to look elsewhere.

My breath left me in a whoosh as his arms came up beneath me and he lunged to his feet with me held aloft. I threw my arms around his neck and held on tight, dizzy with the crazy, wondrous delight that often filled me when I was with him. Minnie yowled plaintively from the screen door. She could wait a minute.

And then a phone started buzzing.

Long ago, Jane Austen was fond of writing universally acknowledged truths about men and women and the relationships they found themselves engaged in. If Ms. Austen were writing my story, my universal truth might include something pithy about the untimely ringing of cell phones.

It didn't take me long to realize two things. One, the cell phone was most definitely mine. Naturally. And two, my purse was sitting on the floorboards beneath the porch swing.

With a resigned sigh, Marcus set me down carefully and allowed me to find my footing before dashing over, grabbing my purse, and tossing it to me. Big mistake. Because even though it was zipped and snapped shut, and even though I caught it, what that meant was that the contents of said large, modern, bucket-style bag were irreversibly jumbled to hell and back.

Without my crutches to lean on, I was forced to stand on one foot and try to maintain my balance while turning the deep handbag right-side up, unzipping it on the go, and then trying really hard to hold on to it and keep it open with one hand while scooping through the multitudinous contents with my other.

Which brings me to my second universal truth. Which is that cell phones, unlike the children of old, must be heard but not seen. I felt around blindly. I sifted through by touch.

I even peered into the dark depths of my bag, hoping to catch sight of the glow of the outer screen. But no luck. It might as well have disappeared through a black hole into another dimension.

Or, it could have slipped into the small rip in the lining that I didn't realize was there, ending up in the neverland between liner and outer shell. Which is where I found it about five seconds after the final buzzing ring tone.

Which brings me to my third universal truth of the hour: a ringing phone waits for no man. Or woman, even.

I pulled it out just as the little glow light blinked out. Within ten seconds, the phone buzzed in my hand once again, notifying me I had a new voice mail message. Marcus fetched my missing crutches while I played it:

"Miss O'Neill, this is Rob Locke at New Heritage Property Management. I just wanted to let you know that we do actually have another party interested in renting the apartment you looked at this afternoon. I hate to appear pushy, but I am going to have to have an answer from you tonight. I would appreciate you calling me back when you receive this message.

"You should still have my card and the rental agreement, but I'll give you the number here: 555-7368. That's 555-RENT. Thanks. Talk to you soon."

I frowned. He needed an answer now? Tonight?

"What's up, love?"

I looked up to meet Marcus's inquiring eyes. "He says he needs an answer tonight. ASAP. I was thinking I'd have a few days to think it over. Now what?" I asked him, hoping for insight.

Marcus handed me my crutches and took my handbag. "Have you even read the lease?"

"I did," I told him, "but there are changes to it that will need to be made—the manager offered a few special incentives to get my attention and sweeten the deal, and they aren't in the boilerplate lease contract he gave me to look over."

The more I thought about it, the more I scowled. I was not pleased with this rush mode I now found myself in. Something about this felt wrong. My BS detector was kicking in. I couldn't help wondering if he was pushing me to make a decision just to seal the deal fast. I mean, just a little while ago, it had sounded as though he didn't have a plan for the evening except playing around with his new-and-improved computer. I just couldn't see him making an impromptu appointment with someone else on such short notice, someone who had now had a full two minutes to review the apartment and was willing to sign a lease on the spot. It just didn't make sense. But, there was also a part of me that worried about missing out on a great deal, waiting too long and letting it slip away, and never finding another affordable apartment.

The question was, which part of me would win out?

At Marcus's suggestion, I called Locke and got through right away. The apartment manager explained again in that same thick, droll voice that he had someone else who was now suddenly interested in the apartment, and he was going to need me to make a crash decision. Right then, if possible. Otherwise, if I wasn't interested after all, he would just get in touch with this second party and tell them it was theirs. Obviously, he wished to give me first right of refusal.

I couldn't rid myself of the feeling that he was lying, that he was gambling on my unwillingness to let a good deal slip through my fingers. And knowing that, feeling the certainty of it down to my very bones, was why I was so surprised to hear myself agreeing to take the apartment . . . just so long as he'd be willing to write in a clause that would allow me to terminate the lease at my discretion with a reasonable amount of advance notice in writing.

"Fantastic!" I heard Locke enthuse on the other end of the airwaves. "And I think I can come up with a clause that will be mutually beneficial . . . but don't go spreading our little arrangement around. There are others who might not take it too kindly that you have special conditions and terms in your lease. I think you'll be the perfect fit for our tight-knit little community. As a matter of fact, I had a feeling about it the moment I first clapped eyes on you. Call it . . . a sixth sense. Call it fate. There was just something about you, Maggie—may I call you Maggie?—that said 'I need this apartment.' Warms the cockles of my heart to know that it worked out for you. I love my job."

Hm. I couldn't help thinking that he was laying it on a little thick. You?

I thanked him, telling him that I'd stop by first thing in the morning to sign a lease that included the details from his earlier offer to me.

"Oh, of *course*," he agreed, "the discounted offer still stands. I am a man of my word. I'll have the paperwork ready for you. All you need to do is drop by the office. I'll have the keys available to you then, and once that little detail is taken care of, you can move in at any time."

Wow. That was fast. "Don't you have to do a credit check or anything of that nature?"

He chuckled in my ear. "No need, no need. You're a friend of a lodge brother. That's good enough for me and for the owner of the complex. See you first thing tomorrow."

I clicked off. Marcus had been watching me the entire time. I met his gaze.

"So," he said. "Tomorrow?"

I nodded as he slipped his arm around my shoulders, wondering why I felt so strangely unsettled about all of this. It had happened so fast. Maybe it just hadn't completely sunk in yet. Maybe I just needed time to think. Maybe the reality of it would hit me later, because just at that moment it didn't quite feel real. I knew I was going to have to reassert my independence in order to give Marcus back the ability to do his thing, so why couldn't I just feel good about successfully finding a solution to yet another life challenge? "He said I could move in any time after signing the papers," I mused, trying to spark up some enthusiasm. "Maybe I can get my dad and some of the guys to help out."

"Great. Sounds good."

He didn't sound very enthusiastic, either. I tilted my head back to look at him. "You sure you're okay with all this?"

"Who me? Yeah. It's fine. I told you that."

"Okay. You just sounded a funny for a minute there."

"Oh. I don't know why. For some reason, I'm having a hard time seeing you there." He laughed at himself, then, and shook it off. "Whatever. Let's go inside, huh?"

Chapter 6

By the time evening came around, I had forgotten all about Marcus's admission of having some difficulty seeing me in this new apartment, and I was too frazzled to address my own strangely conflicted feelings toward what was proving to be a rush job of the highest order. Why did it seem that every time something changed in any part of my life, the world had to instantly switch into spin cycle? And there I was, preparing to put my signature on a document that would cement the change, no turning back.

I slept little over the course of the night, and awakened often. Dreams were part of my problem. Every time I awoke, I was caught up in the snare of yet another dream, struggling to come out of it like a drugged patient trying to come out of anesthesia. I didn't remember much in the way of details, just an overpowering sense of dread, the feeling of hiding but being watched nevertheless. By the time morning came, I was more than ready to be up and out of bed, despite the lovely warm feeling of sharing said bed with the lovely warm body of Marcus. Any other morning I might have lingered as long as alarm clocks and my work schedule would allow, but today I found myself folding back the covers so as not to wake him, ruthlessly dislodging a previously comatose Minnie from the hammock she had made of the coverlet between our bodies, and easing from the bed.

It didn't work, of course. I could swear that Marcus sleeps with one eye open. Or was that his third eye that remains on guard? Whatever it was, he awoke the moment I pushed myself to my feet. Er, make that "foot." With little more than a kiss to persuade him, he made breakfast while I hopped in the tub for a "quick" bath . . . although, if you've ever had a broken leg yourself, you are painfully aware that there is nothing quick about it.

Breakfast was bittersweet as I realized that, even on the nights I slept over, or that he would sleep over at my new place, it wouldn't be quite the same as the last few weeks had been.

It's for the better, I told myself. *Marcus needs this. When he has his degree in hand, he'll thank me for not letting him postpone going back. This is the perfect solution.* I kept repeating those things to myself as we silently drove the five blocks separating Marcus's bungalow from the apartment complex, each of us caught up in our own preoccupied thoughts. Or maybe we were just tired.

September mornings can be a beautiful thing in Indiana. The long, hot, dog days of summer were for the most part behind us, and the occasional rainstorms were returning our grass to a lovely green hue. A welcome respite from the desiccated desert of August, even though we all knew it would be brief. Just a matter of time before the nights, and even the days, turned cool, nipping at the trees and dressing them in glorious fall color. But today, the sun was filtering through green, green leaves with that special soft quality only seen in the early morning hours, and the world around us was preparing for the coming day with the usual sounds of television, garage-door openers, lawn mowers, barking dogs, and aging school buses rattling down the streets. Since we would be stopping before going to the store, I had decided that Minnie would be better off staying at Marcus's for the day—alone, but with her steady supply of friends, the birds, fluttering outside of her favorite window for company, she would be fine.

Marcus pulled his truck into the parking lot I indicated, the same that Lou had parked in just the day before. He looked over at me and smiled. It was encouraging, but I wasn't feeling it. "Ready?"

I didn't say anything. I couldn't. Instead I got down out of the truck, hopping in place on one foot to keep my balance as I reached for my wayward crutches.

"Here, I got 'em." Marcus to the rescue. I was going to miss that.

The sign in the window of the apartment complex office still said "Closed," but the door was standing ajar and appeared to have been propped open. Obviously Locke was waiting for me to arrive and just wanted me to know it was okay to come on in. Girding my loins, I made my way up the sidewalk, my purse bumping clumsily between my side and one crutch with each step. Marcus had offered to carry it for me, but I had refused his offer gently. I needed to know I could do this. I needed to know I could take care of myself. And I needed for Marcus to know it, too, so he wouldn't worry about me overmuch.

Marcus got to the door before me and quickly sidestepped around me to hold it wide so that I could pass through freely.

There had been nothing propping the door open, just the stopper on the hydraulic door hinges that could be set to hold the door for you if you needed to go through with your hands full. The lights in the office were off.

I poked my head in the door. "Mr. Locke?" I called out. "Hello?"

The office, or at least the part of it that I could see, was empty.

Of people.

The mess that met my surprised gaze completely made up for that. My mouth fell open, taking it all in.

"Hooooolllllllyyyyy coooowwww," I whispered, drawing out the words.

Marcus came up behind me and stopped short, too. He let out a long, low whistle.

Someone had done a number on the office. Files had been emptied and scattered over the floor, along with shards of ceramic from broken coffee mugs, and glass, too; drawers had been rifled, and chairs had been overturned and flung about. Worse were the pieces of what appeared to be electronic components, circuit boards, and wires, crunched and battered underfoot.

Marcus swore softly under his breath. "The computer rebuild."

He was right. The computer Uncle Lou had just delivered yesterday was the unfortunate source of the electronic doo-dads and thingamabobs littering the area around the desk. Not to mention the metal casing, which had been beaten into a crunched and dented shadow of its former self.

"Wow," I murmured. "Wow, wow, wow. Who could have done this? Burglars?"

"Why would they destroy one of the only things of value here to be taken, if that were true?"

Good point, that. Offices for inexpensive apartment complexes weren't known for having a lot of high-end stuff around. Lots of low-budget furniture, maybe a computer or two. Not even a lot of cash hanging around. Which meant if the damage was caused by would-be burglars, they were either too stupid to choose a viable target or too inexperienced to know better.

Which meant . . .

I looked around, suddenly nervous, hoping we had not caught said someone in the act. Could they still be there, lurking in the shadows? Hm. Nowhere to hide. Not in this room, at least. There were two rooms leading off, though, and the doors *were* closed. One lead to a bathroom, I knew. The other perhaps to some kind of storage or utility closet? That was my guess, but I couldn't know for sure.

"Should we—?" I asked Marcus, but he cut off the question with a sharp shake of his head. He held up a finger to his lips and took my arm, guiding me gently back out the door.

"Don't touch anything," he muttered, the words understandably terse. "You go back to the truck. Lock the doors. I'm going to have a look around."

Tom had tried that with me once. It had worked. For a little while. This time, though, I really didn't see the need. "It's broad daylight, Marcus. Whoever it was that did this, I'm sure they're long gone. They wouldn't stick around for the manager to arrive and catch them in the act." I paused then as the office hours caught my eye. "As a matter of fact, he should be here already. Maybe he's just running late."

"Maybe."

Why couldn't Marcus sound more convinced? Darn it, now he was making *me* jumpy.

"What is that over there?" He pointed toward the grassy

yard and the obviously new building at its center, with the fenced area beyond.

"It's the new health center that belongs to the apartment complex," I explained. "I saw it yesterday."

"Well, it looks like it's open for business."

He was right. There was a light on inside. Just a tenant working away the pounds? "Should we go see?" He opened his mouth, but I had seen that look in his eyes before, and I quickly said, "I am *not* going back to the truck by myself. Either we both go and check it out, or we both go back to the truck."

Exasperated, he just shook his head. "You are one stubborn woman. Did anyone ever tell you that?"

"Maybe. Once or twice. So what's it going to be, angel?"

He gave a small if reluctant smile at the misquote from his all-time (and old school) favorite movie and let out his breath in a resigned sigh. "Fine. But I go in first. You stay behind me."

"Deal." It was better that way, anyway. Crutches didn't really allow for a smooth, silent ninja entrance.

He was speedier than I was, but then, I think that was his intent. Having long legs on his side, he covered the ground in between the office and exercise center fast, fast, fast, leaving me to follow as quickly as I could manage—no mean feat considering that I had three legs to deal with to his two. I cursed my slowness as I saw him make a sneaky approach from one side of the industrial steel door with its long and narrow window, bending down to look in from a low vantage point. I wanted to call to him to ask him what he saw, but I gritted my teeth against the urge and concentrated instead on just getting there myself, one hop-step at a time. I was even more intrigued when he turned back to me and again held a finger to his lips to caution me to remain silent. I was just within a step or two when he opened the door to . . .

Nothing.

And no one.

I sighed as the tension released from my shoulders. My breath came out more forcefully than I meant for it to, and I realized just then that I'd been holding it. "Whoever it was, they must be long gone by now. They probably didn't even come through here. The place is spotless."

Marcus nodded. "What's through that door?" he asked, indicating a similar door on the other side of the equipment- and mirror-filled room.

"The pool."

"Should we?"

I shrugged. "Why not? And then we should either find Locke or else call the police, I guess, huh?"

"Finding Locke would be my first choice," Marcus said with a wry grin.

"Understood. Well, let's go check the pool area, in case someone heard us coming and went out that way?"

This time we crept on quiet feet toward the door together—or, as quiet as my crutches would allow me to be. The one on the right had developed a squeak a few days before, with only a month's mileage on it. Guess they just don't make things like they used to.

We paused together at the door, our eyes on each other. "Ready?" Marcus muttered, waiting for my nod. "All right. One . . . two . . . three!"

On three, he yanked the door open, and we peered out into the swimming pool area together.

The first thing that I saw was the shoe lying upturned on the perfect, new concrete surrounding the pool. A scuffed loafer that had seen better days, with heels beaten on the edges and soles worn smooth. Not exactly appropriate pool wear.

I had seen that loafer before. Just the day before actually. On Locke.

That feeling of something being off? It was back again. Bigger and better, this time.

"Maggie."

I dragged my attention away from the shoe and blinked up at Marcus. His expression was stoic and grim, but he didn't look down at me. His gaze was focused straight ahead.

The pool.

I hadn't gotten that far yet. My gaze had been snared by the shoe, and immediately my mind had started whirring around why that worn loafer might be there—none of the possibilities good. The best I could come up with is that Locke had interrupted the intruders in mid-destruction and had chased after them, losing his shoe in the process. But now, I was going to have no choice.

I made myself look toward the pool.

At first, I thought someone had dumped some clothes in the water. Or maybe that's what I had hoped. A floating heap of clothes to go along with the single shoe on the surrounding concrete. Like, maybe it was the last laugh of the burglars or intruders or vandals, whatever the case might have been. That could have been an acceptable supposition. Unfortunately, such desperate Pollyanna optimism fell swiftly by the wayside when faced with harsh realities.

Such as the bare foot poking out of the soggy clothing.

"Oh! Oh! Oh!" I whispered in repeat mode.

And that's how my day went swiftly from promising to completely sunk in sixty seconds.

But not as sunk as Locke's.

Locke's day was dead in the water.

Literally.

"Is he"—I had to swallow against the rising gorge in my throat—"is he dead?"

"Yes. His face—"

He didn't need to tell me. I could see it myself, now that I knew where in the heap of soggy clothes to look. Not that I wanted to. Gazing unflinchingly on the face of death was not tops on my To Do list. Ever.

I took an involuntary step back. My heel bumped something as I did so, something heavy. I froze in an instant and looked down at my feet . . . and felt the gorge make the northerly climb again. The thing my foot had nudged was a weight. A hand weight, to be precise. One that matched the set lining the spanking-new racks in the health facility. The thick smear of rusty color on one chunky end of it, though . . . that was different. That was . . .

My head stopped spinning, and I regained control of my faculties long enough to move away from the offensive object, fast, fast, fast.

There was zero chance that this was an accident . . . This was murder, plain and simple.

As plain and simple as a crime like murder can be.

Another murder in Stony Mill.

Criminy.

This hadn't just happened. From the look of him, Locke had been in the water awhile, maybe (probably?) all night long. At least I could feel safe in the knowledge that whoever had done this to him was probably not still hanging around.

Now that we both realized we had breached the scene of yet another suspicious death in Stony Mill, we were loath to move lest we destroy some kind of evidence. I clung to Marcus, my arms locked around his waist, my crutches held loosely as I used his body for support. But more important than physical support, his personal energy was now my shelter from the storm of horror and dismay from which neither of us could hide our faces.

Gradually I became aware that Marcus was not just holding me. I had felt movement just above my head, and I knew he was scanning the area around us. I shook my head, feeling the soft material of his T-shirt rub against my cheekbone. "They aren't still here," I told him. "They wouldn't stay to watch him be found." I don't know why I knew that to be true, but I did. The person who did this was not here.

We stood there a few moments longer just like that, huddled together, before I felt Marcus reach into his pocket and pull out his cell phone. I stood there, within the circle of his arms, listening to his voice rumble through his chest, listening to his steady heartbeat as he gave the 911 operator the address and let them know the "nature" of the emergency.

Nature had nothing to do with this emergency.

The sirens could be heard for miles, wailing, shrieking, clamoring on the clear September air. *Just another day in Stony Mill,* I thought. We had far too many of them. Every time it happened again, I thought, this could be it. This could be the one to break the spell we'd been under. This could be the last. Over. Done. *Finito.* And every time, I was lulled into a tragically false sense of assurance, to dream again, to hope.

I was so afraid that hope was lost to us. That fear sunk in a little more with each bad thing that happened, month after month after month.

A wise man once said, nothing to fear but fear itself, Margaret Mary-Catherine O'Neill. I always thought he was right. Doesn't do to worry, little girl. Keep your head out of the clouds. Stick to the sunshine. The wise, crackly voice of Grandma C came in my ear that time, as real as Marcus next to me, but still ethereal somehow. Tinny. Things were changing in my extrasensory world.

I was only beginning to grasp how. I hoped someday to understand why. For now, all I could do was accept the changes with
some level of grace and dignity. Keep on keepin' on.

Stick to the sunshine.

I was trying to do that, but the storm clouds kept closing in.

And at that moment, so were Stony Mill's boys in blue.
Black and white police cars screeched in from all directions,
converging on the various apartment complex parking lots. I
saw flashes of movement in one or two of the apartments
overlooking the health center and pool area, but then my attention was snapped front and center by the shouts of several
officers now approaching fast with their weapons drawn.

Chapter 7

"Hold it! Stop right where you are!"

"Don't move!"

"You two . . . back up and get your hands in the air!"

Were they . . . were they talking to—

"I said, back up and get your hands in the air!"

Marcus backed up two steps and slowly complied, a sneer of open derision lifting his upper lip. I was a bit slower in my confusion. "What are you talking about? We're the ones who called you. Where's Tom?" Nobody answered my question, so I prodded, "*Fielding?*"

Right on cue, I saw a familiar figure walking up from the side parking lot through one of the apartment pass-throughs, his cocky walk giving him away even at a distance.

"Look, there he is," I said, pointing him out. "I *know* him, all right?" I didn't glance Marcus's way. I hoped he would see the wisdom of my admission. It was certainly better than having a gun pointed in our direction.

Two officers had already headed over to the far side of the pool to check the body. I saw one of them speaking quietly into his shoulder mike as he unclipped something from his breast pocket and reached out with it—it looked like a long, extendo-rod or radio antenna—to lift at the edge of the body.

"Well, if it isn't Maggie O'Neill and her . . . compadre in crime."

The dry humor-but-not present in the too-familiar voice snapped me back from what was going on in the pool. Tom Fielding, Special Task Force Investigator for the SMPD—and my former boyfriend, of course—had stopped ten feet from me and was now standing with his hip cocked out, his hands on his heavy-duty and fully loaded gun belt as he stared at me through his favorite mirrored aviators. The sardonic slash of teeth against the tan of his skin was more a mockery of a smile.

He shook his head at me. "Tsk, tsk, tsk."

My patience had seen better days, as had my nerves. "What do you mean, tsk, tsk, tsk? For heaven's sake, call off your goons, would you? And can I put my hands down? My shoulders are starting to ache." They weren't, not really, but it sounded as good an excuse as any.

"My . . . goons . . . would probably respond better to a request accompanied by a very special, very handy word someone came up with a long time ago: 'Please.' "

I gritted my teeth. "Please . . . may we put our hands down?"

"That's better." With a single nod from Tom, the cops lowered their weapons and holstered them. They did not, however, snap the leather fasteners in place. They were still considering themselves on guard. To his fellow officers, Tom asked, "Anyone checked the property?"

"Hayden and Olds are beating the bushes right now."

"Why don't you four go help out? I'll take over here with Johnson and Kirkland," he said, jerking his thumb over his shoulder toward the two cops closest to the body, one of which was wielding a camera. "Oh, and Chief is on his way. You know what that means."

The cop closest to him nodded. "We'll keep the equipment away from him. Maybe someone else can help steer him away from the pertinent areas. I vote for Olds, since he's the newbie."

"Olds it is, then. Let him know, huh?"

"You got it."

Marcus came up behind me and put a protective arm around my waist as I cleared my throat noisily. "Um, your guys will want to head over to the apartment complex's office."

Tom's attention snapped back to me. "Well, of course, but . . ." His eyes narrowed in obvious suspicion. "What will we find at the offices, Maggie?"

"Well, for one thing, the man whose body is floating out there is the apartment manager, Rob Locke . . . and, well, for another thing, the office is a wreck."

"And you would know this . . . how?"

Before I could say anything more, one of the officers—his name tag read "Kirkland"—came hurrying over, a dripping piece of paper, folded into three, held out in front of him over the extendo-rod in his hand. "We fished this out of the water. It was almost all the way out of his pocket, so I didn't think it would be a problem. Johnson's taking photos of the body as we speak."

Tom went to the supply kit one of the guys had brought over and donned a pair of latex gloves. A frown had gathered between his brows as he carefully gripped the corners and ever so slowly peeled the wet folds apart. The frown deepened substantially as he read the words laser-printed onto the page. His gaze lifted to mine, but his glower didn't lift at all.

"Maggie . . . why is your name on this lease that was in that man's pocket?"

Of course he had the lease on his body. Sigh. Well, it complicated things but only for the moment. I knew I had nothing to hide, and that the facts would bear me out. Besides, this was Tom. He might not be very happy with me at present, but he would never suspect me of something like this. "Well . . ." I began calmly, "that would probably be because I was supposed to meet him this morning to sign the lease for an apartment here."

"Huh. I guess that answers my next question, which was, why in the hell are you here. So, that means you're moving out of loverboy's house?"

I frowned at him. "How did you—?"

At the same time, Marcus's grip on me tightened. "That's none of your business, Fielding, and you know it. You're out of line."

Tom's laugh was caustic enough to stab home the point that he still hadn't forgiven me for breaking up with him for Marcus. Not yet. "I think the dead man in the pool kind of makes it my business. You know, since it's my job. How's about you both make my job easier, huh? I'm going to need to know everything that happened this morning."

I felt Marcus tense behind me, so I turned and put my hand on his chest to stay whatever comment he was thinking about spouting. It was better that I did the talking. "It is really very simple," I told Tom. "I had an agreement with Mr. Locke—the apartment manager—to stop by this morning to sign a lease for the apartment he showed me yesterday. When we got here, we stopped in the office and found that it had been broken into and ransacked. We saw lights on in the health center, so we came this way, hoping to find Mr. Locke. We didn't expect to find him like . . . like that." I gestured weakly. "So Marcus called 911, and we waited here until your guys got here and pointed their guns at us, and . . . well, there you have it."

Tom was writing all of this down. Without looking up, he asked, "Did you see anyone at any time while you were here on the premises?"

I shook my head. "No one. The door to the office was standing ajar when we arrived, but there wasn't anyone there. From there we came directly here, bypassing through the health center. The door to the health center was closed but unlocked, and the lights were already on inside." A flash of an image projected itself onto the blank screen in my mind's eye. "Oh—I doubt this is relevant, but I did see curtains move in a couple of the apartments. But that was after your men got here, so it's only natural, right? Whoever was at home wanted to see what the hubbub was about?"

"We'll be talking to the various tenants in the apartments. Let's you and me get back to the office and the health center. Did you touch anything? Anything at all?"

"The only things we touched were the doors."

Tom arched a coolly assessing brow at Marcus. "And you agree with that?"

"It's just like Maggie said," Marcus told him. "We got here and found all of this, just like you see things now. I called the cavalry in. They threatened us with guns. Good times."

Tom ignored the jibe, but I saw the muscle tic in his jaw. "And neither of you knows the manager in any other way?"

I blinked at him. "Are you seriously asking us if we might have any reason to dislike Mr. Locke?"

"Answer the question." His gaze flicked from the notepad in his hands to my face and back again. "Please."

I huffed out my breath and crossed my arms. "No. For your information, I had never met the man before yesterday afternoon."

"Me, either," Marcus grated out between clenched teeth. "Never met the man."

Tom nodded, saying nothing. Over by the office, one of his guys gestured at him. He lifted his chin to acknowledge them. To us, he said, "I'd like the two of you to leave the immediate crime scene area—carefully—but stick around for more questioning."

As soon as he had gone, I fussed to Marcus, "I should have known. I should have known this was not a good idea. It was just another of my not-well-thought-through plans."

"It's not your fault someone decided to whack the poor guy, sweetness. How could you have known?"

"I couldn't. But I'm starting to wonder about this knack I have for running into bad situations. I mean, who wants to be known for that? Maggie the Jinx? No thank you."

"There's no way you can possibly think you're the problem here," Marcus countered. "You have no idea who this man is or what his story is or who he knows. You just have no idea. Or maybe this really was a burglary gone bad. I mean, we didn't think so, but we really do need to leave this to the professionals, huh? The people with all of the connections, who can really get to the bottom of things. The people who are paid to do this. Like Fielding. Let him earn his salary."

Well, I wasn't sure that any of the men on the Stony Mill Police Department set out to become a cop because they wanted to stop killers in their tracks. I doubted that prospect even lit up their radar screens until this last year. Most of them were just ordinary, stand-up guys who wanted a steady job that involved writing traffic tickets and stopping small-time petty criminals. Protect the populace, keep the peace. Not solving murder after murder. I couldn't imagine any of them even guessing that they'd be signing up for that, not even as a possibility. Least of all Tom. He had, at least, tried to rise to the occasion. I would give him that.

And poor Olds, the newbie cop they had referred to. The poor kid had no idea what he was letting himself in for.

I kept my eye on Tom as he conferred with the one of the guys who had been assigned to working the office crime scene. He glanced down at an object in a plastic evidence bag, then held it up in the bright morning sunlight now coming at an angle through the tree leaves. His expression changed on a dime, and as I watched he said something to his fellow officer and headed back toward where Marcus and I had settled onto a park bench.

"So, you didn't know this guy, huh?" he said, addressing the question to Marcus.

"Nope. I didn't know him."

"Never seen him before."

"Nope. Never seen him before."

"Uh-huh." Tom nodded, matter-of-factly. He held up the plastic evidence bag he'd just been handed by the other officer. "So, maybe you can explain this to me."

It was a part of a circuit board that had come out of the computer Marcus had just built for Locke and that Uncle Lou had just delivered the afternoon before. Clearly visible on the back of the board was a label that read "Quinn Enterprises," with Marcus's home address and phone number listed beneath.

Also encased in the bag were many bits and pieces of other broken computer parts, and in the very bottom, what looked like a crushed USB flash drive.

I opened my mouth, but Marcus beat me to it. "I built the computer for him, but I never met the man. He was an acquaintance of my uncle, Lou Tabor. He was looking for some high-powered computer tech, and I was able to provide it." Marcus shrugged. "In fact, I just finished it. Uncle Lou delivered it yesterday."

"With me," I interjected. "He delivered it when he brought me here to meet with Locke about the apartment."

Tom was once again scratching things down in his notepad. "Uh-huh. The apartment you were about to sign the lease for. Which we found in the dead man's pocket." I knew he didn't *really* believe that I had anything to do with Locke's death, but the way he kept restating the point was really starting to tick me off. "And how did all of that come about, again? All of these weird . . . connections?"

There was that word again. *Weird.* Unfortunately, I really couldn't deny that as fact. Sometimes the way things came about . . . it was weird. I couldn't explain it. Not in any way that a normal, mundane person would be able to grasp and believe in. A very religious person, on the other hand? Well, maybe, although then we'd be drawn into discussions on the wrath of God, when really any godly wrath was simply man projecting human characteristics like revenge and jealousy on a divine being or entity or force that had always stood completely beyond man's comprehension. Even now. Maybe especially now.

I cleared my throat. The only thing to do was try. "Well, you see, it's like this. I found out yesterday that Steff—you remember my best friend, Steff, who lives in the apartment upstairs—well, she's ninety-nine percent sure that she's going to be moving out of town when her fiancé's residency program at the hospital is complete. Which will be soon. So, with her leaving and Marcus going back to school for his degree, I decided now would be a good time for a change of scenery for me, too. A new place, a new perspective on life. You know. That kind of thing." I checked his face, hoping to find understanding there, but all I saw was a closed sort of neutrality. I had to keep trying. "Anyway, Uncle Lou—that's Marcus's Uncle Lou—he mentioned this place, and he kind of arranged the whole meet-and-greet with Mr. Locke, and it was just a big coincidence that Marcus had just built a computer for this guy that Uncle Lou needed to deliver, and with Locke managing an apartment complex that had an available property for me to look at . . . well . . . it seemed kind of meant to be."

"Uh-*huh*." More scratching on the notepad. I wondered if that was a good thing or a bad thing. Oh, for heaven's sake, it couldn't be bad. I had nothing to do with any of this, and he knew me too well to believe that I had. "So, you just came here and looked at the apartment."

"Yes, I did!" I replied, starting to get a little hot under the collar myself. "That is exactly what I did."

"And what was Mr. Locke's state of mind during your meeting?"

"Normal? I don't know him, but he seemed pretty normal to me. I mean, as normal as anyone else seems. I mean . . ." What did I mean? "What I'm trying to say is, he didn't act like anything was wrong. Except . . ." What about the argument with that guy, Hollister? I supposed that was something Tom would want to know, but why-oh-why was I the one who had to witness it? He was tied to Annie Miller's niece. Her boyfriend. Sigh. I really needed to talk to Annie.

Tom was all over my hedging. His sharp gray eyes watched me closely. "Except?"

I wasn't going to have a choice. "Except . . . I did witness a disagreement he had with a very upset tenant while I was there in his office," I told him, reluctance and guilt poking at my psyche all the while. "A man named Tyson Hollister. I don't know if he's the tenant or if his girlfriend is the tenant of the apartment, but . . . her name is Angela Miller. She's Annie Miller's niece."

"You should have mentioned this first thing, Maggie. What was the altercation about?"

The look on Marcus's face said he very much agreed with that sentiment.

I took a deep breath. "It was about the lease. I was trying not to listen—"

"Uh-huh."

"—but it's hard not to unintentionally eavesdrop when someone stands six feet away from you and insists on having it out in your presence!" I finished, a wee bit defensive. "It's not like I was given a choice."

"Hm. Go on."

"Well, evidently Ms. Miller is wanting out of her lease, and Mr. Locke was refusing to allow her an out. Mr. Hollister was adamant that the lease was unethical, not allowing a tenant any way out if they wanted or needed to leave."

"Huh. Unethical maybe, but unfortunately it is standard business practice for apartment complexes these days." When I raised my brows in inquiry, Tom grunted, "I had to sign one, too."

"My apartment on Willow Street allows for the tenant to terminate with thirty days advance notice, in writing," I said. "It's always been that way. I didn't even have to ask for the clause to be written into the agreement."

"Then count yourself lucky. I'm not sure when this particular real estate trend started, but it has caused a lot of problems for a lot of people. All upholdable by law in civil court."

"I guess people just aren't supposed to have emergencies or extenuating circumstances these days."

"You got that right. No excuses." Then, because he had lost the thrust of the inquiries, he cleared his throat and frowned. "Back to the questions at hand. You say that Mr. Hollister was adamant. How adamant?"

"Well, Uncle Lou had to drag him out of the office. There was a little bit of a scuffle. Lou collared him and dragged him outside to get some air, cool down a bit."

"What happened then?"

"Locke and I went to look at the apartment. By the time we were finished, Mr. Hollister was nowhere to be seen." I shrugged. "I figured Lou had done his thing and diffused the situation, and that was that."

"So, this Uncle Lou didn't stay with you the entire time?"

"No, he waited outside until we were done."

"And that was it? That was all there was to the encounter?"

"Maggie," Marcus interrupted softly, "what about the girl?"

Tom looked at him, hard. "Girl?" He transferred his gaze to me. "What girl?"

With all the events of the morning, I'd almost forgotten. "When I was touring the apartment, we—Locke and me, that is—thought we heard a sound. Locke went to investigate the noise, and I stayed in the doorway, waiting for him."

"And?"

"Well . . . as it turns out, there actually was an intruder in the apartment. A young girl. She had been hiding in the front closet, just a few feet from where I stood. As soon as she felt safe enough, I guess, she burst out of the closet and ran. She nearly knocked me down in the process."

Tom took this all in, and by the time I was done, he shook his head. "You know, you live a really . . . *unusual* . . . life, Maggie O'Neill."

I lifted my shoulders in a helpless shrug. "I can't help it. It isn't me. I don't invite it, you know."

Once again, his gaze flicked left to Marcus, then back again. "Uh-huh."

Now he was questioning my lifestyle? *Feh.* I looked him square in the eye. "No offense, Tom, but I don't think I'm the one you need to be worrying about here. Someone killed that man, and it sure as heck wasn't me. And what's more, you know it. I would think you would be more concerned about that person than wasting time harassing your crazy ex-girlfriend." I arched an eyebrow at him for good measure.

"Point taken. So, what can you tell me about this girl?"

"Not much," I said. "It happened so fast. She nearly knocked me over when she came out of the closet like that. I wasn't expecting it . . . but then, I guess, neither was she." I explained how she'd paused just for a moment before she hit the door running.

"Would you recognize her?"

"Well, yeah."

"What did she look like?"

"Young. A teenager. Very blond, almost platinum. Hair in braids, wearing a baseball cap or something like it. Green eyes."

He stopped writing. "You actually noticed her eye color?"

I pictured her face as I was falling backward, as her face had turned toward mine, almost in slow motion. "We had a moment."

"I guess so."

"No, I mean . . . time seemed to freeze for a second there as I was falling, and I locked onto her staring into my eyes. So, yeah, I noticed. The image kind of screen printed itself onto my brain."

"And then what?" Tom asked.

"She took off. Exit, stage left. Locke came out to see what all the noise was. I told him about the girl, he took off after her. But she was already gone, so he came back in."

"Did he say anything?"

I closed my eyes, trying to remember. "He said something about teenage hijinks and that vandalism was always a risk in this business when there were empty apartments at hand. Locke did find a broken mirror in the apartment, though. He was pretty upset about it."

"Anything else that you remember?"

"Only that Uncle Lou knows the girl—he's a teacher at the high school," I explained. "He said her name was Abbie Cornwall, I believe. And . . . we saw her just down the road a little later as we were leaving. She was at the park with her boyfriend."

"Did you say anything?"

I blinked at him. "No way. But Lou was thinking about talking to her counselor at school about the whole thing. He said she was a good kid, but this was the kind of behavior that needs to be nipped in the bud before it becomes a habit."

"Uh-huh." *Scratchy, scratchy, scratchy.* Someone needed to give this man a gel pen. "So, let me get this straight one more time. You were going to sign a lease for an apartment that you had never heard about before yesterday, at an apartment building where a tenant was complaining in front of you about the terms of the lease, where there was a girl hiding in the closet who nearly knocked you over, and the manager said this is all just fun and games, just part and parcel of running an apartment complex?"

Well, when he put it like that . . . I just nodded. What else could I do? It was the truth.

He squinted at me—or was that against the morning sun that was now glinting off his sunglasses? "Um . . . why?"

Marcus looked like he might be wondering the same thing, although he had the good manners not to say it out loud.

"It was a really good deal," I said, coming to my own defense.

"It would have to be," Tom replied.

"Three months' free rent, no security deposit, and a temporary lease to be sure I would like the place before signing my life away."

Tom chewed on this tidbit for a moment, frowning. "Why on earth would an apartment complex need to issue deals like that to entice prospective tenants?" he asked at last. "I've never heard of a deal like that being offered. To anyone. Anywhere."

I started to respond, but all of a sudden his questions had me wondering, too. Now that I had a chance to think without pressure. "He was a lodge brother with Marcus's Uncle Lou. At the Eternal Order of Samaritans. That was his explanation for offering me the special get-acquainted rent deal. It was the same way Lou hooked him up with Marcus for the computer. Lodge brothers take care of their own. I told him I would have to look over the lease. That I would need some time to think it over. That was late yesterday afternoon," I said slowly. "He called me an hour or two later to let me know someone else was interested in the apartment. He said if I was interested, he wanted to offer me first chance at it, but if I was willing to let it go, there was another interested party who was ready to sign a lease, and no hard feelings. I know what it sounds like," I said, avoiding his gaze, "but it felt like the right thing to do last night." At least, I thought it did. Now, though, I wasn't so sure.

"He had another interested party. If that's true, it could be important. We're trying to establish his comings and goings last night. We'll be checking phone records to see who all he had contact with right up to the estimated time of death."

That piece of information would come from the medical examiner, but by the brief glimpse I had had of Locke's face, he had been in the water since last night. At least that was my non-medically guesstimated opinion.

"From what I gathered yesterday afternoon," I told him, trying to be helpful, "he was itching to set up the new equipment from Marcus. He seemed very excited to have it. Whether he had further plans, I don't know."

Tom nodded. To Marcus he said, "I'll need you to write down Lou Tabor's address and contact information. And I need the two of you to stick around a little bit longer, if you would."

I nodded. "Of course."

Tom started to walk away, then turned back on an afterthought. "Oh. One more thing. The flash drive that was picked up from the office. Something you provided him?"

Marcus shook his head. "No, sorry. Never seen it before. It must have belonged to Locke, I would guess. But I'm sure that will be more clear once you access it."

Tom grimaced. "It was crushed underfoot."

"It may still be accessible," Marcus told him. "If the memory chips remained intact within, you may still be able to get to the data."

For the first time I had known the two of them, they

locked gazes with something other than testosterone-driven dislike. Just before he turned away again, I heard Tom mutter, "Thanks," so softly that it might have been the wind.

Might have been. But wasn't.

Could that be change I hear in that non-wind?

A girl could only hope.

Chapter 8

Marcus and I were silent as we continued to wait. And watch. And listen. Shamelessly. I couldn't deny that part of myself that had been roused the moment the investigation started proceeding around us. How could I fight such an intrinsic part of my true nature, an insatiable curiosity about the world as it transpired around me? So while the officers did their things around us, I pretended not to be paying attention . . . but I was taking note of everything within earshot. In detail. I saw the bloody hand weight being bagged as evidence. And I knew that two guys had been enlisted to sweep the office for evidence and prints, just as I knew that two more were going door-to-door at the apartment complex, asking for residents to come down and give preliminary statements about anything they might have witnessed last night, or at any other time, and what they might know about the man who had managed the apartment complex. There were only a couple of residents home at present, but they all came down as requested, each speaking with the particular officer they had been assigned to.

Marcus was taking all of this in as well, I noticed.

He put on his sunglasses when he caught me watching him . . . but it was too late.

"What?" I asked him, transferring my gaze suspiciously back and forth between him and the . . .

Female residents. The young, pretty, female residents of the apartment complex.

"So you've noticed," he said as a lightbulb went off in my head.

"I noticed." I gave him a haughty tilt of my nose. "Your shades aren't dark enough."

He laughed and tipped my chin back toward him. "Your jealousy is showing. Don't you trust me?"

He was right, and I knew it. And the thing was, I did trust him. He had never given me a single reason not to. Not as a friend, and not as a boyfriend. I sighed and made a face, feeling foolish and yet still vulnerable. "They're all very . . . pretty."

"That's what I noticed. And before you slug me," he said, grinning, "what I mean by that is . . . well, what are the odds? It makes me wonder what the rest of the residents are going to look like. Or do you think by some strange chance that the prettiest ones just happened to be the ones who were at home this morning?"

It did seem to be a long shot. "So what does that tell us? That Locke liked to rent to pretty girls?"

He leaned in close to me, smiling into my eyes. "Very pretty girls," he said, giving me a quick kiss on my nose.

Hm. While it was nice to be included in that category by default, my brain was still trying to work out whether that was a good thing or a bad thing to be thought of as pretty by a somewhat seedy character like Locke. A manager he may have been, but the vibe he had given off hadn't been what I would call completely respectable. Maybe it was the tie. Any man who would wear a hula girl on a tie was either a jokester, old and on the verge of senility, or a reprobate.

Or, to be fair, maybe the guy just had an odd sense of humor.

I recognized one of the residents from yesterday's apartment tour. The upstairs neighbor, the teacher with the tight bod and the face full of well-applied makeup. I saw her there amid the others. The officers must have caught her on her way out the door, because school should now be just starting. Lucky her. She stood with her arms crossed and her high heel *tap-tap-tapping*, so I was pretty sure she knew she was late.

"Excuse me," she said, finally bursting in on the conversation the officer was having with the leggy blond just ahead of her, whose teddy-bear-and-daisy covered cotton shift and white pants hinted at an occupation in the health field. "I have to get going. I'm really late. I was expected in a half hour ago."

"Sorry, ma'am," the young officer told her. "We have to ask questions of any and all residents."

"Well, is there anyone else who could take my statement?" she asked. "Anyone at all? I really do have to get to school."

"I'll be finished here with this young lady in just a few minutes," he told her.

She nodded, but I could see the exasperation in her raised shoulders and clenched jaw. I couldn't blame her really. A lot of employers will tell you there is no excuse for lateness, that you should budget in extra time for surprises. I couldn't imagine anyone having the foresight to plan in enough time for a dead body and a police investigation, though. A person would have to be psychic . . . and if a person were "connected" enough to anticipate today's event, they would have made plans to be elsewhere.

Finally the officer finished with the blond and beckoned for the teacher. "Sorry for the delay, miss. I appreciate your patience."

Stepping forward, she nodded. "I don't mean to be impatient, but with budget cuts, the administration strongly discourages absences from its teachers. As I haven't acquired tenure yet, my neck could easily be one on the chopping block if any teaching positions are to be eliminated. You understand."

"Sorry about that. Could you please state and spell your name, and tell me your occupation and your apartment number here."

"Alexandra Cooper." She spelled it for him. "I'm an English teacher at Stony Mill High. I live in apartment 1C."

After writing down all of this information, the officer looked up around him, attempting to locate her apartment and the vantage point that had come with it. She helpfully gestured toward her apartment windows. "Ms. Cooper, can you tell me where you were yesterday evening?"

"I was here, at my apartment. I left for a short time to pick up a pizza from Pizza Sam's and to drop off a library book, but for the most part I was here in my apartment, grading papers with some romantic comedy on in the background."

"And did you see the apartment manager, Mr. Locke, at any point in time yesterday evening?"

She shrugged. "I saw him once when I was glancing out the window, but I try not to see him at all, if you catch my meaning." When the young officer lifted his brows in question to prompt her, she explained, "Mr. Locke was a pleasant enough man, but . . . he was odd. The less time I spent in his company, the more comfortable I was."

"So you didn't have a friendly relationship with him?"

"I didn't have any sort of relationship with him at all," she said calmly. "He was flirtatious, but I think he was that way with all of the girls here at the complex. To tell you the truth, he made me uneasy. But that could just be me."

"How did he make you uneasy?"

She shrugged again. "Can anyone explain the feelings a person gives them? That's just what it was. A feeling."

"Did you see anything last night that, considering the circumstances, might be of help to us in our investigation? Did you see the victim with anyone?"

She shook her head. "Not later. Just as I was arriving home, I saw him come out of an apartment with that girl over there." She nodded her head in my direction. "I imagine he was showing her the apartment in 1A, below mine. She seemed to have been coming from that general direction. And Locke evicted the woman who had been living there with one of my students, just a few weeks ago."

"Evicted?"

"I don't know why. I never asked Abbie. Cornwall is her last name. She's a difficult girl. Rebellious. I see her lurking around here sometimes still. In fact, I thought I saw her yesterday, just down the road, on my way home. You might want to check with her, in the event that she was here later."

"I'll check into that. You didn't see anyone else who might have seemed out of place to you? Any vehicles? Anything at all?"

Her impatient gaze said it all. "This is an apartment complex, Officer. Filled with young women. There are vehicles coming and going all the time, day and night. I can't say that I would recognize a strange vehicle unless it tried to run me down in the parking lot."

"Ever seen Locke with anyone?"

"No."

"What about your neighbors? Ever seen Locke spending time with any of them?"

"No. Listen, Officer, I really think I've given you all the information I have to give. If I weren't already late, I'd be happy to stay and answer any question you can come up with, but I really do need to get to work. I am giving a big test second period, and I need time to run off the copies for the students."

He let her go this time, taking her phone number and asking her to please call if she thought of anything at all that might be of help in the investigation, no matter how small. I was about to approach Tom and ask him if we could be excused as well when someone unexpected crossed my path.

Jeremy Harding.

As in, Liss's ex-brother-in-law.

What on earth was *he* doing here?

I poked Marcus with my elbow to get his attention. "Do you see what I see?"

He leaned close to me, pressing his lips against my ear. "What? Or who?"

Jeremy Harding had been estranged from Liss ever since the previous fall, when his late wife, Isabella, fell victim in the very first murder that had taken place in Stony Mill in my entire lifetime. Liss had very nearly been indicted for the death of her own sister thanks to some sketchy circumstantial evidence . . . but to be completely truthful, her falling out with her brother-in-law had happened well before the real killer was discovered. Theirs was not a relationship based on mutual trust and admiration. And, having met the man once before, I could see why. He wasn't exactly a warm and fuzzy kind of guy. In the meantime, however, he hadn't seen fit to put his postmodern monstrosity of a house up for sale. He and Liss were still neighbors in their respective Victoria Park country homes, both anomalous among their more traditional farmhouse neighbors, though I think each probably wished the other would find a reason to leave.

I didn't have time to wonder out loud why Jeremy Harding would appear at the site of a brand new murder investigation. As it turned out, I didn't need to wonder. He provided that tidbit of information all on his lonesome.

He stalked out into the middle of the proceedings in his expensive suit and dark sunglasses and, using the voice of someone used to presenting a front of authority, demanded, "Who's in charge here?"

Tom separated from the officers who were working the crime scene and came forward. "That would be me. Special Task Force Investigator Fielding. Who are you?"

"Jeremy Harding. I own this apartment complex."

Wow. Talk about strange connections and coinkidinks. Wait 'til Liss heard about this.

While I was trying to process the day's most recent wrinkle, Tom said, "I'm assuming you will be able to provide some sort of identification to that effect."

He took out his identification and presented it to Tom. Tom gave his business card the once-over and began writing down all the information.

"Keep it," Harding snapped. "Just tell me what the hell is going on here."

Tom kept his cool. As a matter of fact, he was cold as ice. "Why don't you tell me what you know, sir?"

An irritable Harding said, "I received a phone call from my

assistant, who had fielded a call at the office from one of your people. All I know is that there has been some sort of accident on the premises, so I hurried over . . . to find all of this. So I ask you again, Officer . . . Fielding, is it? What is going on here?"

Tom had lowered the pitch of his voice, but as they were grandstanding a mere fifteen feet from us, we heard him well enough. "Your manager here has been the victim of an attack."

"Locke?" Harding barked. "Well, where is he? Is he all right? Is he being taken to the hospital? How serious of an attack are we talking?"

Tom cleared his throat. "Mr. Locke has been killed, sir."

Six little words were all it took to strip the bite out of Harding's bark. His mouth fell open. His face paled in the slanting morning light. "Locke is dead?"

"That's what I've been trying to tell you, sir."

"H-how? When?"

"Last night. The medical examiner's office is preparing to remove his body from the premises as we speak."

"Here." Harding closed his eyes and scrubbed a palm down over his mouth and chin. "Here."

"Sir, how much do you know about your employee?"

Harding shook his head. "As much as any absentee employer knows about their employees, I would imagine. We performed the usual background checks as to his work record. His prior experience claims checked out, so we trusted him to perform his job as required."

"I see. Because you see, sir, a funny thing came up when we ran Mr. Locke through our system."

"Oh yes?"

"Mm. Were you aware, sir, that your employee had a prior arrest record?"

Harding's eyebrows shot up. I had to say, mine did as well. When I realized it, I tried harder to maintain the disinterested face of neutrality. "No," Harding was saying. "No, I was not aware of that."

Tom's smile did not reach his eyes. "Perhaps that fact eluded your check. Tell me, sir, what had you managed to find out about your employee during the period he worked for you?"

I couldn't help noticing that every time Tom used the words "your employee," Harding's lips tightened perceptibly. "Decent manager. Turned in his reports and spreadsheets promptly. Didn't appropriate funds for his own benefit. Single. No family that he ever spoke of. Any of this helping you, Officer?"

Tom's expression remained cool. "Not really. What do you know of your employee's schedule yesterday?"

"Nothing at all. Locke maintained his own schedule. He knew what he was responsible for, and that dictated his schedule as required. I wasn't involved one way or the other."

"So you couldn't tell me if he had a late appointment last night."

"Sorry, no."

"The damage in the office. I'll need someone to walk through and categorize what has been destroyed or missing."

At the word "damage," Harding tensed visibly. "I'll do that now. If you're finished questioning me, that is."

"For the time being," Tom conceded. He leaned his head down to speak into his shoulder mike, then told Harding, "Officers Hayden and Olds are working the office. They will assist you. I'll head that way in a few minutes."

Before I could say or do anything to attract Tom's attention, he moved back to the pool area while Harding headed over to the office.

"How long do you think they're going to keep us here?" I asked Marcus.

"I doubt it will be too much longer," Marcus assured me. "They've already taken what information we have. It's not like they don't know where we live or how to get in touch."

"True."

It would have been true, if Harding hadn't reemerged from the office straightaway, clearly on a tear. "Excuse me, but . . . the computer is missing. Locke's computer," I heard him say, faint but distinct.

"Yes, sir," the young officer—Olds?—acknowledged. "The computer was shattered to bits by whoever did this. Or an accomplice. That hasn't been ruled out, of course."

Harding gritted his teeth. "That computer holds key business records," he ranted. "Damn it, I need those files. How am I supposed to piece together Locke's recent receipts and expenditures without them?"

"Gee, I don't know, sir. Shame, too, about the computer. It was brand new, I understand."

"And where are the backup drives? Did they take those, too? Hold on a sec." Harding frowned. "What did you say?"

"I said, it's a shame about the computer, with it being so new and all."

"No, you're mistaken. The computer wasn't new."

"Sure it was, sir. Locke paid for a new one just yesterday, as I understand it. Bought it from that gentleman over there." Officer Olds pointed in our direction.

Harding turned on his heel and, leaving the good officer in the dust, stalked toward us. "Uh-oh," I told Marcus. "Head's up."

Marcus rose to meet him.

"Now you just hold on a minute," Harding commanded,

holding up a hand to stop him. "Yeah, you. I need to talk to you a minute."

"What can I do for you?"

Harding stopped in front of Marcus and planted his hands on his hips. "Well, for starters you can tell me who authorized the computer I understand you provided to my employee here."

Harding was making an ass of himself, but as I recalled, that was nothing new. "Mr. Locke authorized it himself, sir," Marcus explained, the soul of patience.

"Locke didn't have authorization to purchase new equipment. Where's the old computer? You have that, too?"

"No, sir. The computer was a rebuild complete with revved-up hard drive and processor, using the existing chassis."

"You telling me you got rid of my old property?" Harding's face had taken on an ugly purple-red hue.

"No, sir, what I'm telling you is that the computer that was smashed *was* your old computer with some new and improved inner parts."

"Fine. That's just great. That's just wonderful. Computer destroyed, backup externals missing. Christ on a motorbike. I won't pay you, I hope you realize that. Locke didn't have my approval for a big-ticket item."

"Locke already paid me," Marcus said, his smile cold and rock hard. "In cash."

Marcus stood back while Harding let out a string of curse words that would have made my Grandma Cora reach for the nearest tree switch. "That figures," Harding ranted, beginning to pace in small, tight circles, "that just figures. This just gets better and better."

Marcus let Harding sweat things out a bit longer, winking back at me when the tirade became particularly heated, before he said, "If it would help you, I did return the old hard drive to Mr. Locke when my uncle delivered the computer. They were in a large plastic zipper bag. You might have a look around for them. Maybe they came through this ordeal unscathed. It's possible whoever targeted both Locke and the office might not have found them, huh?"

"You think so?" Harding quieted instantly, latching onto the thought. "A plastic bag, you say. Hm."

"If they didn't make the connection, then, yeah. It's as good a possibility as any."

"You might be right, at that. As soon as they let me in there, I'll tear the place apart myself if I have to. I have to have those files." Harding took notice of me there for the first time. "Aren't you . . ." He narrowed his eyes into an assessing squint. "Don't I know you?"

I cleared my throat. "Um, I don't—" I glanced up at Marcus, looking for help and wishing I had blended into the background the instant Harding arrived on scene.

"I do know you. You're the one who's working with Felicity Dow, aren't you?" It wasn't so much a question as an accusation, and the hardness in his voice when he said Liss's name assured that the animosity he'd felt for his former sister-in-law had not cooled over the past several months. "You showed up at the funeral with her."

I had, indeed. I nodded. I had no choice.

"And what, may I ask, are you doing here?"

"I was supposed to sign a lease for apartment 1A," I admitted. "I toured it yesterday, and Locke had asked me to stop by this morning."

"No lease."

I blinked at him. "Beg pardon?"

"No lease. Not for you. We prefer renting to respectable people."

Marcus bristled at this intended slight. "That's not fair—" he started to say in my defense, but I placed my hand on his arm.

"It's all right, Marcus. I'll think of something else. I wouldn't want to stay in a place that wasn't safe. Maybe this was a blessing in disguise. A sign," I said. We both knew the kind I meant. A sign from above. A cosmic sign from my otherworldly Guides.

Now you're talking, Margaret Mary-Catherine O'Neill, the voice of my grandmother intoned faintly in my ear. *You listen to me. I'll steer you right.*

And for once I had reason to trust her. It. Them. Whatever it was that used my grandmother's voice and personality to communicate. For once it really seemed to have my back. The timing of everything in the last two days had been too down-to-the-wire to think it had been left up to chance.

Tom was heading back toward us, an unreadable expression blanking his face. What now?

"Good," Harding said as soon as he realized Tom was coming to talk to us. He hailed him. "Officer Fielding, I told your man that the backup drives are missing as well. I don't know if they're part of the mess that's all over the office floor right now or not, but I need those files. This man here"—he indicated Marcus with a flick of his thumb—"says that the old hard drive was delivered with the computer yesterday. *I need to find that drive.* I'd like your permission to sweep through the office once your men are done to try to locate those parts."

Tom listened with his usual stoic expression beneath the mirrored aviators. "Sorry. I'm afraid that will be impossible."

"But—"

"Need I remind you, sir, this site is now an active investigation. A violent crime was perpetrated on these premises. I'm afraid our investigation takes precedence."

"Officer Fielding, that hard drive is integral to the running of this business—"

"And I'm sure that a day or two to process things won't strain your business proceedings unduly," Tom finished for him.

"But—"

"As soon as we are able to release the area, we will. You'll be the first to know, I assure you."

Harding knew he was at the mercy of the law, and he was experienced enough to realize he had no choice in the matter. Being at the mercy of anyone or anything didn't seem to be a state of being he was remotely comfortable with. He hemmed and hawed and shifted his weight from foot to foot as he considered arguing his case, but eventually his shoulders relaxed and he acceded. "Could you at least ask your men to look for the missing hard drive?" he asked, almost a whine by now. "Not to belabor a point, but I just discovered from this man Quinn that it's possible it was missed by the perpetrators in their war of mass destruction, and if so . . . well, I'm sure you can understand that I'm eager to get my hands on it. Can you at least have them alert me if they are able to locate the hard drive?"

Tom shook his head. "I'm sorry, sir, but I can't make any promises. If the drive shows up, I'm afraid it will have to be taken in as evidence."

"What?!" Harding exploded. "Oh, *hell* no. I am willing to cooperate for the sake of decency, but this I will fight you on, pure and simple."

"Sir . . ." It was a warning, pure and simple. Marcus and I looked at each other, eyebrows raised, wondering whether we should get out of the way.

"This is business I'm talking about. How am I supposed

to conduct business if I can't obtain my own files?" Harding persisted stubbornly. "You want to tell me that?"

"Sir, *I* don't mean to belabor a point, but a man was killed here last night on *your* business property. Need I remind you, he was one of your own employees? Decency doesn't begin to cover what is required here. A little compassion wouldn't be out of line. If there is any chance that there is information on the hard drive that can assist us in our investigation, any chance at all, our team will find it. Then and only then will access to the files be granted to you. Now, instead of wasting my time, I suggest you use your aggravation and impatience for a good cause and give the full measure of your assistance over to our investigative team to solve this crime quickly, hm?" Turning his back on Harding, who was still sputtering, he faced me. "Maggie, you two can go for now. If I need anything more from you, I'll let you know. I will need you to give a complete signed statement up at the PD, but you can do that later today or tomorrow."

I nodded to let him know that I understood. "Tom . . . I hope you find who did this, fast. I know you might not believe me, but it honestly was just a coincidence that I was here today. Nothing spooky, I promise."

He looked at me, but he didn't say anything. At least I didn't feel the outright animosity from him at that moment. Maybe that was another sign that he was softening.

"Ready?" Marcus asked me as Tom walked away. I nodded, more than ready to put some distance between us and Harding and all the negative energy that was sparking like firebombs around him.

Chapter 9

I was silent as we slowly made our way back to Marcus's old pickup truck, Marcus matching his long-legged gait to my slower progress. Out in the parking lot, we saw a city news crew rush Chief Boggs as he exited his police SUV. He must have come by way of Annie's, stopping in for his usual morning treat, if the paper bag in his hand was any indication. The thought made me smile. Mostly because of how easily it could be true. Annie's plate-sized apple and blueberry fritters were well known for being his sweet-spot downfall. I couldn't help wondering what he was telling the reporter. He hadn't even stepped one foot onto the crime scene as yet.

The ride to Enchantments was more than quiet. Marcus and I both fell into a silence born of the strangeness of the moment and the uncertainty of the immediate future. Because all of my plans that had seemed so straightforward yesterday were now all for nothing. How did that always happen? There had to be a lesson in there somewhere. Maybe I wasn't supposed to plan. Maybe I was supposed to learn to go with the flow. Have faith, ask for help, and let things unfold. Maybe.

Or maybe I was just trying to talk myself into it, since I had no other choice.

Could be. I wouldn't put it past me. I'm sure my Guides would even agree.

By the time we got to the store, Marcus had shaken off his silence. He took my hand and squeezed it. "You okay, Maggie?"

"Yeah. I'm all right." I mustered a smile for him. "Despite appearances otherwise, all will be well."

"And all will be well, and all manner of things shall be well," he said, finishing off my quote for me. He wagged my hand reassuringly back and forth. "It will. You know that, right?"

I told him I did as I kissed him good-bye for the day. But I wasn't sure how it would be made right. I was in a funk as I made my way over the threshold into the store I loved so well, feeling as though I'd just lost my best friend. Which was ridiculous. All I had lost was my sense of forward motion, of purpose tied to solution. Which meant I was back to stage one. Nowhere viable to live without taking advantage of Marcus's far-reaching good graces and willingness to self-sacrifice, or taking myself home to face my mother's I-told-you-so. Neither of which were particularly acceptable to me. I knew the apartment was lost to me, and obviously it wasn't as good a deal as it had initially seemed—yes, that was an understatement—but gosh, just having a solution had felt so good.

And of course, flawed a character as he might be, Locke had lost far more than I had today.

I buried all of that and put on my freshest, brightest face. "Sorry, I'm a little bit late," I called out to Liss, who I could hear rattling around somewhere within. I checked the time on my cell phone as I dropped my things on the counter and was surprised to find I was only a minute or two behind the official store opening hours. So much had happened in such a short amount of time that it actually felt much later than it was. I was worried it was nearing eleven. That sort of made Miss Cooper, English teacher, sound a little time paranoid, but I supposed what she said about admin watching their every move was probably true. These were strange and difficult times.

"Is that you, ducks?" Liss called, her voice sounding muffled.

"Yes, it's me," I called back. "I have some terrible news . . ."

"Could you come here and tell me about it, dear? I'm afraid I'm a little tied up at the moment . . ."

I followed the sound of her voice around the stacks to a display area back in the corner that usually held a selection of handmade vintage lace as well as knitwear handcrafted from the wool of sheep raised the organic way by a community of ecowitches in the Scottish Highlands. I wondered sometimes where Liss found all of her more global witchy ties. Her access to the finest artisanry in the witching community seemed positively unlimited. It was probably a moot point. These were the days of info at the fingertip. The Internet had made the world a very small place indeed.

Liss was evidently in the mood for some rearranging of space. I came around the far ceiling-high shelves to find her up on a stepladder, a drill in hand, stretching toward a point on the wall that was beyond her reach. "Liss! What on earth are you doing? Do you have a death wish that I was previously not made aware of?"

"Shh," she said, laughing at herself. "Don't fuss. Just hold the ladder, please."

"Shouldn't we have someone else do that?" I asked her. "Someone taller, perhaps?"

"I would, darling, but Marcus is, generally speaking, my resident handyman, and he isn't here at present. Could you be a love and hand me that bag of cup hooks there?"

"Sure, but don't lean out that way again. You're freaking me out." I put one crutch down and handed her the bag. "What exactly are we doing?"

"Just wanting to hang some pretty swags of twinkle lights over here. I'm thinking on my feet this morning. I was thinking I might make this little corner into a serenity nook for our customers to read or meditate in. Something comfortable and cushioned that they can sink down into and lose themselves in for a few moments of sheer loveliness. What do you think?" she asked, gazing down at me over her gold-rimmed half-moon glasses.

"Well," I told her, "if our customers don't like it, you can send me to the corner any time that you like. I think it sounds wonderful. A haven to escape to when their workday has been trying to beat them into submission is going to go over like the moon over water."

"I think it will, too. I do love giving our customers special moments. Now, what was it you were about to tell me, dear? Bad news, you said? Nothing too terrible, I hope."

I held up a cup hook to her. "There was another murder."

"Oh. Oh dear."

"Marcus and I found the body."

She paused with the drill and looked back at me. "Oh my goodness. What happened?"

I told her how I had decided to take the apartment I'd looked at the day previously, and how that single snap decision had changed the course of my planned new reality. I told her how Marcus had taken me to the apartment complex this morning first thing so that I could sign the lease with all the special deals and discounts that had been promised to me, only to find the office in ruins and a dead man floating in the swimming pool. "Yeah," I confirmed when she shook her head, scandalized. "Can you believe it?"

"My. My, my, my. It never fails to amaze me, the myriad connections that the universe comes up with to create synchronicity in our lives. Not," she said when she saw my face, "that that feels like a good thing when one is in the thick of it. Was it too awful, love?"

"It wasn't fun," I admitted. "His face . . ." I shuddered. "That bloaty look. Like he'd gained forty pounds overnight. And the discoloration." It wasn't anything I wanted to see again.

"Do they know anything yet? Who might have wanted to do such a terrible thing?"

"I don't think so. Not yet anyway."

"And it was most definitely . . . murder? Without question?"

I nodded. When combined with the mess in the office, the coincidence factor was just too great. "It was. I know the police are approaching it as such."

"Ahh." Matter-of-fact realization flickered behind her signature glasses. "So you saw Tom."

"Yes."

"And how did that go?"

I shrugged. "He still hates me."

"Oh, my dear, I'm sure that's not true. The line between love and hate is so very fine. It takes but a moment, a blip in time, to cross that line."

"Yes, well, I think he's treading that line." I made a face. "I would feel worse about breaking up with him if we hadn't been having major personality differences beforehand. And he had been stepping out with his not-ex-wife even before, although I didn't find that out until later of course." He had.

Annie Miller had mentioned an evening date between Tom and his not-quite-ex Julie and had reluctantly clued me in, though at the time she hadn't known exactly what she was seeing . . . only that she had seen him out on an intimate evening with another female who wasn't me. But that was weeks ago, and the past was the past. Or at least I wanted it to be. It didn't mean anything to me now. It didn't matter in the slightest. It didn't burn me at all that his not-ex-wife was pretty and pixie thin and able to wear the kind of clothes that made her look feminine and elegant but would make me resemble the Stay Puft Marshmallow Man. Nope. Not me.

Liss smiled her best Mona Lisa smile and turned back to her work. "Sometimes things happen because they are meant to happen, darling. Sometimes we have difficulty seeing beyond the day-to-day in our lives. We have trouble interpreting the signs."

I knew she was right. Our Guides were always working behind the scenes for us. Only they had the farsightedness to see beyond the traumas and dramas of our day-to-day to the future we were meant to have, and if we listened to that still, small voice within us, they would guide us to our futures with the kind of ease we often longed for but so rarely achieved.

Poor Mr. Locke. Was he guilty of not paying attention to his own still, small voice within? Would his Guides have led him out of this particular danger if he'd but listened? Or was this particular end something that was inescapable, due to the path he'd set into motion with a sequence of choices made, options enacted?

"The apartment wasn't meant to be for you, darling. Obviously that is true. You made a quick decision based on the facts at hand, but your ability to think things through was muddied by the manager himself and his prodding. If it had been meant to be, everything would have gone off without a hitch, things falling into place like clockwork."

The only thing that had fallen into place like clockwork was the accelerating weirdness leading up to Locke's death.

"Tom wasn't meant for you, either."

I gave her a sharp, surprised glance. "No, I know he wasn't." And it wasn't that. It wasn't.

In my mind's eye, I pictured that moment in the hospital, weeks ago, when Tom had walked in on me, with his ex-wife on his arm. The discomfort of the realization that he had gone back to the woman who had broken his heart. The pang of awkwardness—not jealousy, honestly not that—when my eyes met hers and I knew she knew who I was, too.

No, it was much better that Tom found someone whose personal energies blended with his own, rather than clashing with it as mine sometimes did thanks to . . . differences . . . in personal philosophies. And better for me, for all the same reasons.

"Good," Liss said firmly. "Far too often we beat ourselves up for things that are simply part of our lesson plan. Now. Tell me more about what happened this morning."

"I will, if you come down off the ladder and let me make you a cup of tea."

"Aren't you the little manipulator?" she said with a chuckle. "But I think you're supposed to be putting your foot up as much as possible, aren't you? How about if I make us both a cup of tea and you do just that?"

"All right, fine. If you're going to be that way about it," I teased her right back. I hopped along behind her as she made her way back toward the front of the store and the coffee and tea bar that was my favorite home away from home. Annie's café had sent over its usual delivery of plate-sized fritters—

apple and blueberry cream cheese, yum—and a selection of beignettes and cream-filled crepes and scones. Ever virtuous, I turned away from the carb fest that was calling me home by reminding myself that I hadn't exactly been able to work out of late to make up for it. Sigh.

"Tell me. What's your poison of choice this morning?"

I turned my eyes ceilingward, thinking. "Hm. Something soothing and stress relieving."

"I know just the thing. A special blend. I think I'll surprise you."

Liss was the specialist at the shop with regards to the metaphysical healing properties of the gourmet teas and coffees we offered. I knew all of the basics, but Liss's area of expertise was in mixing teas to heal just the thing that ailed you at that very moment. A real gift. One of her many.

Five minutes and she had a steaming teacup sitting in front of me, its aroma wafting up on tendrils of steam, fragrant and warm. She poured her own and sat down opposite me, lifting her cup to her lips. "Ah. That's more like it."

"I'll say," I said, breathing it in.

"This gentleman who was killed. What about it made it seem a certain murder? Isn't it feasible that his drowning was accidental?"

"Well, if it wasn't for the office being ransacked as well, I would say yes. Not ransacked. More like purposely and systematically plundered. The door to the office was ajar when Marcus and I got there. At the time we didn't think anything about it. We just thought he must have been there waiting for me to arrive."

"Plundered. What exactly do you mean by 'plundered'?"

"Well," I said, taking a sip of my tea and wincing as it burned my tongue, "the files had been pulled out and scattered all over the floor. And the computer—the brand new, revved-up, and tricked-out computer that Marcus just rebuilt for him—"

"Marcus?"

"I know, just another one of those weird connections that we were talking about, setting itself up while the rest of us weren't paying attention. Anyway, the computer that Marcus just built for him was smashed to bits all over the floor. Completely demolished. All that gorgeous hardware, gone. A real crime."

"Hm." Liss puckered over her teacup, pondering. "You said it seemed targeted. Why would anyone want to destroy the new computer? If their motive was burglary, they wouldn't destroy something of value. If their motive was solely to kill the poor manager, then why stop to destroy the computer? It doesn't make sense to me."

"Me, either. And I don't know. But it definitely seemed that way to me."

"Interesting. Not to diminish the man's death, of course."

Of course. "There were so many odd things that happened yesterday, too, while I was at the apartment complex. So many odd people. I think . . . I don't know what I was thinking last night when I told the manager I'd take the apartment. It just . . . it sounded like such a good deal, and when he called to say that there was someone else interested in taking it, I guess I just lost all common sense. It was stupid, really. Like the guy who was trying to get his girlfriend out of the lease. He was upset because there wasn't a termination clause that allowed for the tenant to terminate the lease with advance notice, it was all one-sided to benefit the apartment complex. The two of them nearly came to blows."

"My goodness."

"And then he turned out to be the boyfriend of Annie Miller's niece. More synchronicities, I guess. And then!"

"Then? I'm on pins and needles."

"Then, after Marcus's Uncle Lou collared the guy and took him down the block to cool off, the manager and I went to take a look at the apartment itself, and we heard a noise from somewhere inside it. Or at least we thought we did. He walked from room to room around the apartment, and just as he went back to the bedroom, some girl nearly knocked me down as she burst out of the entry closet, where she'd been hiding."

"Dear! Did you actually fall?"

I shook my head. "No, but she scared the bejeebers out of me! I dropped my crutch, and when I looked up again, she was gone."

Liss frowned. "I'm not sure I like this. The apartment that you were looking at was actually broken into that day?"

"The manager said it was probably just teenage hijinks and that's all. That it's just a part of doing business these days. Not much that can be done about it. I'm surprised he didn't set up security cameras to prevent such things, or at least catch the perpetrators."

"Well, he's right about there being risks to doing business, but we have had little vandalism here at the store. Or, we had until this morning."

She had said it so matter-of-factly, so absolutely without drama, that I almost went on to the next part of my story. Instead, I caught myself on an up-breath and looked up at her. "What do you mean, we had a little vandalism here this morning?"

"Nothing to worry about, ducks. Someone left a gift for us on the doorstep, that's all."

"What . . . *sort* . . . of gift?" I asked her, frowning.

"Just a little paper parcel of excrement. Nothing to get excited about. I found it as I was unlocking the door." She gave a delicate pause. "The fact that it was flaming caused a bit of an awkward moment. It would have been even more awkward, were I the type of person to put out flames with my heel, mind you. Thankfully I still had a full thermos of water in my car. I just doused it and got rid of it." She took a sip from her teacup, pondering her effort. "It could have been worse. There were no broken windows or the like. Yes, it could have been much worse."

As much as she didn't like the sound of the apartment, I really, *really* didn't like the sound of vandalism at the store, no matter how "minor" she thought it was. For one thing, vandalism here at the store inferred that someone out there thought badly enough of Liss (at least, I was assuming it was Liss) to go out of their way to do something to antagonize or intimidate her. And I was really afraid that a person who was willing to go that far might be unbalanced enough to take it a step further—to take it to a physical level. A level of harm. But who? Who could feel so strongly about Liss? She was such a wonderful person, so warm and kind and giving.

My bet was on someone from Reverend Baxter Martin's church group, and I had a good idea why. Because Liss was a witch. And she'd been outed, not only through word of mouth but also in the Stony Mill Gazette. Ever since that fateful article appeared this past summer, Reverend Martin, a fundamentalist independent believer who liked to interpret the Holy Bible in his own very special way, had been actively—and singlehandedly—attempting to create a band of devotees to rise against what he had labeled "purveyors of darkness," who in his mind were the source of all the sins of the town. At the top of his list of the wicked: Liss and anyone who associated with her store. And Martin had more ties to people of influence throughout the town than we'd like. He'd been making trouble for Liss at turn after turn, including with City Hall. Could it be that one of his followers was taking his role as religious activist a little too seriously?

Liss saw the concern in my eyes and rushed to reassure me. "Now, now. It really is nothing, Maggie. At least, it's nothing I can't handle."

"Spells? You're talking spells?" I couldn't hold back the frown worrying my forehead. "Now, Liss . . . I know how seriously you take your magick"—after all, hadn't I witnessed enough myself to know that it was real?—"but . . . shouldn't we be talking about reporting it to the police and getting them involved?"

"Actually, dear . . . I already did. To tell you the truth, they didn't seem too very excited about it, although they did take down the information. Perhaps your apartment manager fellow this morning took precedence. In the meantime, I will be doing a full protection ritual with the upcoming dark moon, and you know that I charge my wards daily. Don't underestimate them."

I wouldn't—I'd both seen and felt the effects of them in action. But the wards only protected the property itself. The protection extended itself to the residents therein, but only while on the premises. That troubled me, too.

"You know," Liss went on, fetching a cookie from the tray, "since your apartment expedition went bust in rather a spectacular fashion, you might consider performing a spell of your own if you're still interested in finding a new place to live. Here, have a biscuit. Chocolate cherry chip."

"Mm, my favorite." Cherries from Michigan, what could be better? Um, how about adding them to chocolate chips and chocolate chunks in a cookie? "A spell? What kind of spell? You mean, like a Get Me a Cheap but Wonderful Apartment ASAP Spell?"

She chuckled. "I think your average Home Finding Spell would suffice. After all, a home is what everyone strives to find, don't you agree? And if we don't find one readymade to fit the bill, it's what we strive to create."

I would give her that. "Well, in that case, maybe I'll think about that for this next go-round."

"So you're determined to continue with the apartment quest, then?"

"I have to keep looking," I told her. "I have to find something."

"Marcus?" Liss guessed.

I nodded. "Marcus. He's putting off his classes because I'm there, and he feels like he has to be around to take care of me. Which is ridiculous! But you know Marcus."

"I do, indeed. A closet gentleman. Possibly the last gentleman, Goddess love him." She chuckled, polishing off her cookie and dusting the crumbs from her fingertips. "Have you talked to him about this? Your reasons for wanting a new place?"

"Yeah. I did."

"And how did he take it?"

I paused, thinking about it. "Really well, I think. He was supportive of my reasons for it. It's not *just* because of Marcus, of course. With Steff is leaving town, too, it just makes sense to me . . . I mean, it is a basement."

"Well, then," Liss said, pouring herself another cup. "I would like you to allow me to perform the spell for you on your behalf. To find you a special place."

"A place I can afford."

"A place of your heart."

I nodded, touched by the sentiment. "A place of my heart."

A spell for a home, so that I could go home for a spell. Why not?

"Too bad this apartment didn't work out, though," I said with a sigh. "It really did seem perfect, and such a deal, too. I'm really worried I'm not going to be able to find something affordable, and the whole search will be a moot point because it's just not going to happen."

"I should definitely add in something about affordable."

"And actually, the manager had offered a deal where I would receive three months' free rent and not need a security deposit." When she raised her eyebrows in surprise, I said, "I know!"

"Why on earth would an apartment complex need to be making offers such as that in this day and age, when apartments seem to be at a premium as more and more people lose their homes?" Liss asked. "Does that make any sense to you?"

"Well . . . not really," I admitted. "But as the happy recipient of the offer, it was just too good to pass up. And when he said someone else was interested, I jumped on it. I couldn't bear to lose it to someone else." I sighed then. "And it was all for nothing."

"If the apartment was so perfect, why don't you go ahead with it after all? It's not as though the poor man's murder took place in the apartment you were touring. No harm, no foul. Perhaps you should take the apartment as you had originally planned."

"I can't. Mr. Harding said no way." I had been trying to think of a way to broach the subject, but in the end, the only good way seemed to be the direct approach.

She looked at me strangely. "Mr. . . . . Harding?"

I nodded. "Your former brother-in-law."

"Why on earth would Jeremy have any say in the matter whatsoever?"

"Because he owns the apartment complex. Or Harding Enterprises does, which as I understand it is the same thing."

"Yes, that's the same thing. Jeremy is Harding Enterprises." She shook her head, as though trying to make sense of it and coming up short. "I had no idea."

"Yes, and he recognized me," I told her. "The police called his office this morning, and he came to the crime scene as soon as he got the message. Once he discovered I was there to sign a lease, he told me in no uncertain terms that he would not allow it. No lease for me. It was totally because of my ties to you."

"I'm so sorry, love."

"Don't be. This isn't about you. It's about him. He has some sort of personal vendetta against you."

"Well . . . his whole family life crumbled last year, and he was never comfortable with me as his sister-in-law, so I can see how he might have an issue with me."

"It's ridiculous," I told her.

"But so many matters of the heart don't take logic and reason into account," she replied matter-of-factly. "No one ever said love—whatever type of love—is rational. Even in the best of circumstances."

That was the truth. Just like Marcus wasn't thinking straight about the importance of him returning to classes as planned, all because of his loyalty to me.

"Harding is a piece of work, though," I mused aloud. "After the initial shock when Tom told him there had been a death involving one of his employees, he almost seemed more concerned with the loss of the apartment complex's computer than with the man himself. I'm not kidding. He really did."

Liss chuckled, shaking her head. "That sounds like him."

"He was terribly upset that the computer had been destroyed, upset that the manager had ordered a new computer without his knowledge. He even told Marcus he wouldn't pay him . . . although that was a moot point since the manager had already paid him in cash. Funny, though, that he had done it without his boss's knowledge. I wonder if he used business funds."

Puzzled, Liss said, "I wonder why the manager would have bought a new computer without his boss's knowledge. Usually any large purchase is run through the proper chain of command. Common business practice. If he hadn't died, I have no doubt Jeremy would have had his head on the chopping block anyway, once he'd found out. In a nonliteral sense, of course."

"I don't know," I said, shrugging and shaking my head. "Maybe he thought he needed it and was determined to get it any way he had to. You know, take action and ask for forgiveness later."

"Hm, you might be right. Perhaps he had turned down a request previously."

"Maybe Locke paid for it out of his own funds. That's always a possibility, I suppose." I traced my finger thoughtfully around the gold rim of my antique teacup with its delicate violets painted round. "Although, I do have to wonder why a business computer would have to be as souped up as Marcus said he made this one. Top speed, fair to bursting with memory on the new hard drive. As up-to-date as a piece of computer wizardry could be at this point in time. I mean, I just don't see the reason for the manager of an apartment complex to need anything like that. And why was it smashed to bits? Of course it must mean something to whoever it was that had such bad feelings toward Locke to have taken his life."

"They're certain the two actions were tied together? The police, I mean."

"What else could it be?" I asked her. "The coincidence of the timing is just too great. I just don't see any way that possibility could even be spun. How would that even work? The question is, which came first, the chicken or the egg? The break-in or the drowning? And was that part of it accidental or preplanned or an afterthought?" I considered that for a moment. "Did Locke catch someone in the act? I've heard of burglaries gone bad—not around here, granted—but vandalism? Who would do that? Break into the office of an apartment complex to either steal or destroy *something* and end up killing someone to cover it up? That's like using a ten-pound sledge hammer when a meat tenderizer will do the trick."

"I see your point," Liss said with a prosaic nod. "It would be rather much."

"It's a mystery, that's for sure."

"One probably best left to the police to sort through," she gently reminded me.

I blushed. "Oh, I know. Don't mind me. You know I just like to muddle these things through until I can wrap my mind around them. Call it a personal defect." I giggled as a thought occurred to me. "My mother would call it being a concerned citizen. Of course, she would do anything to pretend she wasn't just being nosy."

"Your mother!" Liss slapped her palm over her forehead. "Good heavens. I nearly forgot."

Uh-oh. "Let me guess. My mother called."

"She did. She couldn't reach you via your cell phone, so she called here."

My purse was still back on the sales counter. I clumped

over to it and pulled my cell phone out of its depths, clicking the button on the side that made the screen light up. As expected, I had new voice mails. Three, in fact. My mother would try up to three times consecutively before she would give up and call the next likely location. Never did she let her voice mail messages speak for her. That would take too much time, and my mother was an active kind of girl.

"Did she say what she had on her mind?" I asked Liss before I even bothered to play the messages. Sometimes with my mom it was better not to. Kept the blood pressure down.

"She said something about turning on WANE-TV. I was going to check it for you, but then I allowed myself to be sidetracked with my little redecorating project."

Since we had no television at the store, the only thing to do was to check the local station on the Internet and hope they had updated their video alerts as usual. Liss reached under the skirted sales counter and pulled out the laptop for me while I situated myself on the comfortable stool, then she wandered away discreetly to give me my privacy. She needn't have bothered. She had heard most every voice mail message my mother had left for me since I started working at Enchantments nearly a year ago. It's not like I could have kept any secrets from her anyway, even if I had wanted to. Not with her uncanny ability to read my thoughts.

After loading the page, I clicked the arrow on the little video window on the station's website and waited the few moments it took while it buffered. As it whirred away, my gaze wandered over to the recent headlines. One in particular caught my eye: "Tragedy strikes again in Stony Mill." As usual, the local media were on the ball. It was a sore point with many a businessman who belonged to the local chamber of commerce. After all the work that had gone into branding the town the self-proclaimed Antiques Capital of the Midwest, instead of being recognized for their efforts with good press, *this* was what Stony Mill was fast becoming known for. Not exactly the angle they were looking for.

The video started playing, so I dragged myself back to the present.

"Coming up next we have an interview with Chief Boggs of the Stony Mill Police Department, who was on scene this morning at yet another brutal murder in the sleepy rural town of Stony Mill. Chief Boggs goes into detail on the town's most recent senseless killing, which has left many residents wondering why their town has gone so wrong. Stay tuned to Channel Three, WANE-TV, and check us out on the web."

It was your typical news update, seen a million times over around the United States on a daily basis. Only this news update had something the others didn't.

It had a fairly distinct shot of both me and Marcus in the background as we were leaving the apartment complex. And thanks to my mother's usual eagle eye, she had seen us.

Explanations would be required. And explanations would bring up questions. Such as, why was I looking for an apartment, and why didn't she know about it, and furthermore, why was she always the last to know about anything that happened in my life? My mother liked to be included in everything in her children's lives. My older brother Marshall had escaped being under her constant observation by moving to New York after college. My younger sister Melanie wasn't any help—she often fed into Mom's need for inclusion by involving her in even the minutest degrees of her life. As a result, Mom left her alone, which meant when Mel didn't want her to know something, she had no trouble hiding it from her. With me, my mother seemed to have a knack for knowing just when to question me, and she was well aware that I was a terrible liar and would have no ability to keep things from her.

Leave it to my mother to have caught my innocent debut on the morning news.

"Oh boy. How am I going to explain this?"

Chapter 10

"What's that, ducks?" The words were muffled, called through teeth loosely clenched around a string of café lights.

"Mom saw the announcement of the murder on the morning news. Guess who was featured in the background as Chief Boggs was being interviewed."

"Oh. Oh dear. You, I take it?"

"And Marcus. We were just leaving the apartment complex at the time."

"Trouble?"

I shrugged. "The usual. She's going to demand to know what's going on."

"If you don't call, she'll be calling here again shortly."

"Don't I know it." Better to get it over with quickly. Like pulling off a bandage that is more sticky tape than anything else. One tooth-gritting rip and Bob's your uncle until the next time.

Customer traffic had been nonexistent this morning, which

was fairly typical for a Tuesday, so after a resigned sigh to re-
lieve my tension, I dialed the number for home, the same
number it had been throughout my life. I was hoping I'd get
lucky, that she would have stepped out to one of her many
ladies' auxiliary meetings and I could tell her I did call her
back, buying myself a little bit of time. But that would be a
postponement at best, and it wasn't happening this morning
anyway—Mom picked up on the second ring.

"Margaret Mary-Catherine O'Neill, it is about time you
called me back."

"Hi, Mom, I love you, too. Are you having a nice day?"

"There is no need to sass me, Margaret. What on earth
were you doing at that place this morning? And how do you
get yourself into these situations?"

And there it was, as expected. The defining characteristic
of my relationship with my mother. Some days, some months,
things were better, but whenever anything went wrong, it always came back to this. "Well," I said, doing my best to keep
any hint of annoyance out of my voice because that only added
to the tension that always simmered between us at some level,
hidden or not, "in answer to your first question, I went to the
apartment complex to sign a lease for an apartment, and in
answer to your second question, how does anyone get themselves into any situation? They wander in. Innocently. You
know. Things just happen."

"To you, Margaret. Things seem to always happen to you."

I sighed.

"I worry."

"Mom, it's an apartment building. How could I possibly
have known the manager was going to run into trouble of
this kind?"

"What were you doing looking for an apartment anyway?
You already have an apartment—which you don't even live in,

I might point out—and a place to stay with this Marcus fellow of yours, even though you don't need it because home would be a much better place for you while you're recuperating."

"It's fine, Mom."

"That doesn't answer my question."

"I was looking for an apartment for a couple of reasons. One, because Steff is getting married and won't be living in Stony Mill for much longer"—*Sob!*—"and two, because I felt like a change might be in order, since she won't be living at my apartment building anymore. There won't be any reason for me to stick with the apartment I have. I just thought it might be the perfect time for a little change," I said again.

"If you need a place to live, I don't know why you don't just move home. You know we have the room."

Eep! Um . . . No. Not. Never. Not in a million years. "You probably should save it for Mel," I told her. "She might need it." It had been only weeks since Mel had been unceremoniously and rudely, well, dumped, for lack of a better word, by her cretin husband, Greg Craven, a family law attorney who specialized in divorces and personal estate management and who now seemed determined to use his experience against her. Maybe he'd locate his misplaced family values before it was too late, but it didn't seem likely. Mel had been hanging tough in the family home in the pricy Buckingham West subdivision with the four daughters Greg seemed to have forgotten about, but who knew how long that was going to last. Regardless of community property law, the plain fact was, things were expensive, Mel had five mouths to feed including her own, and she didn't have a job. I just hoped she had found a really good lawyer who wasn't one of the cretin's cronies-in-law.

"Hm. Well, as much as I hate to admit this, you might just have something," Mom admitted. "Things have been tense. All Greg's fault. He won't talk to her except through his lawyer. Why does he even need one, since he's one himself?" she fussed.

"I don't know."

"It's like the Greg we knew all this time wasn't the real Greg at all."

"Hopefully Mel's attorney steers her right. Any man who would leave his wife at the birth of their newborn twins without a word of explanation deserves to be taken for everything he's worth."

"Yes, well, let's get back to the subject at hand. We were talking about you. What on earth, Margaret? How does one go from looking at an apartment to being a witness to yet another murder? I don't know what this town is coming to. It's almost like Lucifer himself has decided to take up residence here in Stony Mill and is just digging his spurs into the unwary."

The Devil came down to Stony Mill? Seemed to me he'd have a lot more fun in a bigger, better playground, but who was I to judge?

"I didn't witness a murder. I mean, Marcus and I happened upon the poor man, but we didn't witness the murder."

"You—? I think I'd better sit down for this." And I heard her breath huff out of her through the mouthpiece, just to let me know she wasn't simply being overly dramatic.

"Are you all right, Mom?"

"I would be if my oldest daughter would keep her nose out of trouble."

"Now, Mom. You know that's not fair."

"What happened to the arrangement you had with this Marcus person?" she asked, ignoring my claim. "Trouble already?"

Maybe it shouldn't have bothered me so much to hear the

whisper of hopefulness in her voice. It was no secret that Marcus wasn't, at least by outward appearances, everything my mother hoped for in a man friend for her oldest daughter. But it did. "No, Mom. Not trouble already. Not trouble at all. Things are going really well."

"Then why get a new apartment right now?" she persisted. "You're already living in sin together. Not much more damage can be done as far as that's concerned."

"Gee, thanks."

"Oh, you know what I mean. And stop changing the subject. Why get a new apartment now?"

I sighed. I didn't really think it was any of her business, but how do you say that to your mother? "Because," I admitted finally, "he is putting things off because of me being there with him."

"What sort of things?"

"Important things. Geez, Mom! Do you have to know everything?"

"Now, Maggie," she said, switching to the more familiar tone to soften me up, "you know I am just concerned about you. And with good reason, I might add."

Hm. "I'm fine. It's not like we had anything to do with the apartment manager or his death, you know."

"I'd like it noted, I didn't say that you did. But think of the way it must look to other people. And this isn't the first time you have somehow become embroiled in the unfortunate actions of others. Combine that with your boss's . . . reputation." The emphasis on this last word left no question whatsoever to her meaning. "You must see why others would look askance."

"No one would even notice, Mom."

My mother sighed. "Oh, Margaret. You just don't understand. This is a small town."

Didn't I know it.

"Now, what about this apartment? Did you already sign a lease? Does your father need to find someone to get you out of it?"

"I've got it handled, Mom. Honest. You don't need to worry."

"I wasn't worried at all until I saw you on the area news report in connection to a murder."

All right, fine. So I could kind of see how that might be a little worrisome. "Sorry. It wasn't my intention to be on TV at all. It's not like I was dying to be interviewed or anything."

"Yes, well, see that you aren't dying to do anything," she snipped archly. "It's bad enough that my daughter is involved on the fringes of any of these . . . incidents. You keep your eyes open. I don't want to have the sheriff knocking on my door in the middle of the night one of these days."

"Don't worry, I don't plan on it," I said, laughing . . . but was there an edge to my voice that even I didn't want to acknowledge. Could anyone really feel completely safe these days? When normal, everyday people were biting it throughout the normal, everyday courses of their lives? For all of Reverend Martin's fears about Liss, it struck me as deeply ironic that none of the murders our town had endured had involved the supernatural or witches or magick in the slightest. And still the good reverend and his followers could not see that what they really should fear was the secret darkness hidden deep within themselves and the people they knew.

"What will you do, then? If you aren't going to be staying with Marcus?"

"I don't know," I answered truthfully. "Things happened so fast with this apartment, and then to have this happen as well . . . well, it threw a wrench into the works, and all of my plans came crashing in. Don't worry, though. I'll think of something."

What that something was, though, that was the question. The problem never left my mind for long as the workday passed us by in a flurry of lunchtime customers, decorating Liss's conceptual serenity space, logging in new inventory, and shipping out Internet orders. I held down the fort while Liss carried out the preparations for the special ritual she would perform to reenergize the protective wards she had placed on and around Enchantments. Marcus texted me just after lunch to check on me, bringing the problem straight back to the forefront of my mind. What *was* I going to do? I found myself flipping through a copy of *Magick for Practical Uses* to find a good example of a house spell that I could customize and make to serve my own needs. With the new moon, it was the perfect time to lay my wishes on the line and state my needs and hopes and dreams.

At least Tara and Evie's arrival after school brought a much-needed distraction. Liss had disappeared up to the loft to gather supplies and prepare for her protection ritual. All I had been doing was worrying and mulling and worrying some more anyway, and the two girls had a knack for brightening up the space with their schoolgirl antics and intense energies. Tara Murphy was Marcus's teenage cousin, and a wild child if ever there was one. With her chunky ink black hair and bright eyes, slim build, and feisty attitude, she was approaching womanhood and her senior year in high school with the same vibrancy of spirit she applied toward everything. What that meant, in most cases, was a smartass wit that left some adults cold . . . but they didn't know her biggest secret: that deep inside, where few dared to look, her bluster disguised a heart as soft and sweet as one of Annie

Miller's caramel custard cups. It was just that a person was well advised not to let her know that you knew.

Evie Carpenter, on the other hand, didn't care who knew she was as sweet and empathetic to the sufferings of others as all get-out. She was an unrepentant earth angel and a powerful, developing psychic with connections that put my paltry attempts to shame. With fine golden hair stretching in loose waves to her waist, and a temperament to match, she was as stereotypical in appearance as they come. But Evie wasn't ready to shoehorn herself into anyone's molds. She was already hard at work blasting her mother's notions of what a good daughter should be by using her mother's own rules to assert her independence. I for one was glad to see her having some success with her efforts to become her own person. After having spent so many years straining against my own mother, it was heartening to me to know that Evie could escape that same limiting fate if she wanted to.

Tara's backpack made a dull thud as it hit the scarred antique wooden counter. "Hey, Fluffs," she said breezily. Coming around the corner, she peered over my shoulder and read a bit. "Ooh, whatcha cookin'?"

I pulled the book away from her reach and held it protectively against my abdomen. "Do I read over your shoulder?"

She held her hands up. "All right, all right, sheesh. I was just asking. No need to get your panties in a twist, Fluffs."

Fluffs, Fluffster, Fluffmeister, and any number of other variations on a theme with Pagan meaning were her favorite nicknames for me. Labeling me a Fluffy Bunny Pagan from day one had been her fairly derogatory way of observing and calling me out for my preference for acknowledging only the light in life, which to badass Tara's dark faery perspective meant I was leaving out a very important part of the universal balance. And who knows, she could be right. But I was far more comfortable with lending energy to the good in the world. It didn't mean that I couldn't see the darkness that kept nudging at us, searching for purchase, and name it for what it was. I just refused to cater to it. Since Tara had gotten to know me better, the nickname had softened into a way of expressing ironic affection. At least most of the time. One could never be one hundred percent certain when it came to Tara.

She sauntered over to the café counter as Evie, who had been trailing behind her, seated herself on the counter with a little heave-ho and a wiggle. Reaching into the glass case, Tara pulled out a pair of white chocolate chip cranberry cookies, jumbo size, and grabbed two paper napkins from the neat stack by the tea boilers.

"I mean," she said, handing Evie a cookie and a napkin, "it's no skin off my freckled nose if you want to read up on magick but not practice it regularly. I'd be happy to leave you to your fumbles if you want. Otherwise, I was going to offer to help you out."

Evie giggled. "You know, Tare, I think that's the first time I've ever heard you admit to your freckles. You usually pretend they don't exist."

Tara stared her best friend down. "Yeahhh. Keep it up, Evil. You want to keep that cookie or not?"

Evie made the zipping motion over her lips and held her cookie protectively. But it didn't stop her from grinning broadly at me as soon as Tara's back was turned.

"And you can wipe that smile off your face, too," Tara grumbled without turning around.

I shook my head, marveling at their simpatico connection. "How did you know she was smiling?" I asked her.

"I could feel it," she said with a shrug. Like it was no big thing. And with Tara and Evie, it wasn't. "So, the whole apartment thing didn't work out?" she asked. "You decided not to take it?" At my questioning stare, she shrugged. "Uncle Lou mentioned it."

No use pretending she hadn't seen the spell I'd been reading about. I set the book down on my lap. "Actually, I did decide to take it after a call from the manager last night, telling me there was someone else interested in it and could I please make a decision right away so that he would know what to tell them."

"Oh." Tara looked at me, waiting. "So, why do you need a Home Finding Spell?"

"Well, it could be because I changed my mind. Or, it could be because your cousin and I stumbled over the manager's dead body this morning when I went to sign the lease."

Tara blinked. So did Evie.

"Well, not stumbled, per se," I continued on as though this were the most normal conversation in the world to be having, and there I was having it for the third time that day. "He was in the pool, after all. Swimming with the fishes. But not. I didn't see any fishes in the swimming pool. Only the dead manager."

"Wow," Tara mused, staring at me. "And here everyone keeps insisting that working out is supposed to be *good* for you. I'll take my chances with vegging out in front of a good video game."

"He was actually *dead*?" Evie squeaked, her faint eyebrows arching high. "And you *found* him?"

"Yes to both questions," I confirmed. "It was not fun."

Evie held out her hand toward Tara, palm up and fingers waggling expectantly. "By the way, Tara . . . A-*hem*. I think we're forgetting something." She wiggled her fingertips some more.

Grumbling under her breath, Tara dug in the pocket of her backpack. She pulled something out and tossed it at Evie. It landed on her lap with a green, fluttering trajectory—a folded dollar bill. "You know, I should know better than to bet Evie when she has one of her feelings," she told me. "Dumb of me. We heard the sirens this morning, and she swore it was another murder."

I gave them the short version of the details I had mentioned earlier to Liss. It seemed easiest that way.

"What are the odds?" Evie asked to the store at large.

I didn't know, but it seemed to me that the odds of it happening in Stony Mill were getting better and better all the time, and that worried me.

"So, old Tom is probably fit to be tied that you're involved in something like this again, huh," Tara observed, as spot-on as usual.

It wasn't a question. It didn't need to be. "He certainly wasn't thrilled to see me there," I admitted.

"Who do they think did it?"

I shook my head. "I don't know. The guy felt a little off to me, but what can you do? A lot of people give off that kind of energy."

"Off? Off how?" Evie mumbled around the crumbs of a big bite of cookie. She turned red and swallowed hard. "Sorry. Bit off more than I could chew."

Some days, I felt much the same way. "I can't explain it, really," I told her. "Seedy, a little bit, maybe?"

"Who would have messed up the guy's office that way?" Evie puzzled. "Seems to me if someone wanted to rip the guy off, they wouldn't have broken the computer. They would've sold it."

"Well, obviously whoever did it *meant* to demolish the

computer," Tara said. "Think about it. No one would have just smashed it unless they had a reason to."

"And it was new, too," I added. "The guy hired Marcus to rebuild the old one into a supercomputer. Through Big Lou," I told Tara. "Your dad actually knows the guy from his club."

"Maybe the guy had enemies somehow," Evie suggested.

Tara rolled her eyes. "Well, obvs he had enemies if someone was willing to kill him, Evester."

"What do you know about the guy, Maggie?" Evie said, ignoring Tara's teasing jibe.

"Not much," I admitted. "He did have an argument with a tenant while I was there. The guy—Hollister—was pretty hot under the collar. Lou had to take him down the block to cool off. He looked like he would have liked to throttle Locke. That's the manager, Locke."

"Well, there you have it," Tara said. "Maybe that's the guy. Maybe their argument continued later on, after you left."

"Maybe," I said. "I'm not sure, though. I happened to run into him awhile later at Annie-Thing Good, when Lou stopped there to pick up dinner for you and your mom. And . . . as it turns out . . . this Hollister guy has connections to her niece. Annie's, I mean. I sure hope it wasn't him. Annie seems pretty fond of him."

"So you don't think it could have been him?"

"I just don't know. I don't want to think so, because I like Annie a lot, and I'd hate to see her hurt by something like this." The very thought made me feel gloomy. And then I remembered something I was going to ask them. "Oh! I almost forgot. Do either of you know a girl named Abbie Cornwall?"

"I do." Evie waved her hand. "She's in the grade below me."

"Yeah," Tara said, "isn't she going out with JJ?"

Evie nodded. "Perkins," she confirmed. "Since last spring."

"JJ and Charlie hang out sometimes," Tara put in.

They both looked at me suddenly with a question punctuating their brows. "I was just wondering," I told them.

Neither one of them looked as though they believed me.

"All right, fine. I ran into her yesterday. Or should I say, she ran into me."

Dual puckered brows deepened.

I sighed. "While I was looking at the apartment. She was hiding in the closet of the apartment I was looking at and nearly ran me down when she burst out of it to run away. I didn't know who she was, but we saw her just down the road with a boyfriend—"

"JJ," Evie said helpfully.

"JJ," I echoed, "and Lou recognized her. Evidently she and her boyfriend are both on his track team. Or they were last spring. So," I said, "any ideas why she might have broken into an empty apartment?"

"Blond girl, pretty thin, great taste in eye makeup?" Tara clarified.

I had to laugh at the last. Tara's taste in heavy mascara and eyeliner was a source of contention between her and Marcus and Lou both. "Yes. Same girl."

"I think they used to live down close to Marcus's place. Is it that old apartment building down south?"

I nodded. "New Heritage. They have been renovating it for a while, from what I understand. Everything is pretty much new, except for the outside."

"That might be the place. I don't think she and her mom have a lot of money."

"Lou said her mom was a single mother. And the apartments were reasonably priced, even without a special dis-count on the monthly rent."

Evie waved her hand at me. "I have JJ in my Spanish class. I could ask him tomorrow."

"Or we could do that right now," Tara said, arching her brow meaningfully and patting the laptop. "I have him on my Friends list."

A customer approached the counter just then with a ques-tion about whether the wooden benches crafted by fellow N.I.G.H.T.S. member Eli Yoder could come in other finishes or wood selections, which required me to track down Eli in order to find the answer. No, not by driving out to his farm. By cell phone. It never failed to amuse me that Amish Eli was business minded enough to own a cell phone . . . but then, I suppose in this day and age, even the Amish have to be reachable in some way by their customers. Technology waits for no businessman. In the meantime, I chased the girls off to the office to log in the day's new inventory receipts.

By the time I was finished with the customer and had said my good-byes to Eli, Evie had poked her head out from be-hind the deep purple velvet curtain that separated the front of the store from the back office and was waving at me to come back. After looking around to be certain no customer would be left stranded, I met her at the doorway.

"JJ was online. He wants to know why we want to know."

"Know what?" I asked, still distracted by my previous mission.

"Why we want to know about Abbie."

Flustered, I frowned. "What did you two do, ask him straight out?"

"Well, we really didn't think it through for long," Evie admitted. "I'm sorry, Maggie. But what should we tell him?"

"He says yes." That was Tara, aka the girl behind the

purple curtain, who evidently had taken matters into her own hands. Evie pulled the curtain back so that we could talk to her. "I told him a friend of mine might be moving to the apartment building, and wasn't that where Abbie lives? He said yes . . . and no." She made a face then to make it clear just what she thought of cryptic responses.

"What does that mean?" I asked her.

"Yes, that is the apartment building, and no . . . meaning not anymore . . . because she and her mom were kicked out by some jerk in the front office without any warning."

The information jibed with what Locke had said about evicting the previous tenant . . . and hadn't the other tenant, Alexandra Cooper, said something about Abbie? Oh, but . . . "Something isn't making sense here to me. Abbie wasn't eighteen. Locke had been very clear with me, stating that children under the age of eighteen were not allowed. It's supposed to be an adult community. Even the brochure he gave me said so."

Tara tapped something out on the laptop keyboard, then waited. "I don't know anything about that, but it was definitely the same place," she said after the laptop dinged at her with a response from JJ. "He says . . . first the guy was always hanging around, pretending to change lightbulbs or wash windows outside, until Mrs. Cornwall told him they could do it themselves. Then Abbie accidentally broke the mirror in the room they shared, and he showed up at their door and started threatening to add the replacement of the mirror to their month's rent. Mrs. Cornwall," she read, "told him that he should stop peeping in their windows and pay attention to the other pretty girls he rented apartments to. I guess he didn't take that very well."

None of it made much sense, other than it seemed that JJ was saying that Locke liked to rent to pretty young women, which was something I had already noticed. But why would Mrs. Cornwall's comment have brought about their eviction? Something wasn't adding up.

"So she lived at the apartment and was evicted. Why would she have broken into the apartment yesterday?"

"Maybe she left something in the apartment that was important to her and she wanted to find it," Evie suggested.

"There didn't appear to be anything in the apartment," I told her. "At least nothing I saw."

"Maybe she'd already retrieved it?"

"Maybe." But I wasn't convinced.

"Do you want me to ask JJ?" Tara asked.

"Um, you'd have to explain to him how you knew she was there," I reminded her.

"Good point." But she was typing something in anyway, I noticed. "I'm asking him whether he heard about the manager being murdered," she explained even though I didn't ask. And then there was a blip and she sat up straight in her chair. "Hey!"

"What's wrong?" Evie asked her.

"He just logged out. Without a word!" She shook her head, making her choppy pixie hair sway. "So rude. What is the world coming to these days?"

What indeed.

Chapter 11

Before I left work for the day, I consulted with Liss about the components I needed for a good Home Finding Spell. She had completed her protection ritual and looked a bit tired, but was glowing with light. She started tucking small bits and bobs into little paper envelopes: a polished amethyst crystal, a tiny stopper with individual usage amounts of patchouli oil, rose hips and buds, and cinnamon sticks. "These should do the trick," she told me. "Dress your candle with the patchouli oil, and make sure it's not so large that it takes more than a day to burn down. Did you work on your intentions?"

I held up a piece of paper I had printed off. "I've got my list of wants right here. I know what I want; I know what I need. I'm just worried I won't find anything that fits into those guidelines and is affordable."

"Tut, tut! None of that, now. Lending energy to your fears just makes it more difficult to get past them in your reality.

Focus on what you want, and keep that light burning brightly. It will bring you more of the same. Focus on what you don't want, and . . . you'll get more of the same. Most people learn that the hard way. Some never understand it at all."

It was the Law of Attraction that she was referring to, and it was something I had always understood on a certain, nebulous level but rarely had paid attention to until a situation got so extreme that I had no other choice but to listen because I was out of other options. Like attracts like. Positive attracts positive, negative attracts negative. Change your outlook, change your day-to-day experience, change your future, change your world. Now that I was more conscious of it, I was working to enact it more into my life by making better choices and opening myself to the change that appeared for me to reach out and experience. That was key, too—being open to the change and allowing it to happen. Not being too afraid to experience something different and unfamiliar. Allowing yourself to stretch and grow in new ways of being. Change was scary, but it was exciting, too. It all comes back to you and your outlook.

Meeting Liss had been the first, sparkling moment of change hovering like a firefly on my spiritual horizon. The question at the time had been, would I be courageous enough to accept? I was, and I did. Each change brought more coming along on its heels, a slowly accelerating flow of them. Slow, to allow me to get comfortable with the idea of how each one fit into my life and made it better before another one came along to begin the process of expansion all over again. I didn't start out a full-blown sensitive. I had abilities, yes, that I had denied almost into oblivion. It was the act of opening to even one of the abilities that allowed me to open to even more. And I was opening more all the time. Accepting more all the time.

The Law of Attraction at work.

But how did the Law of Attraction apply to Stony Mill? Did that mean that a large number of the normal, everyday, churchgoing folk of Stony Mill had a nose for darkness beneath all their goodness and light? Is that why all of these murders kept happening? Were we drawing the darkness, unwittingly or not, to ourselves on a large scale? Because things that happened on a broader scale had the energies of the masses contributing to them. Which is what made predictions on a large scale easier than on a personal level. One person could change their life in the course of a single day. A community, however, couldn't change so quickly. It had the energy threads of any number of people feeding into it, so to revise a course already set into motion by countless individual actions long before would require coordinated change on a mass level. Much more difficult to enact.

I just hoped it didn't mean the town was doomed by its own dark secrets.

And I still wasn't sure that the Stony Mill community's own sinister energies were the underlying cause of all the tragedies the town had suffered in the last year. A part of it, certainly. But all? I just didn't know. And what you don't know, in a situation like this, *can* hurt you.

Casting a spell for a nice new home was unquestionably a simpler proposition.

"Last, but not least," Liss said, tucking in a tiny satin pouch in a bronze color, "a charm bag. What herbs you don't use will go in here, and you're to carry it on your person as much as possible to charge it with your energy and intent. Now remember, you don't have to rhyme your spell if you don't want to. Sometimes that makes it easier to repeat, but it isn't necessary. Besides that, just visualize, visualize, visualize. Oh!" Taking me affectionately by the shoulders, she looked into my eyes and beamed at me. "I feel like a proud mama whenever you take it upon yourself to do one of these." She chuckled at herself. "Without the labor pain. Naturally."

I laughed.

"You know . . ." Liss's face took on a thoughtful expression. "I might just have to cast one of these myself. Not for a new home, but a new car. That's another story. Never, ever buy a car during Mercury Retrograde," she cautioned. "I've certainly learned my lesson. From now on I will wait until Mercury is once again firmly and irrefutably direct in its orbit."

Liss's Lexus had been giving her fits for as long as I had known her. For such a lovely luxury vehicle, it had come with more than its share of problems.

"What kind of car are you going to look for?" I asked her.

"I have no idea. Perhaps I shall let it find me instead," she replied with an airy wave of her hand. "Just like your new home will find you." And she smiled. Knowingly.

Well, I had no idea how that would work, but I knew enough about Liss that it would all the same. Just. Like. Magick.

Marcus came to pick me up just then, so I said my good-byes and left to go off and do a little magick of my own.

I was silent most of the trip home, my mind full of the events of the day.

"Penny for your thoughts."

"Hm?" I glanced up to discover that we had pulled up to the curb, and the truck motor had been switched off. "Oh. We're home."

"Uh-huh. At least I am. I think you've been somewhere else, though."

I smiled at him. "I guess I have."

"Worrying?"

"Maybe."

But he knew me better than that. "Worrying, definitely. I thought I told you not to do that," he teased.

"I know, I know," I groaned. "I can't seem to help myself. Liss and I had a chat about it today, too. Lending energy and focus to negative things. I'm going to try harder not to do that. I know it just makes matters worse. Sometimes the execution is more difficult than the good intentions." I glanced over at him shyly. "Marcus . . ."

"Maggie . . ." he said, the lilt in his voice meant to lighten the air. But I had something to say, and I needed to be sure he heard me.

"I really want you to go back to finish up your degree as planned," I blurted.

"I know you do."

"And I'm really afraid that I'm messing that up for you. Because of"—I reached down and rapped my knuckles on my flamboyant cast—"*this*. Stupid bad luck and bad timing."

He took off his sunglasses and sighed. "I know. It's no big deal for me to postpone it a little while," he said, taking my hand, "because I know myself and I know it really is only a temporary deferral. But . . . it seems to mean a lot to you—"

"It does," I said quickly.

"—so . . . I give you my word, Magpie, we'll find a way so that I can start classes Monday as previously planned. All right?"

"All right." And I knew he meant it, which meant the world to me. "I'm not sure how, but I know if anyone can make this work out, you can. I, uh"—I felt a blush heating my cheeks—"I even talked to Liss about it. She recommended a Home Finding Spell to bring the perfect place my way. I have the stuff for it right here." I patted my handbag, which I'd been holding protectively against me.

He raised an eyebrow, and a slight smile touched one

corner of his mouth. "You're willing to go the spell route? Wow. This must be serious."

I made a face. "You aren't the only one who can spell."

"Evidently."

"And besides, it isn't for anything dire, something I could fumble," I explained further, "with my shortage of experience."

"Well, why don't we take your . . . *stuff* . . . inside and work it together? If that's okay with you."

Okay? It was more than okay.

He came around and helped me inside, carrying my things for me. As we crossed the porch, it hit me all of a sudden just how much had happened in the last twenty-four hours. It felt more like days. "Wow."

Marcus, who had been in front of me, nudging open the screen door with his elbow, tossed a saucy grin over his shoulder. "Thanks. I try."

I giggled. "Not you."

"Oh. Break my heart. No, don't worry. The crumbling edifice of my ego will recover. Eventually."

"I'll be the first to admit, you're pretty wow, too. But I was thinking about the day," I said as I clumped my way through the door he held for me and across the threshold. Minnie came running around the corner, meowing up a storm, and wound her way around my feet and crutches. I stopped so that I wouldn't trip over her and reached down to scratch her behind the ears.

"Why don't you go sit down and put your feet up—doctor's orders," he said when I made a face, "and I'll pour us some iced tea."

I had to admit, putting my casted foot up high on a pile of pillows and leaning back felt really, really good. Much better than I would have thought before Danny laid down the law. Maybe the good doctor did know what he was talking about. Who woulda thunk it? And it was even better when Minnie launched her fat little body up onto the sofa, pranced all over my prone and inert figure, and then settled herself down on my chest, purring in my face with her eyes closed blissfully. Aw. The little rascal missed me.

"Hey!" Marcus protested when he came around the corner with two glasses of tea. "She took my resting spot."

"I guess you two will just have to work out a schedule," I told him, laughing.

He set the tea down on a coaster on the glass tabletop and then brought me my bag. "In case you want to set up on the table."

I took out the bag of goodies Liss had sent home with me, as well as the piece of paper that stated my wishes. After asking me about a candle, Liss had decided to assume I wouldn't have one at my fingertips and had included a small white votive in with the rest. Marcus slid the table closer to me so that I wouldn't have to reach so far. I opened the bag to take things out, but Marcus said, "Hang on," and went off down the hallway, returning a moment later with a silky cloth that he spread out over the glass surface of the coffee table. "Altar cloth," he explained when I turned questioning eyes upon him.

"Oh." A thought occurred to me suddenly. I cleared my throat. "Um, Marcus?"

"Hm?"

"Where do you usually work when you cast your spells?" I asked shyly, tilting my head to gaze at him sideways.

"Actually," he said, spreading the silken scarf over the table before placing the bag of goodies on top of it for me, "I honestly don't cast very many spells."

I blinked. I wasn't expecting that. "Really?"

He laughed at my surprise. "Really. I guess I just don't see the need to. Most of the time I feel that I'm perfectly capable of bringing things about on my own or with the help of my Guides. And with a certain level of patience."

"Patience is something I'm not always good at," I admitted.

"Sometimes casting spells comes off as pushing the issue or trying to control the outcome of things, in my mind, when most of the time a simple heart-to-heart with your Guides can do so much more. Just sitting back and letting them do their thing on your behalf," he told me with a shrug. "I like to let them take the wheel and see where they'll take me."

"Like with me?"

His smile was enigmatic enough to rival the Mona Lisa's. "Maybe."

"Well, did you ask them about me or not?" I persisted.

"That," he said, leaning in and kissing me on the nose, "is for me to know and for you to forget about."

"You did!" I laughed. "You did. Admit it." And then I sobered. "Poor Tom. He never had a chance, did he?"

Marcus finished setting out the spell components on the cloth but said nothing. He didn't need to. We both knew the answer to that. Tom and I, we were just not meant to be. We were too different. He was *Law & Order*, and I was *Practical Magic*. His days were all *C.S.I.*, and mine were *Bewitched*. He thought all psychics were Miss Cleo, and I wanted to learn to bend spoons like Uri Geller. He thought Stony Mill was Mayberry born again and was dreadfully confused by the reality that it wasn't, and I was beginning to think Stony Mill and Eastwick were next-door neighbors, and when the Devil finally decided to poke his head out of the shadows and let the rest of us see him for what he truly is, I wasn't sure I wanted to be around. We were different.

Different people. Different priorities. Different worlds.

Except now his world was crashing up against mine, and now my problems were becoming his problems and his problems were becoming my problems, and that, my friends, was not good. For any of us.

"What are you asking for in a home?" Marcus asked me.

"Oh, you know. Just a place to call my own that is *not* in a basement and has plenty of natural light, allows pets, is safe, very affordable, close to you"—he smiled at that—"and has a good feeling to it. You know. Nice."

"You could stay here," he suggested.

I smiled, a little sadly. "We talked about the reasons why—"

"But we didn't talk about alternatives that would allow us both to do what we need to do and get done what we need to get done."

"What . . . alternatives?" I was trying not to get too excited. Sometimes it was better not to get your hopes up too soon.

"Well, I talked to Liss on my way to pick you up—"

"You did?" It must have been before she and I gathered spell components, because Marcus had arrived just as we were finishing up.

"—and she knows how opposed you are to getting in the way of my continued education . . . even though you aren't—"

I waited, raising my eyebrows to urge him on and wondering how this was going to play out.

"—so, Liss suggested that she could drive you to and from work for as long as it takes you to get your cast off and drive again."

The little dickens! She hadn't said a word! No wonder she was acting so pleased with herself while gathering up all the herbs and things. She knew the spell wasn't going to be necessary. A spell that worked in advance of even working it . . . it didn't get any better than that. Negative reaction time. Awesome. I hoped her car spell worked just as well. Not to mention the protection ritual. That one was especially important, as far as I was concerned.

"Liss," I said, "is incredibly closed mouthed when she wants to be."

He grinned. "She is at that."

"So . . ."

"So, what do you think?" he asked, letting his excitement for the prospect bubble over.

"Is she *sure*?" I asked him, worrying. "I mean, I know she probably thinks nothing of it, but I don't want to be a burden to anyone, let alone my boss, and . . . oh, gosh . . . it would solve a lot of problems, wouldn't it?"

"So that's a yes, then?"

"That's a . . . maybe . . . I have to talk to Liss first. I have to know, *for sure*, that it won't be putting her out."

He just smiled at me. Knowingly. As knowingly as Liss had earlier. And then he kissed me, and I forgot what I was so worried about.

The doorbell rang, breaking into the momentary reverie. I sighed as his lips left mine and grumbled, "Darned door-to-door salespeople."

Marcus rose to his feet and peeked past the curtain on the front window, where video camera equipment still pointed outward, even though it had been weeks since the last time he'd thought he saw anyone—meaning Tom or his cronies—scoping out the house. What can I say? We'd both been a bit too preoccupied to bother ourselves putting it away. "Uh-oh."

Uh-oh?

He went to the door and yanked it open. "Well, well. Look who it is."

Standing just outside, his finger raised toward the doorbell as though he had been about to ring it again, was your favorite police officer and mine, Tom Fielding, in all his aviator-sunglassed glory.

Chapter 12

My mind was having a hard time wrapping around what I was seeing. Why would Tom be standing at Marcus's front door?

Tom gave a self-important little cough to clear his throat and took off his sunglasses, tucking them into the collar of his white tee. He was doing his best to appear official, and yet there was an air of uncertainty to him, a self-consciousness that niggled along my emotional pathways, making me feel a little nervous as well. "I have a few questions to ask you, and I was hoping this would be a good time." And then his gaze traveled down to Marcus's bare feet before drifting past him to see me, relaxing supine on the sofa, and his uncertainty hardened perceptibly.

Oh, snap.

There was something about the appearance of a man's bare feet that to me felt somehow . . . intimate. I couldn't help wondering if Tom was thinking that same thing. Especially when paired with me, lolling about on the sofa with a distinct lack of lip gloss. My hand flew to my hair, hoping it was at least presentable.

I sat up a little straighter. Or, as straight as the soft cushions and pillows would allow.

A glower settled in between Tom's brows. He snapped his gaze back toward Marcus, who appeared to be mulling over the statistical probability of success of turning Tom summarily away.

Yeah, I didn't think it would work, either.

All he could do was grit his teeth and reluctantly open the door a little bit wider. "By all means, come on in, make yourself at home."

Tom stepped over the threshold with all the enthusiasm of a man who knows he has a job to do and it's not going to be pleasant. His hands flexed around the edges of a bulky expandable file folder he was transferring back and forth between his hands.

"Hi, Tom."

He didn't look at me. He just waved the folder in my general direction.

"Why don't you sit down?"

Because that would make this seem like a social call . . .

I heard the thought, plain as day. But did I imagine it or project it on him? Or was it real?

I'd never know, because there was no way I was about to ask him.

Marcus closed the door, and I could tell by the tension in his shoulders that he felt as though he'd just invited the enemy to sit down to a friendly meal. He came to stand next to me, his thumbs catching hold of his belt and hooking there as he eyed Tom, who still hadn't taken a seat and was standing next to the armchair on the opposite side of the coffee table.

Obviously it was up to me to break the ice. For my own sake. "Marcus, why don't you get Tom a glass of iced tea?" I suggested pleasantly.

Tom's eyes left Marcus and settled on me. With relief? "This isn't really a social call, Maggie."

"I have no doubts about that, Tom," I replied dryly. "But it doesn't have to be difficult. Does it?"

Tom and Marcus eyed each other a little longer, and then Marcus went off without another word to the kitchen, returning a moment later to find that Tom had, indeed, done as I'd bid and was now seated on the edge of chair and was waiting for him. It wasn't the most relaxed of perches, but it was a start. Marcus set the glass down on the table in front of Tom and then sat down in front of my reclining body on the narrow shelf of sofa leftover, his left hand looped loosely but protectively over my knee, just above my cast. I know Tom noticed.

He flipped through the file folder, selected a page, and laid it across his precisely positioned knees. Then he took his flip notebook out of his breast pocket, opened it to the next free page, and laid it down as well. He looked up at the two of us.

"Well. What a day, huh?"

If he intended to confuse us, it was working. On me, at least. "Yeah. Big day." I glanced over at Marcus.

"I, uh, I brought forms for you. Both of you. I'd like you to fill them out with what you told me this morning. Your version of events. Your statement as to what happened." He handed them over to us.

"Now?" I asked.

"That won't be necessary. But if you could get them in to me as soon as possible, I would appreciate it. If you run out of room, you can attach an additional piece of paper. Just be sure to initial all pages and sign and date the form where indicated."

"Gotcha. Can do." I waited for him to go on, but he didn't. And Marcus wasn't helping. Finally I asked, "Is that all?"

"Actually . . . no." He fidgeted with the wire fastener on the spiral notebook, tracing the spaces with his fingertips. "I, uh . . . oh, hell. There is no easy way to do this, so I'm just going to come right out and say it."

"That might help," Marcus said, finding his voice at last. "At least it would help us get the show on the road." I nudged him lightly with my knee and felt his hand tighten over me. Minnie, disgusted with the repeated disturbances of her glorified slumber, turned to give Marcus a reproachful sneer and then hopped down to the floor to watch the proceedings from a distance deemed safe and disturbance free.

"What do you need from us, Tom?" I asked.

He hesitated for what seemed like forever. "First, I have to ask for your sworn secrecy," he said. "You can't tell anyone. If you can't promise that, then I'll have to come up with another solution."

"Solution to what?" I prompted gently.

"Sheriff Reed spoke to the state crime lab this afternoon. Their medical testing facility is running on schedule, but there have been staffing cutbacks due to budget cuts at the state level, and the IT group is swamped. They are pushing back time lines for the completion dates of all tests submitted to them, saying it could be months . . . which means that our investigation into Robert Locke's murder is at a standstill. Unless . . ."

Both Marcus and I waited, but I think we both knew what he was about to say.

"Unless we find another, private-sector source to use as an outside contractor." He lifted his gaze to meet Marcus's neutral stare. "Which is what brings me here today. *You* have friends in high places."

"Oh yeah?"

"Yeah." Tom nodded, tapping the tip of his pen repeatedly against the notebook. "When your name came up, I have to say, I was surprised. And . . . well, never mind. But Ledbetter is insistent, and he's convinced both Boggs and Reed that you and your computer magic are the way to go." Ledbetter was the district attorney, so his opinion went a long way when suggestions were made toward an investigation. Tom's expression said that he couldn't believe it but was trying very hard to work with his superiors on this and not against them.

"That must have been hard for you."

The words slipped out before I even knew I had opened my mouth. Marcus and Tom both looked at me curiously, and I cringed inside. Stupid empathic sensibilities. Sometimes they were more trouble than they were worth.

"Yes, well . . . it's my job. I'll do what I have to do," Tom said. And then he cleared his throat. "So, what do you say? Are you interested? You would be doing a good thing for the county. The sooner we get this murder solved and put behind us, the better off we all will be." More nonconvincing convincing.

"What ties do you have to Ledbetter?" I asked Marcus out of curiosity.

He shrugged. "I built new computers for his legal team last spring at a substantial discount over buying name brand at a retail outlet . . . which meant his budget was more than enough to allow everyone to be upgraded. It made for a very happy team. And I also solved a networking problem they'd been patchwork fixing for the last couple of years because no one understood enough about the security parameters. Good thing, too—their firewall was a joke. They're lucky no one hacked in just because it was so laughably easy."

Marcus let Tom wait a good long minute. So long that I was starting to feel uncomfortable with the silence myself. "I don't know," he said at last.

Confusion registered in Tom's steely gray eyes. A muscle in his jaw clenched, just once, and then relaxed forcibly as if by sheer dint of will. "I don't understand."

But Marcus was not ready to relent. "The computer stuff is a business I run, Quinn Enterprises Ltd. It isn't a charity. Not even for the county government."

"We're prepared to pay you your usual fee. All we need is a quick turnaround, guaranteed."

"Hm," Marcus said finally. "I start classes on Monday. That doesn't give me a lot of leeway, but I think it can be done. What, exactly, do you have for me?"

"I need your sworn confidentiality agreements first. One for you and for Maggie." He flicked a glance in my direction. "Normally Maggie wouldn't be included in this special arrangement at all, but as she has medical issues at present and is staying with you at your place, the DA has agreed that this is enough of an extenuating circumstance to warrant simply obtaining her agreed-upon silence in the event that she is privy to information simply by living in the same house." From the file he removed two prepared agreements and handed them over as well.

"Well," I said, not certain any of that could be considered

flattering, "it's not like I'd be out spreading the word about all of your confidential information anyway, Tom."

"Well . . . I'm sure you wouldn't mean to. But people do tend to talk if they're not reminded not to, Maggie. I'm just saying."

I felt my lips compressing in annoyance and disapproval. "I honestly don't see how that's a fair assessment of the situation. Or of me."

"It's not meant to cast judgment or to be derogatory in any way—"

"And yet somehow it is," I returned quickly, resisting the urge to cross my arms over myself. Meanwhile, Marcus was there beside me, smirking and sitting back for the ride.

"You're being unreasonable."

"I don't see why it's so unreasonable. Maybe I just don't like being labeled a gossip."

"I never said you would do that intentionally—"

"Oh, so it's just that I'm not smart enough to realize when I'm going to spew information all over? Look out, room, she's gonna blow?"

"What? No, no. That's not what I meant. I mean, look, this is my job, Maggie."

"To serve and protect and defend. Yeah, I know. Whatever it takes."

Tom had had enough. "Look, are you going to agree to this or not? Because if not, it's no skin off my nose to go back to the DA and tell him it just didn't work out. I'm more than happy to go out and find an alternate solution. The only reason I went along with this in the first place is because Ledbetter was so dead set that this would be the perfect answer for all concerned. Quinn here makes a little money and serves a greater purpose, we get answers about what data's on the stuff we recovered, and *bam*, murderer hopefully identified. Win-win."

I was fully prepared to nudge the conversation back to the issue we had just been discussing. Marcus, on the other hand, decided enough was enough. "All right," he said, cutting in and cutting off anything else I might have been ready to say.

"You'll do it?"

"Yeah."

"Well, all right, then." For the first time since he walked through the door Tom relaxed back in his chair. "Signatures first. Then we'll talk about what we need you to look at."

Marcus avoided my questioning glance, but he was already signing his, so it would have been pointless for me not to sign as well. Finishing his signature with a flourish, Marcus handed his pen over to me. I signed the agreement. It wasn't like I would ever, *ever* go against the request for confidentiality, regardless of the issues I had with Tom. It hurt my feelings that he would think so poorly of me when I had given him no reason for so little faith. But then again, Tom was a cop, and if there was one thing I'd learned from my time with him, it was that cops of some experience lost the ability to trust your average citizen on the street, even those they had known personally for years. They viewed everyone as possible perpetrators of some crime or indiscretion, suspected everyone of secret deviance or vice, unless proven otherwise. With modern-day cops, it was no longer a case of innocent until proven guilty. It was guilty unless proven otherwise. An unfortunate occupational hazard.

Marcus had handed me his agreement to place with my own, so I tossed them down on the tabletop for Tom. "There. Two signed confidentiality agreements. Hope it helps."

He reached for them. "It's a start."

I think that's when his mind first registered the items Marcus and I had spread out on the coffee table just a short while before he'd arrived. The *click* was almost audible in the still room.

"What—" And then he recoiled instantly. "What is that?" His gaze went from one item to the next and then back again.

"Nothing."

"It doesn't look like nothing. It looks like something."

"Nothing . . . to worry about." My voice lifted up at the end, more like a question than a statement. Darned insecurities.

"I'll tell you what it looks like," Tom said, his stubbornness coming out in a big way. Of course that was nothing particularly new. "It looks like something occultish."

Tom placed anything and everything paranormal or outside of the realm of the everyday, mundane world into the occult category. But he meant it in a bad way. As though every witch and pagan out there could be compared to a more ruthless magical practitioner who was just in it for power and control over another. Because that was the fear of every mundane when it came to magick, or abilities they didn't have. That it would be turned and used against them, and they would be defenseless to stop it. Witches, to him, were consorts of evil, trafficking with all sorts of things that he wasn't sure existed, but didn't want to come in on the wrong side of, just in case. He was all for stacking the deck on the side of righteousness and piety and moral standing. I, on the other hand, believed in the Light. It didn't always mean the same thing. Take Reverend Baxter Martin, for example. The perfect example.

Marcus was in no mood. "What it is, is none of your damn business. Now, are you wanting my help or not? Because if not, you can get the hell out of my house."

Tom shrugged. "Fair enough." The expandable file folder came out again. He inspected our signatures and dates on the confidential agreements and then carefully filed them within. And then, he pulled out a clear plastic bag. Inside it was the crunched thumb drive that had been found among all the scattered computer effluvium in the office. He held it up. "This was found on the floor of the office this morning."

A faint smirk touched Marcus's lips, barely contained. "Yes, I know. I was there, remember?"

Tom ignored him. "We want you to do what you can to read the data on this, safeguard the files to prevent their loss, and try to resolve any corrupted data that you possibly can. Since the computer was specifically targeted, what we're hoping is that we will find something on there that can be tied to a motive for the killing. Right now we're just trying to piece together as much information as we can, just trying to talk to as many people as possible who might have seen something, anything, to try to recreate his last hours. Maybe there's something on this that can help, too."

"Sounds straightforward enough."

Tom took something else out of the file folder and handed it to Marcus. "Here's a letter for you, signed by Chief Boggs, Sheriff Reed, and District Attorney Ledbetter, giving you permission to do all of what we just talked about." He cleared his throat. "It, um, also gives you immunity, in the event that something of a certain, um . . . nature . . . shows up. At least with regard to what you might find on the drive."

There was something in between what he was saying that he was purposely leaving out. I could feel the presence of it, hovering there, waiting for someone to acknowledge it. "What exactly does that mean, something of a certain nature?" I asked, watching his face closely for the telltale hint of what he was hiding. Marcus was watching, too. "Immunity from what?"

I could tell he was struggling with how much he thought we should know versus how much we might need to know. Finally, he must have decided to just lay it all out on the line. "There are . . . things that could potentially be on the drive. Things that might be unpleasant. We just have no way of knowing for sure until we are able to gain access. And if it is blank or the files are corrupted or unrecoverable, well, I guess we'll cross that bridge if we come to it."

Unpleasant. Unpleasant, how? Who were we dealing with here? Robert Locke was just your everyday, average, slightly creepy but mostly harmless apartment manager . . . wasn't he?

Marcus just came straight out and asked him.

"He has a record," Tom said, "for something that happened quite awhile ago. He never did time for it— somehow he seems to have gotten off lightly."

"A record for something he did in Stony Mill?" I asked.

Tom shook his head. "No, it was elsewhere. If it had been here, we'd have thrown the book at him."

Small town, swift justice. That sounded about par for the course.

"Seriously, what sort of thing are we talking about?" I pressed as he seemed hesitant to answer concretely. "Something unpleasant, something he had a record for. I mean, that could be anything."

Marcus seemed to have picked up on . . . *something* . . . out of all the somethings, though. "I think that the answer is in the need for immunity. Why would anyone need legal immunity for something relating to a file kept on a thumb drive?"

Think, think, think. What would a person keep on a thumb drive? Well, just about anything they wanted to back up. Documents, music, photos . . .

Photos?

"He likes porn?" I asked hesitantly. "But that's not illegal."

"It's not illegal *if* it is a photo of a person who gave her consent to be photographed . . . and is of a certain age."

"Child pornography?" I squeaked. "He was arrested for child pornography?"

Tom nodded and said, "Distributing. But I didn't say a word. You did not hear that from me."

"How on earth did he get out of serving time for something like that?" I wondered aloud. "You're right, we would have thrown the book at him. The biggest one we could find."

"How? I don't know. My guess is that either his family had enough money or status or power—or heck, all of the above—to buy his way to a plea agreement. Or that he has friends in high places. Or both."

I couldn't fathom having so much of any or all of the above to be able to get out of the punishment for an actual crime. I tried, but the concept just boggled me. I was getting stuck somewhere between rich bitch and skeeving diva. But the male versions of those, naturally.

The trouble I was having with that was, Locke didn't seem the rich-and-connected type. Those were not high-quality duds he was rocking. And the shoes? My grandmother had a saying about a man who didn't care enough to take care of his shoes, or who couldn't spare the time to iron the major wrinkles out of his shirt. "Man like that can't be troubled for anything good." Maybe she was right. Maybe it was more than just laziness, which is bad enough of a character flaw on its own.

"So, you're thinking that we might find incriminating

evidence on the thumb drive, since the computer itself is a bust," Marcus said.

"Yes. With any luck."

"What about the old hard drive? I gave it to Uncle Lou to deliver with the computer."

I thought back, trying to remember if I'd seen it, but there was nothing in my memory banks about him delivering a zipped plastic bag with old computer parts within it. "Lou left me out in his car while he went back in to talk to Locke. I assumed they were going to talk computers."

Tom focused on the one thing I hadn't thought to mention before. "He met with Locke alone?"

"Yes. But only for a few minutes," I rushed to say when I saw the wheels turning in his head, "and then he was back out with me."

Tom had picked up his spiral notebook and pen and was writing something down. "Tell me more about your uncle, Quinn."

"Now, hold on just a minute," Marcus protested. "You can't think my uncle—"

"I'm not inferring anything of the sort," Tom assured him. "But I need to know what connections the victim had. Any one thing could be important."

Marcus looked at him a good long while before answering. "Lou is in an organization with Locke. You know, like the Masons? They are lodge brothers. It's how I connected with Locke in the first place. Members frequent the businesses of other members. Keeping the wealth in the family, so to speak. Church members do the same thing. Locke was looking for computer equipment, my uncle fixed him up with me. That's all there was to it, as far as I am concerned. I'm sure my uncle would tell you the same thing."

"I'm sure."

But he didn't sound as convinced as I would have liked. At least he didn't seem to believe Marcus was being duplicitous in all of this.

"If your uncle handed the old hard drive over to Locke, then it's possible Locke stowed it somewhere. That's what I'm hoping will come out of this. That maybe the perp didn't realize the computer was brand new and thought they were destroying the only source of evidence that might connect them to the victim. But we won't know unless we find it. I'm hoping by the time the guys are done working the scene for evidence, this missing hard drive will show up. And if it does, we may send some more business your way."

It was the typical "You scratch my back, I'll scratch yours" trade-off—which wasn't such a bad thing, when I thought about it.

"Well, we'll see how that works out," Marcus said. "In the meantime, the thumb drive. I'll get to work on it right away."

Tom handed him the bag. "Remember: protect the files. Recover what you can, but protect the files."

A thought occurred to me. "You know, the owner of the apartment complex—Jeremy Harding—seemed awfully upset about not having access to the computer. And he seemed pretty excited about the possibility that the data might still exist on a hard drive somewhere."

Tom frowned at me. "You know Harding?"

"Not really. Well, kind of. I guess." I blushed. "He is related to Liss. Or was, before his wife was killed last year. Does that make them no longer legally related, once the common family member is no longer in the here-and-now? Or does it depend on one's emotional perspective? I've never quite figured that out." And then I saw the look on his face, and my face went even hotter. "Well, maybe that doesn't matter right now."

Tom was still frowning. And thinking. "You're right, though. He was. It could be explained by the fact that he's used to getting his way. People with money often are. But . . . maybe. It's worth checking into." He flicked a glance in Marcus's direction. "I'll be talking to your uncle as well. But don't read anything into that yet."

"Harding was also upset because he hadn't authorized the computer," I continued. "That could be looked at two ways. Either it was because Locke hadn't followed his rules of purchasing equipment—and this is a likely scenario because Locke seems to have paid for the computer on his own—or Harding didn't want something that was kept on that computer to fall into the wrong hands. Neither one screams murder, though, does it?" I made a wry face.

"Lucky him," Marcus quipped. "And I'm going to say he definitely paid for the computer on his own. He paid me in cash. A business entity doesn't pay in cash."

"No, you're right," I said. "It would have been a check for sure." And then, as another thought occurred to me, "I wonder if Harding knew about Locke's past."

"Yes, well, I think we're getting a little ahead of ourselves here," Tom replied coolly. "Not to mention I think we're also forgetting something."

"What's that?"

"The fact that I am the police officer, and you are not. I want you to remember that, Maggie. This is my job, and for your own safety, it's important that you remember that."

"I know, I know. You don't need to worry about me, Tom. I mean, have you *seen* this thing?" I asked, raising my cast aloft. "I'm not exactly in prime investigative shape, am I?"

"Thank the good Lord for small favors," Tom muttered.

It was no secret to me that he didn't appreciate my knack for being in the wrong place at the wrong time, and neither did he admire my aptitude for reasoning through detail if said details entered into the general sphere of my consciousness. But I couldn't exactly help it that people talked. Nor could I help it that I had the uncanny tendency to stumble into situations that later are deemed relevant. I mean, really. Was that my fault? Call it fate. Call it luck. The worst luck in the world.

"Do you have any idea who did this?" I asked.

He shook his head. "No. Not at present. But I wouldn't tell you if I did. All I can do at this point is talk to all of the people who have been seen with Locke recently, or who have been known to have taken issue with him. Explore every possible connection. Take statements, and try to prove them against cold, hard facts. Today everyone is a suspect." He smirked at me. "Even you, Maggie."

That surprised me. "Me?"

"You saw Locke yesterday afternoon, preceding his untimely death. You even spoke to him later in the evening, arranging to meet him."

"To sign a lease! I wasn't even aware of his existence before yesterday afternoon. You can't be serious." And then I saw the amused glitter in his eyes. "Oh. You're not serious."

"Not really. I just wanted to see what you'd say."

"It was a joke."

"I guess you could call it that."

Not a very good one, but hey—when it came to humor, Tom was a little out of practice.

Ba-dum-bump.

It was about this time that Minnie decided she had had

enough standoffishness. None of us saw her winding, secretive path. None of us registered her movement at all. Not until . . .

"*Gah*!" Tom recoiled as a solid fifteen pounds of flying black fur landed not-quite-gracefully on his shoulder from behind in what could only be termed a sneak attack. "What is it? Get it off, get it off!"

"*It* is Minnie. My cat," I reminded him in a soothing voice. "You've met her before, don't you remember?"

His eyes wild as they stared in the direction of Minnie's round, full-jowled face, which was in turn staring intently at him, he said, "Oh yeah. She was smaller then, wasn't she? Not quite the size of a puma?"

"Well, she's grown some. She was only a kitten then."

Minnie chose that moment to investigate his ear while he sat there, stiff as a statue. "What does she think she's doing? Oh God . . . I think she's tasting me."

"Licking, Tom. Maybe she likes the scent of your aftershave," I teased.

"No. No, I'm pretty sure she's just testing the flavor of her next meal."

Marcus was much nicer than I was. He relented, rising to take Minnie from her newfound perch. Although, if the look of pain on Tom's face and the accompanying ripping noise was any indication, he didn't bother to unlatch her claws before lifting her away. "Come on, Minmeister. You've done enough terrorizing for the day." He lifted her to his chest as he carried her off down the hall, her jewel-toned eyes, one blue, one green, staring keenly over his shoulder as though she just might be plotting her imminent return.

Tom, you have been warned.

For all of his tough-cop sensibilities, Tom looked as

though he might actually be worried. "What have you been feeding her?" he asked me.

"Just a little kitten food." I fluttered my eyelashes, the soul of innocence. "Of course she takes down a cow or two most nights, but . . . kidding!"

"I don't know what's gotten into her," Marcus said, shaking his head as he came back into the living room. "I set her down on her favorite windowsill to listen to the birds, but she kept trying to escape me. I actually had to close her in the bedroom." And as if to demonstrate his claim, we could all hear the thumps coming from the hallway. No, she wasn't throwing herself at the door. More like hooking her claws beneath the door and flicking hard, thereby rattling the door in a decidedly annoyed fashion. It was a good thing house cats were small. If they were any bigger, it could get scary fast.

"Maybe she just likes Tom," I suggested helpfully.

"I don't know," Tom hedged. "I still think she was working up her appetite."

Despite the obvious tension that existed between the three of us on a personal level, we still found ourselves meeting each other's respective gazes and chuckling. Which for me turned into a case of the giggles when I could not get Tom's reaction out of my mind's eye. "Oh my goodness . . . You should . . . have seen . . . your face!" I gasped in between.

"Well . . . she did kind of come out of nowhere," Tom said in his own defense. "I mean, you seriously might want to think about putting her on some sort of diet, Maggie. She could do damage, landing on someone like that."

Wiping away the tears from my eyes and trying to get myself under control before a new fit could hit me with that image (*I will not picture it, I will* not *picture it*), I let out a deep, shuddering breath. "Whew! Okay. I feel better now."

And I did. Amazing how a simple shared laugh could rid the air of days' worth of accumulated negative energy. A catharsis for the soul.

Stony Mill could do with more of it.

Chapter 13

When Tom had gone, Marcus set me up with fresh iced tea and a whole bunch of DVR'ed Magnum episodes, a secret project he'd been working on for me to bring my *Magnum, P.I.* addiction out of the dark ages of VCR and into the twenty-first century. He fluffed the pillow behind my head, restacked the cushions beneath my ankle, and with a kiss on the nose told me in no uncertain terms to mind my manners and stay put in healing mode. But even with Magnum for company I found myself unable to get into my zone. How was I supposed to focus on Thomas Magnum and his lovely dimples and eye crinkles and ridiculously heartwarming laugh when I knew Marcus was at his worktable just down the hall? I closed my eyes—I could picture him there, his hair tied back low at the nape to keep it out of his way, the superbright work lamp switched on and flooding the area with light, a hands-free magnifying glass showing him the details, while behind him three large flat-screen monitors awaited him at his computer hub and server station. The boy was tech-ed out to the max, and he liked it that way. And he was good at it. Very good. It was the real reason I was so psyched for him for wanting to go back to school to finish his degree with an eye toward teaching as his end goal . . . just like his Uncle Lou. Marcus's talents with technology were the kind that *should* be shared with the next generation, and he had an amazing way of connecting with his young cousin and Evie. He would make a great middle school or high school teacher. I had no doubts about that.

I just hoped this project for the PD went quickly, so it wouldn't interfere with his class schedule.

I had spent all of forty minutes with my virtual crush Magnum, trying to be good but scarcely hearing a word he said, not even noticing when he sidled up to the curb in his favorite piece of red hot rod, before I decided I would check on Marcus's progress.

I got up as quietly as I could and made my way on crutches down the carpeted hall.

"I hear you." Marcus's voice drifted out through the open door.

I appeared in the doorway and stood on one foot, cast in the air behind me. "I wasn't trying to sneak," I denied. Okay, fibbed. With a straight face, even.

"Good thing. It wasn't working. By the way, you're dribbling glitter on the carpet."

I looked down. "Oh. Heh. You'd think it would be done coming off by now. The girls really went to town with the glitter and bedazzling, though. I find it everywhere."

"I don't mind," he said, grinning. "At least I can always find you from the trail of sparkly stuff you leave behind."

"Ha-ha." I crutched my way to the desk and hovered peering over his shoulder. "So. How are things going?"

"Curious, are we?" He laughed. "I'm going to have to do a little work on it before we'll know one way or the other whether the thing will even be accessible by any computer."

"Oh." I tried to hide my disappointment, but it didn't work as well as I'd hoped. "So, probably not tonight, then?"

His smile teased me for my impatience, but at least it was indulgent. "We'll see. If you've given up on following doctor's orders for the day, you could go throw my dinner together, woman." His blue eyes twinkled. "Or you could just go sit down and I'll throw in a frozen pizza for the both of us."

"Hm. I'm not an invalid, you know. I'm perfectly capable of throwing a frozen pizza into the oven."

So I did. With Minnie's help. She helped me enjoy my Magnum marathon, too, purring away in a compact black ball as Marcus worked late into the night.

Marcus was still playing around with the thumb drive when it came time for him to drop me off at the store in the morning. He and Liss had arranged that she would start picking up and dropping off on Monday, his first day of class. He was a bit behind because he had convinced himself that he would just put everything off, and I was little worried about that—he still needed to buy books, for instance—but he was a big boy, and I knew he would find a way to work everything out. He didn't need me to nudge or remind him.

Still, it was hard to get through my day without wondering, what was he doing, had he had any success, was he pulling up files right at that moment? A curious mind is a terrible thing to waste.

Liss walked over to Annie's for lunch, leaving me to cover the counter. "I'll just pop over and get us some soup, how does that sound?" she said. "I could use the fresh air. A walk is just what I need to get my creativity flowing." She was still putting the finishing touches on her brand-new serenity space. It looked perfect to me, posh and cozy and delicious, but Liss was a perfectionist, and for her final details she would need to find her zone. For that she required some fresh air, some activity . . . and maybe a fresh-from-the-oven double fudge caramel cheesecake brownie. Hold the guilt.

I was just packing up the last of the white chocolate cherry cookies that had been fresh that morning for Devon McAllister, who had dropped by to get Liss's advice on a situation that had come up at Grace, the religious college his father had insisted he attend despite the fact that Devon was a square peg to the school's round hole. He was without a doubt one of the most informed young men of his age that I had ever met, a true scholar of anything paranormal, and he had never come across a conspiracy theory he didn't see some merit in. Once upon a time, I had thought conspiracy theories were modern fairy tales that bored people told to spark some intrigue in their very colorless, insipid existences. I had since revised my opinion, but I certainly didn't embrace the conspiracy-theory magnum opus the way Devon did. But that didn't make me more right than him. In fact, his devotion to his cause and the underground newsletter that thrived because of his energy both amazed me and put me in awe of his dedication. I was also put in awe of his ability to down a cool dozen of Annie's large specialty cookies in one sitting, but that was just part of his charm.

"I brought the latest newsletter, by the way," he told me, slapping one down on the counter. "You really need to read it. Awesome stuff in there." He patted the top page like a proud papa.

"Thanks, Devon. You know I will. I have lots of reading time these days."

"Still with the cast?"

"Still with the cast." I resisted the urge to sigh. It was what it was. It would be off soon enough. I just had to be patient.

The front bell jangled with its usual brassy cheer. Liss came barreling down the main aisle toward us with far more speed and forcefulness than she usually employed. Her eyes were bright, her hair was windblown, her cheeks were pink, and she was breathing heavily. "Ducks! I ran all the way. With any luck the soup is still in its containers. Hello, Devon, how are things?" She pushed the paper sack over at me, using the countertop for support as she tried to regain her breath.

"Things are great!" Devon enthused. "I brought a few copies of the latest for you. Maggie's got them. But I wanted to talk to you about something. I've been spending a lot of time at the library lately, digging through some of the historical tomes for the area. There is some fascinating stuff in there. Enough to make me kind of think people here have always been whacked."

Liss laughed at the unsympathetic viewpoint. "That's lovely, dear."

"No, really. I also found a history of my family's roots in Stony Mill that had been left to my father through his grandmother. Some of it is written as a diary type of entry. And the things she writes about—in so many words—could have been written today."

"Things such as the family's social and community life?"

Devon shook his head, his dark eyes shining with a curious zeal I recognized. The hunger to understand. To *know.* "No, ma'am. Odd things. Things they couldn't explain. The dead rising. End-of-days kinds of things. At least, that's what they attributed it to. The Devil living and playing amongst them."

"Well, glory be," I half joked, though truthfully I was fascinated by the find. "Looks like maybe I should put my reading time to better use." Anything that could shed some light on the state of the town's eternal soul was a good thing in my eyes.

"Indeed," Liss said pensively as she took a seat next to Devon. "It never really occurred to me to look into the town's history for anything more than a reason for the disturbances. Never once did I think that perhaps some of this had happened before."

"Do you think maybe your dad would mind if I borrowed that family history of yours when you have read your fill?" I asked. "I'm going to have an awful lot of free time in the evening in the next few weeks, with Marcus going back to school."

"Sure," Devon said. "I mean, he'd probably say no . . . but what he doesn't know won't hurt him. I'll just tell him I'm not done with it yet if he asks. He probably won't ask, though. He spends more time at his special lodge meetings after he finally does leave the bank than at home, since Mom left. How anyone can spend so much time with buddies playing cards, I'll never understand. It's not even for money." He shook his head, baffled.

Lodge meetings . . . I wondered if it was the same lodge that Uncle Lou belonged to. Stony Mill was small enough; there couldn't be too many of these special brotherhoods around . . . could there? Maybe I'd ask Lou.

Devon made his good-byes, saying he had to get the rest of the issue to the post office and still needed to grab some lunch before getting back for his afternoon class.

When he'd gone, Liss gave up on all pretenses of feminine decorum and respectability and pushed her hair back off her forehead where it had flopped down over one eyebrow, fanning herself with the nearest stack of napkins. "Good Goddess, it is warm outside."

Which reminded me. "So, why did you run all the way from Annie's? Feeling the need for a stronger form of exercise?" I teased her as I picked up the paper sack and pulled out the cups of soup, still intact despite their jostling.

"Oh! My dear." Her hands made a dramatic flair. "I took a moment to speak with Annie while I was there, and she was quite distraught, I must say. Her niece evidently has been put on suspension from her teaching position, just yesterday. Something about inappropriate behavior, or the suspicion thereof, which Annie says is complete and utter bollocks. She said Angela is the soul of propriety and very aware of her place as role model for her impressionable students. Now she has to wait for a formal hearing by the school board in order to state her case."

"Poor Annie!" Poor Annie's niece, for that matter.

"And now her niece's boyfriend is being questioned in connection with the murder of your apartment manager fellow as well."

The movie screen in my memory flickered to life and I pictured Tyson Hollister getting physical with Locke right in front of me. "Oh, that's not good."

"Annie is quite fond of the young man and is certain he isn't involved. Just as certain as she is about her niece's innocence. She is worried, also, because this is a small town . . . well, she is afraid that racial bias might come into play among certain representatives of our bureaucracy, with Tyson being . . . you know."

Racial bias was an ugly secret in Stony Mill, as it was in

many other small towns throughout the Midwest that had never been remotely integrated in their entire history. Or maybe, just maybe, it was prejudice against being new or different, as much as it was about the color of one's skin or the place of one's birth. Around here, the same families were born, lived, and many died within the spatial confines of this area. Sure, some moved away, and occasionally others moved in (though they would always be considered outsiders), but by and large, people stayed to themselves here, marrying into each others' families, raising their kids together, occasionally divorcing and marrying someone else who had grown up right here as well. It was the way that small towns worked. But . . . "I don't think she has to worry about that with Tom. I really don't. For what it's worth. I just spoke with him last night, and they haven't focused on anyone in particular. I'm sure they're just questioning the boyfriend, the same way that they would any other person who had dealings with Locke in the days before he was killed."

Liss's expression sharpened with interest behind her half-moon glasses, which she had just slid into place. "You spoke with Tom?"

"Yeah."

"Last night, you say?"

"Yeah . . . oh, hold on now, wait just a minute. He stopped by Marcus's place to ask Marcus to help the PD out with a technical aspect of the investigation."

Now she looked even more interested. "Oh, really? Now that *is* something, isn't it? When only a few weeks ago they could scarcely bear the sight of each other. Time does heal all wounds."

"Well, I don't think they're likely to be found sitting around a campfire tossing back beers and comparing the local football stats anytime soon."

"I can't believe Tom found the wherewithal to ask our Marcus for help."

"Well . . . technically speaking it was more the district attorney. And Chief Boggs and Sheriff Reed," I amended. "But DA Ledbetter was probably the driving force." I told her about the work Marcus had done for the DA's office and how that job had turned into this one.

"So, what goes around, comes around?"

"Exactly."

"And what does that mean for the investigation? What type of work is Marcus doing for them? Something computer related, obviously. Hm." She tapped a fingertip on her chin. Suddenly she angled a direct look at me over her glasses. "You did say the new computer was demolished, didn't you?"

"I did. Smashed to bits, all over the office. I can't really say what he's doing, though. Tom made me sign a confidentiality agreement."

She nodded. "I understand. But even without you telling me anything, I suppose I can assume he's looking for files. What sort of files, I wonder? Was your Mr. Locke known for something of a shady nature? Something someone might have killed him for?"

I shrugged helplessly, wishing I could tell her more. "As far as Annie's concerned, the only problem between her niece or her niece's boyfriend and Mr. Locke had to do with their wanting to break the lease and being held against their will. That was the only thing they argued about when I was there, at least. For Annie's sake, I hope that's true. I really do. I know she loves her niece Angela, and she seemed pretty fond of the boyfriend, as well." I grimaced. "I feel bad. I was the one who had to mention Tyson Hollister's argument to Tom. When he asked me to describe my dealings with Locke the other afternoon. Their argument did get pretty heated and might have resulted in a few punches thrown if Marcus's Uncle Lou hadn't been there to break things up. But to kill someone, over a disagreement like that? I just don't know. It seems a huge jump . . . but I suppose stranger things have happened." Boy, had they ever. And Stony Mill was full of such strange happenings.

The cups of soup were waiting for us. I flipped off the lids. The scents of chicken, cream, carrots, celery seed, and tarragon rose to greet me. "Yum. I'll just heat these up for us," I told her, turning around to reach for my crutches. Then turning back and realizing my logistics problem.

Liss laughed. "How? No, you need to prop your foot up for a bit. Why don't you go over to the serenity space and ponder the changes for a bit? Maybe you can tell me what the space is still calling for. And then we can have a nice, peaceful, serenity-filled lunch."

We did, too. And we enjoyed it.

Later in the afternoon, the two of us were sifting through voluminous amounts of packing peanuts, trying to track down by touch the precious gems hiding within, when we heard Tara and Evie breeze into the store. "Back here!" I called out to their hellos as they attempted to locate us.

I felt their presences before I turned to greet them— their energy levels were always raised, which I supposed was probably the natural state of a teenager high on life. "How was school today?" I asked without turning around.

"Fine. Mrs. Lancaster gave a pop quiz, which utterly sucked . . . for the people who weren't prepared. I aced it, of course."

I heard Evie groan as if in pain. "I read the chapters she assigned, but I guess I was one of the unprepared ones. I've been having so much trouble concentrating lately!"

"It's no big deal. She'll let you take a do-over. You'll ace it next time. And hey! We brought you a surprise, Maggie," Tara said, all in a quickie blur.

"Aw, that's awfully sweet of you," I said, turning around to find . . . not quite what I would ever have expected.

Because my surprise was Abbie Cornwall, eyeliner, Chuck Ts, and all.

"Um, hi," she said, raising a hand in a shy wave and then biting her lip.

"Hi," I said right back, while my gaze darted first to the left to meet Tara's and then to the far right to peer at Evie.

"It's Abbie Cornwall," Tara said, a little unnecessarily. "Abbie, this is Maggie O'Neill."

"Uh-huh," Abbie said. And then didn't say much else. Which was only adding to my whole sense of the bizarre about the encounter.

Liss jumped in to save the day. "Well, hello there, Abbie dear. It's nice of you to stop in today. Do you like tea? Most girls your age haven't tasted a good cup of tea. Would you like to try one?" She squinted down at petite Abbie in assessment mode. "You look like a blend of oranges and spice and maybe a little zing that I will keep to myself."

"Um . . . sure?" Abbie said, obviously not quite certain what to make of Liss, who today was wearing a dress that was straight out of the early Edwardian era and probably unlike anything the jeans-and-sneaker-clad teenager had ever seen before.

Liss tottered over to perform her tea magick, leaving me to stare at the girls, wondering what on earth had brought us to this moment.

"Abbie has something to say," Tara finally said, nudging her forward when it became apparent to all that Abbie wasn't going to say anything without a little prodding.

She cleared her throat. "S-sorry for all the trouble the other day."

"You didn't know I was there?" I offered helpfully.

She nodded. "I just wanted to get out of there before the jerk came back out. I heard him stumbling around back there, dragging his knuckles."

I laughed at the image. It was probably irreverent of me, considering the knuckle dragger she was referring to had ended up dead the next day. "You didn't mean to nearly knock me over."

"Nope."

"I didn't think so." The two of us sized each other up while Evie and Tara watched. "You know, Abbie, the police are going to want to talk to you about that day. Not that they'll think you had anything to do with what happened— um, you have heard what happened?"

She nodded.

"Anyway, they're going to want to talk to you about it—"

"They already have," she said. "They called me to my counselor's office this morning. I thought it was for my annual consult, but nope. I guess you must have been the one that turned me in, huh?"

"Well, I did mention our brief encounter. Not to get you into trouble, but in the event that perhaps you had seen anything or knew anything. I know the cop who is leading the investigation, and I'm pretty sure that right now they are looking for anything that can help them."

"Tea!" Liss called from the café counter.

"Ooh! I've been thinking about this all day!" Evie turned to hightail it over. Tara followed. Abbie hesitated a moment. I mouthed, *Over there*, to her and indicated the counter with a nod of my head. She followed suit, uncertainty making her scuff the toes of her Chucks over the old uneven floorboards.

Liss had poured four cups, steaming hot, and they were waiting for us with the usual accoutrements of honey, pure cane sugar, cream, and ground nutmeg on standby.

"There you are . . . Abbie, is it?" She nudged the cup at the girls' school friend. "Good for everything that ails you. Try it with honey—just a dollop—and a dash of nutmeg. Go on. Try it."

I could tell by Abbie's face that tea wasn't her usual drink of choice, but she lifted it to her lips anyway. The surprise in her eyes was a delight I never grew tired of. "Yum!"

Liss beamed. "Ah, my dear. I'm glad that you like it. It always makes me especially happy to introduce the genteel pleasures of tea to a new generation."

"So," I said when given the opportunity, "you said that the police talked to you at school, then?"

Abbie nodded glumly. "I am going to be in so much trouble when my mom finds out."

"She doesn't know that you were at the apartment complex?"

"I was supposed to be at school. I ditched." She met my eye, a ferocity in her own. "But I'm not sorry. I just wish I'd found it."

"I'm sorry. I'm a little lost. What were you looking for exactly, and how did you come to be there? You obviously had a reason."

Abbie took a sip of tea, bracing herself. "I used to live there. My mom and me. That was our apartment last summer, and that jerk of a manager booted us out. My mom and me, we were homeless for three whole weeks before she lucked into a new place for us. That guy didn't care, though.

He just said we broke the terms of the lease, so it was at his discretion."

I frowned. "Broke the terms of the lease. How? Oh. You mean the age thing?"

Abbie nodded. "But it was the only place we could find that my mom could afford, so you can't blame her for making him believe I was over eighteen," she said urgently. "And it was a stupid rule anyway. It's not like I was going to make any trouble at the complex. Anyway, I didn't do anything wrong. Except for the breaking into the apartment thing, which technically speaking wasn't *breaking* in since I had a key and everything. It's not my fault the jerk didn't think to change the locks."

Teenage sensibilities. Wasn't it wonderful the way the mind worked?

"Why did you break in . . . I mean, go back?" I asked her, curious.

She shied away from the question. "I didn't find it. You guys got there before I could. And he got what was coming to him, as far as I was concerned," was all that she would say. "After the way he treated my mom, and . . . everything . . ." Her voice trailed off.

The answer troubled me. A lot. What did she know? And my thoughts kept coming back to her boyfriend, JJ, who had logged off from his conversation with Tara rather than reveal what he knew. And I hoped desperately that neither of them had anything to do with it.

But my questions slipped away from me when I heard my cell phone ringing away back in my purse in the office. The rousing strains of the *1812 Overture*, trumpeting triumphantly away. I had changed it to something less . . . extreme . . . several months ago, but Marcus had changed it back to my ring tone for him and only him one day after I broke my ankle. He said it brought back fond memories, and who was I to complain when he was being romantic?

"I'll get it for you, Maggie," Evie offered, sliding from her stool and racing toward the back of the store without even waiting for me to thank her or protest. She found it in my purse with much less trouble than I usually had and came running back out in record time with it suspended in front of her. "It's Marcus," she whispered. Unnecessarily, since it was still ringing and there was no way Marcus would have heard her, and he wouldn't have minded in the least if he had.

I quickly grabbed it and clicked Send before the call could go to voice mail. "Hey!"

"Hey, sweetness. You free?"

"For you, yes."

"Hmm. I like the sound of that. So, is it all right if I stop in?"

"Yes, of course." My heart started beating faster; I knew it couldn't be just another social call. Could it have something to do with his project for Tom, so quickly? Anticipation settled in all my nerve endings "Aren't you going to give me any hints?"

"Nope. You're just going to have to be patient." I could hear the smile in his voice.

"Fine," I said, pretending to pout. "What time will you be here?"

"How about now?"

Chapter 14

I heard the store's back alley entrance open and close, followed by the booted footsteps my ears were attuned to pick up anywhere. "Excuse me, everyone!" I sang out and hurriedly crutched my way toward the office. We met in the middle when he flung back the violet-hued velvet curtain.

"Sneaky," I said. "Very sneaky."

"I was already here."

"So I see."

"I figured Liss wouldn't complain."

"And you were right, ducks," Liss said, waving at him. "Are we all set for next Monday?"

"We are indeed. Or at least we will be as soon as we buy our books." He looked at me and grinned. "I love using the royal 'we.' "

Liss laughed.

"Mind if I steal Maggie away for a few minutes?" he asked her.

"Of course not. Steal away." She returned to the girls at the counter, smiling to herself.

"So . . ." I said. "Where to?"

"Any suggestions?" he asked. He flicked his gaze over my shoulder. "Little pitchers and all that. Including an extra today, I see."

I nodded. "I'll explain in a minute." I called to Liss to let her know I'd be outside a few minutes, and then I followed Marcus out the back door.

"So?" I said, my natural curiosity getting the better of me. He indicated his truck, which was parked in my usual but currently unused space behind the store, and held the door for me while I slipped inside, out of the sun.

"All right, I'm in," I said when he entered from the driver's side and closed the door behind him, rolling down the window. "Are you going to tell me or not?"

"Not." As my face fell, he relented and said, "I'm going to show you."

He reached behind the seat and drew out a big, heavy duty envelope. A big, *fat*, heavy duty envelope.

"*I*"—he said, his voice pumped up with pride—"managed to get the thumb drive operable."

His proud moment was my proud moment. "As if there was ever any doubt. So . . .?" My eyebrows lifted expectantly. "Was it important?"

"I think so. And I think it makes it that much more important that Fielding and his crew locate the old drive or any backup drives that may be hanging around Locke's office or apartment. Makes me wish I had done a full backup on my own, but once all the files were transferred from the old drive to the new with no errors, there was no need."

"What was on it?" The suspense was killing me. A part of me wanted to see . . . and a part of me was cringing at the uncertainty of what he might have found.

Without a word, he opened the envelope and handed me

a stack of papers, upside down. Slowly, I flipped the stack and turned it lengthwise so that I could see properly without my mind having to make that small adjustment.

It was a photo of a young woman. The photo was a little grainy, as though it had been taken from some distance away, with lines across it, and the apparent subject, the young woman, was in a state of half undress, bra and panties only to cover her bits, her blond hair draped over her face as she bent down to her upraised leg to slip off a shoe.

"Locke had a girlfriend?" I proposed, hoping beyond hope. Except it didn't seem like the kind of pose a girl would adopt when trying to be sexy for her boyfriend. There was something altogether too casual about it, even unaware. Like she had just gotten home and was getting ready for the shower and had no idea a camera was recording the event.

I flipped to the next page in the stack and tried not to be surprised to find it was another photo.

Another partially clad woman.

With brown hair.

In other words, not the young woman in the first photo.

This pic, too, seemed to be shot from a distance but zoomed in, with the same type of fuzzy lines in the foreground, although perhaps from a slightly different angle. And again, the girl was seminude, wearing nothing but a towel around her waist, her arm raised to bare her breasts as she pulled her hair from her neck as she faced a mirror that showed all, but only from the mouth down. Just below her collarbone was a tattoo of what looked like a bird.

Both women were quite lovely in form. Enviably so. The faces, though, in these two photos were not captured.

There were more pictures of each of them, many catching them in the middle of doing very innocuous things. Brushing their hair. Their teeth. Putting on a pair of boots. Sitting cross-legged on the bed, typing on a laptop. Darting naked from the shower with hair wrapped turban-style, as though on the hunt for fresh undergarments. Sometimes their faces were shown, sometimes the focus was more on their bodies. Okay, always on their bodies. The faces seemed to be extraneous details. And then there were the shots that were more . . . risqué . . . like when they brought male company back to their place, and the usual activities ensued. Then the sheer volume of frame-by-frame pics became really intense. And not once did I get the impression that these sessions were staged for the camera. Not once.

The hair on the back of my neck had risen, prickling its way up to my scalp. A warning.

There were more women, too, in similar situations. This had been going on for some time.

Who were they?

There was a sameness to the photos that leapt out at me, the deeper into the pile I traveled. The rooms. There was a similarity to them. A sameness of design. Different bedding, but the angles of the rooms seemed to match, even when the angle of the photo did not.

"It's enough to make you want to keep the curtains and blinds closed at all times, isn't it?"

I let my breath ease out of me, realizing for the first time that it had pent up with all the intense discomfort I had felt flipping through some other woman's sexy-times photo op. "No kidding." I shuddered, releasing even more energy. "Creepy. He had quite the thing for naked women. Multiple naked women."

"Well . . . most men do," he admitted, not entirely apologetic about it, either.

I laughed in spite of myself. "True."

"But there's a difference to these pictures, I think."

I nodded. "Because the women had no idea they were being photographed. That is what you were getting at, isn't it?"

"Yeah. Exactly that."

"The sameness in the photos. Did you notice that, too?"

Marcus nodded.

"It's because they were taken there, at the apartments. The mirrors. Did you get far enough past the ever-present boobage to recognize that the mirrors were all very similar? Big, heavy, over the bed . . ."

"I did, in fact, notice that," he said.

"Good. Anyway. The apartment I looked at had that exact same kind of mirror. Now, I didn't go through the other apartments, obviously, but it can't be a coincidence, can it?"

"Like Liss, I don't believe in coincidence."

"The mirror in the apartment I looked at was cracked. Like it had been hit with something. Maybe when the previous tenants had moved out, I don't know. I didn't like the mirror at all. Locke told me he'd put it on the repair list. I asked him if it couldn't just be removed, and he refused. He said it was a built-in, so it would have to be repaired. I didn't question him."

"Hm. I mean, it could be part of the original design of the apartments, I suppose. You did say they were an older place that was being remodeled. Maybe built-in mirrors over the beds are common to that design era."

"I think the brochure said they were built in the seventies. I don't know if all of the apartment buildings were constructed at the same time or what, but I'm guessing they were. I seem to remember riding past them years ago on one of the many townwide bike excursions that Steff and I made as marauding teenage girls, looking much the same. The apartments, not Steff and me. So . . . maybe. But if they were being remodeled to bring them up-to-date, the way that Locke suggested to me that they were, why would they leave a design element in that was so very outdated?"

Neither of us had an answer for that particular question. Chalk it up to poor taste or bad advice, I guess.

"What comes next?" I asked him.

"I take these to Tom, along with the copy I made of all the files. And we'll see what he says."

"Do you think he'll be surprised?"

"Does anything seem to surprise him? Really?"

Hm. He had a point.

"I thought Tom said he had a record for child pornography. How on earth does this fit in with that?" I wondered.

"I don't know. We'll let Tom worry about how to connect the dots, huh?"

We'd been out here long enough, so I told Marcus I was going to have to get back. He kissed me quickly and told me he was going to go pay a visit to Tom at the police department. "I should be back in time to take you home, no problem," he promised. I watched him drive off, waving as he pulled away, and then went back inside.

The group at the counter had been joined by a party of one, I noticed. I made my way over. The addition was a woman who might have a few years on me, but no more than that. Brown hair, medium length. Pretty enough, but perhaps a little tired, if the strain around her up-tilted eyes was any indication. Jeans, sturdy tennis shoes, a thin jersey hoodie . . . this was a down-to-earth working woman, with a worldliness in the lines that were starting to etch themselves into her forehead and between her brows. There were hundreds of women like her in town. Never would they be a part of Mel's coffee clique. They had more important things on their mind. Like day-to-day survival.

"All taken care of?" Liss asked, smiling.

I nodded. "I think so." I wished I could confide in her about what Marcus had found. She had been my sounding board on everything for almost a year. I trusted Liss with my life. She was the most conscientious person I knew, and she was also the most connected, spiritually. And with that in mind as we found our way through these troubling times, in my opinion the more she knew about everything that was going on in this town, the better I felt. Knowledge was power. Forewarned is forearmed.

But I couldn't. Not with the confidentiality agreement binding me as effectively as any spell. I had given my word . . . and no matter how hard it was to keep things from her, I had to uphold that promise. "Abbie's mother has come to pick her up," Liss told me. "Becky Cornwall, meet my assistant and right-hand woman, Maggie O'Neill."

Becky Cornwall held out her hand, and I shook it. "Nice to meet you," she said.

Abbie had transferred her gaze to the floor the instant I came back into the store, an obvious effort to lie low and deflect attention.

"My daughter tells me that you're the one that found Mr. Locke's body, Miss O'Neill," she said, getting straight to the point. "I hope it wasn't too awful. I know that the police spoke with Abbie today with her school counselor present. I assume that means they will be in contact with me, too. Guess that's just how it works these days."

Surprised, I glanced over at Abbie. "Oh, I wasn't aware she—"

"Told me? Yes. She can be headstrong, but she's a good girl."

I nodded my understanding. She was a teenager. Head-strong came with the territory. "From what I understand they are trying to speak to as many individuals who might have had contact with Mr. Locke as possible. And since Abbie and I both saw him the day before he died, it was inevitable that we would be among the first."

She looked confused. "Abbie saw him?"

"Yes, at the . . . at the apartment building that day . . ."

Behind her, Abbie cringed. Evie and Tara were frantically shaking their heads. *Uh oh.*

She looked at her daughter. "I thought they questioned her because we used to live there."

"Now, Mom, before you get all psycho about things, just remember . . . the guy kicked us out. For no reason." Abbie Cornwall pleaded for understanding.

Her mother looked stunned as realization dawned. "I can't believe you . . . you went back there? Didn't I tell you, never go back?"

"I know, I know. Mom, geez. I was safe." Abbie met my gaze. Stared me down, actually.

"And now this . . . this murder. Abbie, tell me you're not mixed up in this. You and JJ. Tell me."

"Mom! You know we're not. It wasn't about that. You think I could ever do something like that? I'm not crazy, I'm not violent, and I'm definitely not stupid. Sheesh. And JJ would never—he was on standby to protect me, Mom. To make sure I was okay. And for your information, JJ was at the high school gym, working out on the weight machines, when the cops said it was all supposed to have gone down. There were a lot of guys there. You can ask any of them."

"That may well be, but I still think you and I and JJ need to have a talk. Tonight."

I cleared my throat. "Mrs. Cornwall, unless the police find some evidence to the contrary, there's no real indication that Abbie had anything to do with Locke."

"Ms., not Mrs.," she corrected automatically. "I never married." Frustration tightening her already thin features, she raised her arm and pushed her hair off her face and shoulder. As she did so, her thin jacket slipped from her shoulder. Before she could pull it back on, a colorful bruise on her shoulder caught my eye. Not a bruise. A tattoo of a hummingbird poised over a daisylike flower. Just under her collarbone.

Becky Cornwall was one of Locke's ladies. I was sure of it.

She saw me looking and blushed, straightening her jacket. "I got it when I was just a little older than Abbie is now. Stupid, stupid, stupid. I always have to cover it up. Gives people the wrong idea, you know?"

Liss chuckled. "Don't all of us girls do silly things at that age? I'm convinced these are the things that remind us of our true selves when we've become lost in time and duty and responsibility. They remind us of who we are when we let ourselves be free and frivolous and playful. That's not such a bad thing as one heads into one's crone years."

I laughed, too. "You know, I don't care how old you get, I don't think I'll ever be able to see you as a crone."

She pretended to be wounded by my words. "Oh dear. And I do try so hard, too."

Ms. Cornwall relented but only slightly. "You're right. Now is the time for them to make mistakes if they're going to. I just wish she'd listen a little more closely."

Abbie looked down at her feet. "Sorry, Mom."

"Never mind that now. Go on and start the car for me, would you? We'll talk later."

For some parents, that might come off as a threat, but I didn't get that vibe from Becky Cornwall at all. She waited until Abbie hit the front door before turning back to us. Tara and Evie took that hint that she wanted to talk to the grown-ups of the group and sidled away.

"I appreciate you telling me about her being there, Miss

O'Neill. Raising a teenager is hard enough these days without people keeping secrets from you because they don't want to rock the boat. Lord knows the kids keep enough secrets on their own time. Straight talk. There's not enough of that these days." She hesitated a moment and then admitted, "Well, not that there ever was. If there'd been more of that with my parents back then, maybe I wouldn't have ended up an unwed single mom at the age of seventeen. Not that I regret having her, but . . . I want more than that for Abbie."

I nodded. "I understand completely. But you are right, she seems to be a nice young girl. She obviously respects you. You've obviously done a good job of raising her, despite the wrinkles in the fabric that occur along the way."

"Thank you. I appreciate you saying that. But when I said she can be headstrong . . . she should never have gone back to that place. The manager threatened to sue me for misrepresenting myself on the lease and lying about Abbie's age. I know, it wasn't the best thing to do," she said hurriedly, frowning to demonstrate her own contrition, "but raising a daughter on one salary isn't always easy, and . . . we needed a place to live that I could afford. I tried to explain when Locke confronted me, but he wouldn't listen. We were living out of my car for three weeks in May—I'm afraid Abbie has never forgiven him for that. Or Miss Cooper."

"Miss Cooper?" I echoed.

She nodded. "The upstairs neighbor. A teacher at the high school. I guess she recognized her and mentioned it to Locke. I don't think she meant anything by it, but when Abbie found out, she flipped. She thought Miss Cooper had told him on purpose, because of some joke she told in class that didn't go over too well. I don't know, though. I have to say . . . once I found a new place for us and could breathe again, I was almost glad it happened. I don't know why, but

I never really felt safe there. Sometimes our things would move around. On our dressers. In our closets. Even when both of us were gone. It was the strangest thing. I never knew quite what to make of it . . ." Her voice trailed off, and from the way that she shrugged and then bit her lip, I knew she was embarrassed by the inherent "weakness" of her uncertainty. I wondered what she would say if she knew that, nine times out of ten, a person's instinctive nervousness comes into play for good reason? That, like a mother's instinct for her child's well-being, such things are instances of intuition kicking in, and a person would be well-advised to heed the warning. "And then, when Abbie kept hearing things . . ."

"Abbie was hearing things?" I echoed. "Where?"

"In the bedroom. My bedroom. You see, she still gets nightmares that scare the bejesus out of her, so sometimes she'll still to this day crawl into bed with me when she can't stop shaking. I never minded. I mean, it's always been the two of us, on our own, her and me against the world. I always felt like I had only borrowed time with my girl anyway. But when she kept hearing sounds . . ."

"What kind of sounds?" Liss wanted to know.

"Odd sounds. Clicking. A strange whirring, like the wind in the walls, whispering at us. I actually started thinking I was hearing them, too." She shook her head self-consciously. "Funny, the way imagination spreads from person to person in the dark."

But was it just imagination? Or were they really hearing something . . . there, in the darkness? Whatever it was, I didn't have the sense that it was spirit related, despite my momentary worry early on when Tyson Hollister and Locke were arguing. From what Becky Cornwall described, they could easily have been hearing something . . . mechanical.

Not the heating and cooling systems. Those sounds would have been familiar, heard so often as to become nonexistent to a resident. They wouldn't even have registered. So what was it that Abbie and her mother were hearing that had been freaking them out?

I really wanted to ask her about the photos, but . . . no one was supposed to know. There was no way I could broach the topic with her without going against my confidentiality agreement with Tom. My lips were tied. Sealed. Whatever.

Becky Cornwall was just leaving when I heard Tara exclaim from the back office, "What are you doing back here? You just left!"

"I thought I'd grace you with my presence doubly, cuz. Make your day truly special."

Marcus! But what was he doing back here so soon?

"You wanna make my day special, you coulda just brought me a brownie or something. I am starved. S-T-arved. They had fish sticks for lunch today. You ever had fish sticks at the high school? It's like glue. Rolled in corn flakes. Yum, let me tell ya."

He laughed. "Sounds awesome. Where's Maggie?"

"She's in there. Same bat counter. You know the drill."

"Yeah, I know the drill. Thanks, sweet stuff."

I waved to attract his attention as he swept back the curtain. "I thought you went to talk to Tom about the—" I mouthed the word "pics."

"He wasn't there. Janeen at the station said he's out at the apartment complex crime scene with the team."

I raised my eyebrows. "She just went and told you where he was?"

"I . . . haff . . . vays." He waggled his eyebrows at me.

I laughed. "I'll bet."

"So . . . what are the odds that you could come along with me?"

"You're going out there to talk to him?"

"You got a better idea? Things always go more smoothly between the two of us when you are there to run interference."

On second thought, it wasn't really a bad idea. And if I went along, I could assuage my need to know firsthand. That was so much better than rehashing the details later and risking missing something.

I cringed as I recognized in the bent of my thoughts the same behavioral patterns that I saw in both my mom and my sister. Not to mention half of Stony Mill proper. I ought to be ashamed of myself. For all the trouble I'd given my mom and Mel for their gossip chain over the years, at that moment I realized I had somehow managed to follow suit in my own special way. I was becoming my own worst nightmare.

Could it be? Was I really . . . a gossip-aholic?

It might require therapy.

Extreme therapy. Because it was too late for gene therapy.

I checked the display of antique clocks on the far wall opposite the counter. "It's about that time, actually," I said. "Can you wait a few minutes while I clean up?"

"Sure, take your time."

I performed my usual, end-of-the-workday tasks, but since the store would be open late tonight on Liss's watch with Tara and Evie in supporting roles, those tasks were greatly shortened. We were able to call it a day in no time. I told Liss I'd see her in the morning, waved at the girls, who were busy sorting through aging stock to get things ready for the town's upcoming Sidewalk Days Sale, which always drew scads of people for the fun, and gathered up my things.

We were on the road in no time, heading away from the river and more deeply into the south side of town.

"I hope he's still there," I fretted to Marcus, "or we're going to have to track him down."

"No use calling, we're almost there."

We drove past the little community park Lou and I had seen Abbie and her boyfriend JJ holed up in after her escape from the closet. Just a few blocks more and Marcus was pulling into the parking lot. At first glance it appeared that every black-and-white in the county was on-site, parked one after the other in front of the office. "Thataway," I said. Unnecessarily, but it still made Marcus smile.

"Ya think?"

We parked at the far end and got out, Marcus matching his pace to mine as we made our way up the sidewalk beneath the leafy canopy of the overhanging trees. The door to the office was propped wide open, the yellow and black police tape pinned back to one side, out of the way. To our right I saw a couple of officers chatting or comparing notes in the pool area.

No Tom.

Wordlessly Marcus jerked his head toward the office and raised his eyebrows in question. I nodded. We headed in that direction, waiting for someone to see us and, perhaps, to stop us from going farther. No one did. By the time we were to the point where we could actually see within the office itself, we had slowed to a creep. We paused on the sidewalk just outside by unspoken mutual consent. I know I, for one, was hesitant to just barge in, but I could see straight in through the open outer door and couldn't help noticing they had the door to the utility room open. Voices filtered out to us.

"—Johnson found it, sir. It was locked in a drawer—"

"—knew we'd find it sooner or later. Quinn said he was

instructed to return it to the victim with the rebuilt computer—"

That could only mean the original disk drive. They'd found it. I turned to look at Marcus. With everything that he found on the thumb drive, I couldn't help wondering what more might be found on the hard drive itself.

"Anything else turn up that could shed some light on his past?"

"Not yet, sir. The guy lived here in this tiny room, and it's like he didn't really have a life. No personal stuff besides clothing. No letters. Some bills, though his room and board seemed to be built into his job."

"Bank activity?"

"Still no statements for you, sir. I expect we'll find it all on his computer. I did find a notebook that contains a list of passwords to online accounts. You'll probably find it there."

"Kind of out of character, for what we know of him, don't you think?"

"Guess he had the same trouble remembering all his different passwords the same way the rest of us do. It was locked away with the old hard drive."

Tom came into view then, his back to us. "I'm going to take this and the hard drive and get on it. I want you to continue here. Nothing goes undisturbed. And don't let Harding in here. He's been on my case constantly, trying to get in here. At this rate, even when it is safe to give him access to his files—assuming they're found on the drive as expected—I'm tempted to hold off as payback for the harassment."

"Gotta be a law against it, heh?" his fellow officer quipped. It was the young guy . . . what was his name? He looked over Tom's shoulder and saw us standing there. "Oh, hey. We got company."

Tom turned and glanced warily over his shoulder. Seeing

Marcus and me there, he spoke quietly to the man before walking our way. "Hey. I wasn't expecting to see you here."

Marcus held up the thick envelope and waved it back and forth.

Tom's eyebrows rose. Recovering himself, he slipped on his sunglasses to hide his responses. "You got in?" he asked, his tone cautious.

"I got in," Marcus confirmed. With only a little added self-satisfaction.

"And?"

Marcus handed over the envelope. Tom took it, unwinding the cord closure, and removing the stack of printed pictures. His brows knit together, and he let out a long, low whistle.

"Is that what you were expecting?" Marcus asked him.

"I don't know what I was expecting . . . but this kind of takes the cake, doesn't it?" He started flipping through. I kind of wished he hadn't put his sunglasses back on, so that I could see the thoughts flickering through his eyes. When those glasses weren't in place, his eyes revealed far more than he could ever know. Or maybe he did. Maybe that's why he hid behind the mirrored aviators so damn often.

He let out another low whistle.

"Is that for the enormity of what this means to the investigation, or is that for the chickie pics?" I couldn't help asking.

The briefest saucy grin was my reward. And then he smothered it, covering it with his professional, all-business mask. "My entire focus right now is the investigation, Miss O'Neill. Obviously. It is my job."

"To serve and protect."

"Bet your ass."

I waited until he had flipped through more of them. "Marcus and I noticed something about the pictures."

He stopped flipping and glanced up at me, over the rim of his shades. "You looked at these?"

No sense in denying it. He would have accused me of it anyway. Besides, I'm sure if he really thought about it, he would have known I would. "Uh-huh. All of them."

He sighed. "All right. Let's have it. What did you notice?"

"They were all taken here. At these apartments."

He frowned, going back to the beginning and taking a closer look. "You know . . . I think you might be right."

"I did tour an apartment, you know. I have no idea if the others resemble the one I walked through—though I have a good hunch that they do; all apartment complexes seem to follow their original pattern—but if so, then yes, they all look to be taken here."

"Hm." He flipped some more, slowly, paying attention to detail. "And did you notice anything else?"

I cleared my throat. "I think the ladies in the pics are all residents—current or past—of these apartments."

"And why do you think that?"

"Because I met one of them today."

Tom and Marcus both stared at me.

Marcus spoke first. "You didn't tell me that!"

I bit my lip. "It was kind of last minute, and then you came by and asked me to ride shotgun, and . . ." I lifted my shoulder in a helpless shrug.

"Never mind that now," Tom interrupted. "Who do you think you recognized?"

"Her name is Becky Cornwall."

"Cornwall, Cornwall . . ." Tom frowned, thinking. "I know that name. Where do I know that name from?"

"She and her daughter Abbie used to live here." I supplied the information helpfully. "In the apartment I was looking at, actually."

A lightbulb seemed to go off for him. "Ah. I spoke to her today. At the high school. She's the girl who was hiding in the closet and nearly knocked you over."

"The one and the same."

"Kids these days. I warned her about that sort of behavior, too, while I was at it. It's not something we're interested in pursuing. Too many irons in the fire right now. There was no damage perpetrated. Looks like stupid kid stuff to me. I hope we haven't come to the day when kids can't mess up a little bit anymore without being thrown into the pokey." He tilted his head toward me. "How did you fall into meeting her mother?"

Fall into. Ha. The same way I seemed to fall into everything these days. Unwittingly. "She came into the store to pick up Abbie."

"Uh-huh." There was a pregnant pause while he waited.

"Abbie was at the store with Tara and Evie," I explained further.

"Uh-*huh.*"

"The girls . . . they confronted her about her unintentional assault on me, and I think they probably convinced her in their own special coercive ways to come in to apologize to me in person." I laughed, knowing that Tara was incapable of being anything other than her usual forceful self, which made Evie's energies softening everything out all the more important. "So, anyway. She apologized, we all got to talking, then her mom came to pick her up, and we all got to talking some more."

"Talking."

"Yeah."

"You seem to do a lot of that."

I was not going to rise to his bait. "It's called being personable, Tom. And caring enough to listen when people seem determined to talk."

"Yes, you're very good at both of those things, Maggie."

It wasn't a slam, but I wasn't sure it was a ringing endorsement, either. Meh, whatever. I'd take it on face value for now.

"So . . ." Tom said thoughtfully, going back to the photos. "Which one is Abbie's mother?"

I reached for them and sorted through them until I found one that showed the tattoo on her shoulder. "This one. This is Becky Cornwall."

"I'm going to ask the guys who have been interviewing the tenants to go through these and see if they can pick any out of the current crop."

"Good thing none of these are of Abbie herself," I commented. "Nude or seminude photos of an underage girl, that is not cool."

"And certainly not out of the realm of possibility, considering his past record," Tom admitted. "Time will tell. Or should I say, the original computer drive will?" He held up a baggie that contained the previously missing piece of equipment, an excited light in his eyes.

I was interested, too. After what had been discovered on the thumb drive, what would be found on the original hard drive itself?

"What do you say, Quinn?" Tom raised an eyebrow above his silvered shades. "Care to do a little more work for the hometown PD?"

Marcus nodded slowly, all business. "I think I could do that."

"Same deal as before. The confidentiality agreement is still in effect." He locked eyes with me. "For both of you."

"I don't think that will be a problem," Marcus replied. "Do you, Maggie?"

I shook my head. It wasn't quite the truth, because I would love nothing more than to mull things over with Liss, but that didn't matter. I wouldn't break it. "Not for me."

"Good. You got into the thumb drive fast enough. This should be a cakewalk for you, since there doesn't appear to be any damage whatsoever, although there is always the possibility that the files could be password protected."

"I should have something for you ASAP, then, depending on your objectives."

"What do you mean?" Tom asked him. "Just to be sure we're clear."

"Well, if you want me to sift through the entire contents of his computer, then that would, of course, take much longer than searching for relevant JPEGs and other items of possible interest and copying the lot of it to an external hard drive that you could plug into and search through to your heart's content."

Tom made up his mind even faster than I did. "Option number two. Do your thing and search for things that might show up on an initial survey for possible interest, but copy everything over to an independent drive so that I can do a more in-depth search as time allows."

"And bill the county my regular rate plus expenses, such as the external drive, correct?"

"Deal."

Tom gave an ending-the-conversation-now nod and started to walk away. He paused in midstep about ten feet away and turned back. "One more thing."

Surprised, Marcus and I both waited for him to say what he had to say.

"You know computers, but . . . I hear tell that you worked in Intelligence in the military. Is that true?"

Marcus nodded. "Very."

"Think you could take a look at something?"

I started to follow, but Tom said, "It's kind of cramped quarters, Maggie. Would you mind staying outside?"

Would I mind? Of course I minded. Marcus and I were a team, like chips and salsa. Like witches and magick. Like, *What is Tom thinking making me stay outside?* "No, of course not," I lied pleasantly through gritted teeth. "I'll just be here, then. Waiting. Around. No problem."

Marcus aimed an apologetic glance my way—over his shoulder as he followed Tom's lead. I sighed, fidgeting with my crutches. I should probably find a place to sit down. Prop up my ankle. But if I stayed where I was, I ran the chance of maybe, possibly overhearing some of what was going on inside the office.

I was focusing so hard on eavesdropping, I mean, overhearing the goings-on inside the office, that I completely missed any sounds leading up to:

"Did I hear them right?"

Chapter 15

I whirled around—albeit clumsily—at the voice behind me, only to find Alexandra Cooper standing there, in the shade of the tree. This afternoon, the clothes she was wearing—close-fitting yoga pants that showed off her supertight abs and glutes, topped off by a zipped-up hoodie jacket that would have had me dying of heatstroke—gave a clue as to her intended destination. But with her thick, long hair down and a face full of makeup, I couldn't help hoping she had brought along a hair tie and a towel. She was going to need it. Hair sticking to sweaty face while working out? *Bleah.*

"I'm sorry?" I asked her, distracted by the multitude of visuals.

"Did I hear them right?" she repeated. Her glance bounced off toward the office, then back at me. "They found pictures? And a hard drive?"

"Um . . . well . . ." My mind was whirring, uncertain how

to process this direct assault on my agreed-upon promise of confidentiality. "I mean . . ."

"So, it's *true?*"

"Um . . ." I was going to have to do better than that. "Is *what* true?"

"There had been a rumor floating around the place that the creep was taking photos of all of us." She jerked her chin in the direction of the office. "Locke. I can't believe it. I can't believe he actually was. I was so sure it was just one of those silly rumors perpetuated by silly little girls fresh out of college and off on their own for the first time."

"Um, well, I think you'll have to ask Special Task Force Investigator Fielding about that."

"You heard him as well as I did, I'm assuming. Since you were a part of the conversation," she pointed out.

"Um . . ."

She huffed out her breath, putting her hands on her enviably trim hips. "It makes sense. Now. Because what would you expect from a man like our illustrious apartment manager? Standing in his private room in his office, getting his jollies from being no better than a sleazy peeping Tom. Good Lord, I hope they're careful with their evidence. Things like that can ruin good people."

"Who—exactly—had been talking about Locke taking pictures around here?" I asked her, my curiosity having gotten the better of me. "Was this something that was conveyed to the police? It's the first I've heard of it."

"Well, unless I'm mistaken, you're not a tenant," she said, lifting one well-manicured eyebrow.

"No," I agreed, "I'm not."

"So you wouldn't have heard anyway, would you?"

"No. I guess I wouldn't have." She probably wouldn't

believe how I knew what I knew to begin with, so there was really no need to explain.

Her blunt demeanor softened then, slightly. "I guess it's all just part and parcel of who he was, though. Not a big surprise, considering his past." She sighed. "All water under the bridge now, though. Perhaps we can all just chalk this one up to divine justice. Something to think about, eh?"

"Oh, yeah. Definitely. Something to think about." I was still caught up in the thought that someone amongst the residents of the complex had found out that Locke had been photographing them. Why was that just a "rumor"? Why wouldn't someone have reported it, if they'd known or even suspected? I said as much to her.

"Why? Maybe the person couldn't prove it but wanted to warn the others anyway," she suggested with a dispassionate shrug. "I mean, it was no secret that he had an eye for a pretty girl. He even offered me a package deal to sign a lease here when I mentioned that there were several places I was looking at. His offer made it hard for me to turn down." Her mouth twisted. "I really wish I hadn't listened, now. All of this has been . . . pretty intense."

"What about Abbie?" I asked her. "Could she have been the one to start the rumor?"

"Ah, Abbie Cornwall. A-slash-B student, most of the time. Could be all As if she wanted to. Did she start the rumor? I don't know. She and her mom weren't here long. Locke took a comment I made in passing about her being my student and put two and two together about her being underage as far as his lease was concerned. Booted them there and then. Abbie seemed to take it pretty hard. I'm pretty sure she blamed me; Locke told them how he'd figured it out, the jerk. Just blurted it out without a thought as to how it sounded. It certainly didn't help my relationship with Abbie at school." Her mouth twisted in a grimace that was meant to double as humor. She paused then, as though considering whether she should say more. "You know, it occurred to me last night . . . I *had* been seeing her around the complex lately. Quite a lot, actually. I know it probably means nothing. At least I hope it does. I *hope* she didn't do anything that might get her into trouble." She cocked her head to one side thoughtfully. "She lived in the apartment you were looking at, you know. I saw you coming out of it that day, so I'm assuming you were here for a reason," she explained.

I nodded my confirmation. "Yes, I was looking at the apartment."

"Lucky you." When I raised my eyebrows at the wry comment, she prodded, "Well, you didn't sign the lease, did you?"

"No. I never got a chance to. That's why I was here that morning. That's how I found his . . . body. Marcus and I."

"I suppose he offered you a special deal on the rent?"

She was very forthright. Surprisingly so, considering we were strangers caught up in an even stranger situation. Maybe that came with being a teacher and dealing with teenagers, day in, day out. A kind of coping mechanism? "Well . . ."

"Don't worry, it's not like it can come back to bite you now that he's dead. I knew I wasn't the only one he offered the deal to. What I could never figure out at the time was, why?"

"What kind of a deal did he offer you?" I asked, curious. Locke had told me it was because of Lou being a lodge brother. Was that not true?

"He cut the rent and offered me two months' rent free," she said without even blinking. She raised a hand and carefully smoothed back her already carefully arranged hair, and then self-consciously plucked to straighten the bangs back out over her forehead. "You?"

So. Not just because of being lodge brothers, then. "Something quite like that, actually," I admitted without going into detail.

She nodded matter-of-factly.

"I, um, don't suppose you found the apartment through someone who knows him from his lodge?"

Confusion knit her brows. She shook her head. "I heard about it through another teacher. Her niece had just signed on to live here. And before you ask, yes, with a special rent deal. It was exactly what I was hoping to hear from him when I came to look at the apartment. Good, safe, clean places are hard enough to come by. Add low rent into the mix, and—like I said—I couldn't turn it down."

"Why do you think he was offering these deals? I mean, like you said, good places are hard to find."

She tilted her head to one side and angled a measuring gaze my way. "Well . . . this is just a guess, but . . . you're an attractive girl. Have you seen any of the other tenants?"

"One or two, from a distance." And a few in pics, all too up close and personal.

"They're all quite pretty," she commented. "Young. And if the rumored pictures are true . . ." She shrugged. "You do the math."

Marcus and Tom came out of the office just then, and our conversation came abruptly to an end. "Well, I'd better get my workout in, now that they've cleared the health center for residential traffic. Thanks for the info," she said, waving as she melted away.

A workout. Never my favorite thing, but after being relegated to inactivity for weeks at a time, even a stair machine was starting to sound good. And much safer than the stairs at the hospital when all is said and done, *letmetellya*.

"So, you'll get back to me as soon as you can?"

"You got it." Marcus held out his hand, and I held my breath as seconds stretched interminably. Finally, Tom with jaw set reached out and slammed his palm against Marcus's in a testing, gauging, testosterone-filled handshake.

Aw. Look at the two of them, making nice. Maybe there was hope for a truce yet.

Tom barely gave me another glance before he moved off toward his next task. I waited for Marcus to offer a clue, any clue, about what Tom had enlisted his help with. Marcus just looked at me, a patient and enigmatic smile lifting one corner of his mouth.

Maddening.

"Well?" I asked him finally.

"Ready to go?"

I crossed my arms, tapping my fingers against my biceps. Not. Budging.

His smile widened. "You are so cute when you're mad."

"Not working."

"And persistent." When I set my jaw and stared patiently into his eyes, he finally relented. "Okay, okay. He wanted me to take a look at some electronic equipment they found locked away in the back room."

"In the bathroom?" I repeated, confused.

"No, *back* room. Which was actually set up as a bedroom and private space. Locke sure kept it locked up tight. Can a man's name be a glimpse into his character?" he mused. "A sign?"

A bedroom? I had thought the additional space, besides the bathroom, was a utility room or something of that nature. Why, I don't know. It just never occurred to me to consider it in a more personal way.

"He lived there," I said, trying to wrap my mind around that. Come to think of it, one of the officers had said something about that. It just hadn't registered.

"Sure seemed that way to me."

"Is that . . . normal . . . for an apartment manager? I guess I'd always expected that they only worked on the premises unless they had an apartment—a regular apartment—within the complex. Not just a room connected to their office."

"I don't know. But that's what he did. Twin bed and all." Wry amusement twisted his mouth. "Some Lothario, huh?"

"Except for what we now know of him. And we still don't know if it had a connection to the reason for his murder." Except if not that, then what? Was it enough that Locke had a secret past? And was that past tied to his present? It certainly seemed, through the synchronicity of the thumb drive being discovered in the wreckage of the office, damaged but still viable, that the universe was pointing us in that direction. And then a sudden thought occurred to me, and I tilted my head to one side and squinted at him: "Wait a minute, he wanted you to look at what? What *type* of electronic equipment?"

He grinned at me. "Wondered when you were going to get around to that. It was video equipment, and what looked to me like a gaming system that had been modded to be a central media server. Low tech but very efficient. And . . ." His voice trailed off, a major tease.

"*And?*"

"It appeared to me, based on a very cursory examination, mind you, that our Mr. Locke had customers for his . . . product."

It took a moment for it to sink in with me. I had been thinking of Locke in terms of a simple, lower-level businessman, an employee of a larger business entity, and not a very important one at that. Not someone with customers. And in the blink of an eye, that vision of him was forced to change. Customers. "For the photos?" I asked him, my voice faint.

"And possibly video," he suggested.

"Video! Of what?" The pictures he'd grabbed off the thumb drive swam into view in my mind's eye—grainy, sordid. *Secret.* "He had videos of the women as well?"

"That would be my guess."

"What sort of videos? Oh, don't tell me," I said, closing my eyes and cringing. Such a violation of trust. "I don't want to know."

I couldn't help thinking back, remembering the moment I'd first seen him, coming out of the room I'd assumed at the time was the bathroom. Turning to lock the door behind him. It hadn't struck me then how odd that gesture had been. It sure as heck did now.

"That's not for sure. It's just an educated guess. Hopefully we'll all know more once I have the data off this old hard drive, hm?" He raised the zipped plastic bag for emphasis. "And speaking of which . . ."

He had a job to do. And my job was to stand by and watch, one gimpy foot in the air. Where was the glory in that? Sigh.

"No wonder he handed out steals and deals to his prospective tenants," I commented as we made our way back toward the truck, feeling a tad bit gullible for nearly falling for his spiel myself. I could have been featured among those photos as well. Who was he selling them to? How did he market them to his "clients"? Ugh. The whole notion of it made my skin crawl. Sleazy, sleazy, sleazy.

Marcus paused, one hand on the passenger-side door handle. "To more than just you?"

"I spoke to one of the tenants today, while you were in with Tom. A teacher. Oddly enough, she would have been my upstairs neighbor, if I had actually taken the apartment," I told him, marveling at the coincidence. "She told me Locke had offered her a similar deal. Lower rent, a couple of months rent free. And she made it sound as though it was pretty likely the two of us weren't the only lucky recipients of such a deal."

Marcus shook his head. "The guy really had a racket going on, didn't he?" He helped me up onto the seat, then handed me my crutches and waited until I had them situated before closing the door and coming around to his side.

"Quite the con artist. I guess he was making up for the loss in rent revenues by lining his own pockets and letting the apartment complex take the hit. Harding must be so proud."

Marcus laughed. "I'll bet."

His cell phone rang. He grabbed it from the charger and held it to his ear. "Hey, Unc. What? Um, yeah, of course. She's right here." He looked over at me and held out the phone. "So, care to tell me why my uncle suddenly wants to talk to you more than he wants to talk to me?"

I shrugged prettily. *"I . . . haff . . . vays,"* I muttered, waggling my eyebrows as I emulated his previous claim in a seriously bad attempt at a Russian accent.

He handed the phone over with a lecherous sweep of my body that took my breath away. "Oh, I know," he agreed, "I know."

I cleared my throat as I answered the call. "Hello there."

"That you, Maggie?"

"It is."

"Well, thank goodness. I've been trying to reach you."

"You have?" I asked, surprised. I reached into my purse and

pulled out my cell phone. Whoops—powered down. Guess I should have charged it earlier. "Oh, sorry about that. My phone shut itself off."

"It happens. It's been one heckuva day. Hey, listen. Coupla things here."

"Shoot."

"You didn't sign that lease, did you?"

The question took me by surprise. "Well, actually, no. I didn't. I didn't get a chance to. The whole dead-man-in-the-pool thing kind of took the wind out of my sails just a mite." That probably sounded flippant, but it was the truth. "And then the owner took issue with me working with my boss and refused to honor any lease agreement that Locke might have offered me, so that was the end of that. I'm not worried, though. Everything happens for a reason. I firmly believe that."

"Thank goodness," he repeated, and he really did sound relieved.

Curious now, I said, "Can I ask why?"

I heard a sigh over the airwaves. "We spoke with Abbie Cornwall this morning."

"I know," I told him.

"You do?"

"She came into the store today to apologize."

His relief had morphed into confusion. "Excuse my French, Maggie, but how in heaven's blue blazes did that come about?"

If that was as French as Uncle Lou could get, I could only surmise that it was as a result of holding himself in check as a schoolteacher and role model for so long. "I'll give you a hint. One of them is related to you."

"Tara." He filled in the blank easily. He didn't even sound surprised.

"And Evie. The two of them are a force to reckon with when they get together."

"Don't I know it." His sigh wasn't frustrated, depressed, or resigned. More an acknowledgment. "Listen, Maggie. There's something about that place that is ringing all my bells. I just don't think it's a good idea for you to get mixed up in a place like that. I knew I had to say something."

"Aw, thanks," I told him, touched that he'd thought enough of me to want to look out for me. "Harding, the owner, kind of eliminated that as a possibility, even if I had wanted to follow through with it after finding Locke . . . which I didn't."

"Harding? Jeremy Harding?"

I was getting that feeling again, the one that crept along my nerve endings like a breath of cool air. "Do you know him?"

"I know *of* him. He's a member of my lodge, too."

The Eternal Order of Samaritans lodge again. Why did that feel so portentous to me? Oh, maybe because the place hadn't hit my radar at any point in my entire life . . . even though it must have been a part of Stony Mill history for a while because that kind of organization didn't just come and go in the night. And yet in the last few days, I'd heard of it in regards to Uncle Lou, Devon McAllister's father, Locke himself, and now Harding, too. Had Harding mentioned that he and Locke were lodge brothers? I didn't think that he had. In fact, hadn't he made it sound as though he didn't know Locke very well at all?

"I have to say, I'm glad. You'll find another place. One that feels right, that doesn't have a pall of doom and gloom hanging over it." He sighed again. "It wasn't just Abbie. One of the middle school teachers was suspended today, and it sent a shock through the entire teaching staff."

"Oh, that's too bad," I said, only half listening because I was wondering whether Harding's connection to Locke could have been more than what he made it out to be. "What happened?"

"There were . . . photos . . . of her taken in compromising situations that were making the rounds of the students. Cell phone to cell phone, email to email, and I'm sure other forms of round-robin communication I am completely and blissfully unaware of at my advanced age, and I would like to keep it that way, mind you. No one knows where the kids got the pictures, but word in the teacher's lounge was that the principal and assistant principal had been working all day, interviewing kids and trying to track it back to its inauspicious beginnings. Regardless, it doesn't look good for her. The administration is quite clear on the need for teachers to view themselves as role models for the kids and to conduct themselves accordingly. Kids —especially at the middle school age—are so impressionable."

Photos. Compromising photos. Oh boy. "What's going to happen to her?"

"They suspended her, with pay for the time being, pending an investigative hearing. Of course she insists she has no idea where the pictures came from or how someone could have taken pictures of her in her own place without her knowing about it, but, like I said, admin isn't very forgiving. They will just argue that she shouldn't have put herself in a situation where something like this could have happened. The pictures had to come from somewhere."

All of a sudden, I remembered a comment Liss had made in passing just that morning. "Lou . . . who was the teacher? What was her name?"

"Miller," he said, giving the name I in that moment fully expected to hear. "Angela Miller."

Annie had been beside herself, Liss had said. Her niece suspended from her job. Something about inappropriate activity, but Angela was obviously the soul of propriety from the lips of Annie herself, and you know what? I believed her. "Oh. Oh, that's not good."

"Nope. Not good at all," Lou agreed. "Colleague of mine mentioned in passing where she was living. Turns out, she lives at that same apartment complex. Forgive me for saying, it's all a bit too much, in my mind. Place must be cursed. Hey, listen. Gotta run. I'm glad you didn't sign. Load off my mind. That's not the sort of thing you need to get yourself mixed up in. You have enough to deal with, with your ankle and all. Tell Marcus good-bye for me, wouldya?"

He signed off, leaving me chewing on my lower lip as I considered what he'd told me.

"Penny for your thoughts? Or should I adjust for inflation and the economic crash?"

I looked up. We hadn't budged from our parking spot. Marcus was watching me, the soul of patience as he waited for me to come back to earth.

"What would that be now? A dollar? Five?" he wondered cheekily. "Hm."

"If it's five, you will in future catch me thinking more often," I said, laughing.

"Yeah, me, too. So, you gonna tell me what Uncle Lou was calling about, or is that going to be one of your little secrets?"

"He was calling to warn me away from the apartment complex."

"Kinda late for that," Marcus said, "but well meant, I'm sure. Despite the fact that it was his find to begin with. Maybe he feels bad about that."

"Maybe. He said he just had a bad feeling about it after

talking with Abbie. He also mentioned in passing that a middle school teacher had been suspended today."

"Yikes. That doesn't happen very often around here. For good reason?"

"Because pics were being circulated of her."

One thing Marcus was incredibly good at was reading between the lines. "What kind of pics?"

"The kind that can get you fired if you're a teacher at a middle school and are required to behave as befits a role model for the kids."

He drew a deep, measuring breath, in through his nose, releasing it through his mouth, long and slow. "We're talking about the same thing here, aren't we?"

I nodded. "Uh-huh."

"I don't suppose this teacher lives at the same apartment complex?"

"Uh-huh. We need to take another look at those pictures, Marcus. And see if anything else turns up on the hard drive Tom wants you to get into."

"Why all the interest, Maggie? We could just let Fielding do his job."

I nodded. "We could do that. But this is for Annie."

He looked at me, not understanding.

"It's Annie's niece who was suspended."

"Oh," he said, realization dawning. "Shit."

I didn't have to say another word.

Our course of action decided, Marcus set it into motion. "What was he saying about Harding?"

"Oh, nothing. Just that Harding was a member of his lodge," I replied airily.

"And that means something." He didn't sound convinced.

"I don't know. But . . . don't you think it's odd that all of a sudden we keep hearing about this lodge?"

"What do you mean, keep hearing?"

I explained what had just occurred to me. "And then Devon's dad, too. And now Harding. And he certainly didn't mention that connection to Locke when he spoke with Tom about how well he knew him."

"Just because they're in the same organization doesn't mean they're best buddies or anything like that, Maggie. I mean, I know you want to connect the dots, but sometimes they aren't really connections. They're just dots. Look at Uncle Lou."

Oh, I wish he hadn't mentioned Lou. That was one big sticking point as far as I was concerned.

Because I knew Uncle Lou.

And Uncle Lou wasn't the kind of man who would participate in anything unethical.

And belonging to an organization certainly wasn't a crime.

It was just a series of coincidental nonconnections. They meant nothing.

"You're right," I conceded. "It's nothing."

He reached over and squeezed my hand. "I know you want to help Annie. Let's go take another look at those pics, huh?"

Chapter 16

Back at his bungalow, Marcus set me up on the computer while he readied the old hard drive for reactivated service at the worktable behind me. The grainy pics were easier to see on the screen of his oversized HD monitor as opposed to the smaller format of the printed shots. Much easier. I could make out far more elements of the rooms . . . and on the girls.

"Wow. You didn't say you had seen all of this in so much . . . crisp . . . detail."

He grinned over his shoulder at me. "Jealous?"

I angled a saucy pout in his direction. "Why would I be jealous?"

"Exactly my point."

I have to say, that was one thing I liked about Marcus. He always knew what to say to make a girl feel good about herself.

I picked out Becky Cornwall straightaway without even

a shadow of a doubt. I don't know why I didn't recognize her
instantly when she walked into the store, why I had needed
the tattoo to clue me in. It seemed so obvious now, looking at it. The way she held herself, her shoulders drawn up
toward her chin as though constantly on guard, even in a
relaxed setting, was very distinctive. Even without clothes
on. As though she sensed the camera there, even though she
didn't. There were none of Abbie Cornwall, though. I was
especially glad for that. One of the girls was wearing the
kind of white, soft-soled shoes popular with nurses and gran-
nies nationwide. But no granny I knew had a body like that.
She also had shimmering blond hair that was pulled up into
a thick, looping bun at the nape of her neck. It shouldn't be
too hard to pick her out from the list of tenants.

None of these were the person I was looking for.

I found her soon enough, about halfway through the
lengthy list of file names. As soon as I saw her, I sat up straight.
How did I miss seeing it before?

There were numerous shots of her. Quite the pretty little
thing she was, petite, with pale alabaster skin and long
strawberry blond hair that curled in spirals down her back.
There were also a number of very, *very* intimate photos of her
with Tyson Hollister doing what young lovers did best when
they were alone in a private setting, away from prying eyes.
Too bad the eyes that were prying were secreted away. Out
of sight, but not blind. Most definitely not blind, I thought,
counting the number of pictures of her. And the collection I
was sifting through were only the pics from the thumb
drive. Who knew what Marcus would find on the hard drive?

"Do you see what I see?"

"Beautiful redhead, check."

"Do you think she resembles a young Annie Miller?"

His eyebrows rose. "You're right. So this must be Angela Miller, you think?"

I nodded.

"So, am I right to assume that you're thinking the pics that were making the rounds of the kids at the middle school can be sourced to Locke?"

"That's what my gut is telling me, yes. You?"

He stared at the photo, allowing his gaze to soften as he turned inward, breathing deeply. At length he said, "Yeah. I think you're right on the money."

"So now the question becomes, what do we do with this information?" I asked. "We can't just let Annie's niece be fired for something that was none of her doing. Victims shouldn't be targeted for their victimization, ever. It wouldn't be right."

"Are you suggesting that we show them to her?"

"We can't," I admitted. "Not without Tom's okay."

He made a doubting grimace. "Hm. That's not likely to be forthcoming. His priority is the murder investigation. Understandably so."

"Leave Tom to me," I said with more confidence than I truly felt. Hey, fake it 'til you make it, right? That was my motto, anyway.

"I had every intention to."

I called his cell phone, knowing it was late, knowing he might just be off duty, knowing I could be interrupting, and yet unwilling to wait until morning.

"Maggie?" came his voice through the speaker without preamble. Caller ID, obviously. Which meant I was still in his contact list. I wondered if I should feel special, that he hadn't deleted me yet. "What's wrong?"

"Hi, Tom," I said, waving away the rude faces Marcus was

making. Cheeky devil. "Nothing's wrong. I just . . . we came across something that I think you should know about."

"Something with regards to the thumb and hard drive Quinn is cataloguing for me?"

"Exactly!" I said with some relief. "And . . . well . . . a little more than that, maybe."

"Oh, yeah? How'd this happen?"

"I'll explain it when you get here. Can you come?"

I waited a full five seconds while he considered whatever it was that he needed to consider. "Um . . . yeah. Give me a few minutes."

It was a little more than a few, but who was counting? Marcus went to answer the door so that I wouldn't have to get up. Minnie was as grateful for his helpfulness as I was. She had circled her way onto my shoulders shortly after I had sat down, and there she stayed draped there like a live, rumbling, black fur stole.

Marcus showed him back to the computer room and waited. Tom stood in the doorway, looking around at the organized library of electronic equipment. "This is the bat cave, huh?"

It might as well be, tonight.

He came in and leaned against the worktable behind me, crossing his arms as I turned to half face him. Marcus came and leaned against the desk beside me. Presenting a united front, as it were.

"So, what do you have for me?" he prompted.

I cleared my throat. "You know the pictures that were on the thumb drive found in the wreckage of Locke's office?"

He raised one brow rather than giving me the obvious answer.

"There was an issue at the middle school today."

Tom waited, not a single muscle flexing.

"That involved pictures."

Slightly more interest now. "What kind of pictures?"

"From what I understand, the same kind of pictures that Locke had been taking."

He kept his expression neutral. "And you think this is related to the investigation . . . why?"

"Because the subject of the photos was a teacher. One who lived at the apartments. Annie Miller's niece, Angela, in fact."

He forgot all about poker faces as he considered this. "I think I'm going to need you to explain. In detail."

"Marcus's Uncle Lou was telling me about his day, and he happened to mention that a teacher had been suspended today," I told him. "At the middle school. Evidently there were pictures of her in compromising situations that were making the student rounds, and someone found out about it and reported her. She was suspended for the pictures and for not conducting herself in a manner befitting a role model of young teens, pending an investigative hearing in front of the school board. Tom, it was Angela Miller, Annie Miller's niece. Annie was adamant when she told Liss that her niece was the soul of propriety, and that this was all some terrible mistake. And," I said, pausing for emphasis, "as you know, she lives at the apartments." I turned to the computer and pulled up the first photo I wanted to show him. One of the worst. "I'm pretty sure this is her. She looks the spitting image of Annie, albeit half her age. But who's counting. And"—I made a face—"I'm pretty sure neither Annie nor Angela know about these. My question is, how did kids at the middle school get ahold of Locke's handiwork?"

Tom barely glanced at the photo. "I interviewed Angela Miller yesterday to take her statement. That picture is definitely her. And her boyfriend, Tyson Hollister."

"School kids, Tom. How?"

"I don't know."

Marcus cleared his throat. "What about our theory that Locke had customers for his secret hobby? Do you think he would have been selling them to kids?"

"Would kids have had the money? Doubtful. I checked his bank account. He was receiving money transfers from several different accounts. Pretty little sums, too. Kids wouldn't have access to money like that. In any case, I have a list of account numbers and an interview with the bank manager tomorrow morning. The people whose names appear on those accounts are going to have a bit of explaining to do. It's not illegal to purchase pornographic materials where adults are involved. But where the subjects are unaware they are taking part? That's another story entirely."

"So you think we're right?" I asked him. "That the photos responsible for Angela Miller's suspension are likely to be sourced back to Locke?"

"I think that's a fair assessment, yes. Timing is everything, and the timing of this is too specious to be considered coincidental."

"And . . . do you have any particular suspect you're focusing on yet for Locke's murder?" I couldn't help asking.

"You know better than to ask that."

But I couldn't let it go. "What about Tyson Hollister? Annie seems to think he's trustworthy. Just misunderstood."

"He told my investigating officer that he had taken Ms. Miller out for dinner and a movie the other night when Locke was attacked. I checked his story. He has the credit card receipt for both the meal and the cancelled ticket stubs for the movie." Tom shrugged. "I believe him."

"Any of the other tenants?"

"They all seem more victim than suspect at this point. I

don't know, Maggie. I just don't have enough information to go on at this point."

Hm. A thought occurred to me. "You know . . . one thing you might find out is whether any of the bank account people had middle school kids. That at least would explain Angela's situation."

"I'll make a point of it."

"Good. Because I'd hate to see her get fired over something that wasn't even her fault."

"I see your point. But I have to be careful. This is evidence in a murder investigation. Unfortunately, if it comes down to that, it trumps Ms. Miller's wrongful persecution." He looked us both in the eye. "And don't make me remind you that you have both signed confidentiality agreements. I don't expect any of this to get out in any way, shape, or form."

"Neither of us have said anything to anyone. And we won't. Right, Maggie?" Marcus prodded.

"I made my promise. I will stick to it." Oh, but it would be hard, if Annie's niece did end up losing her job because of a creepazoid like Locke. Angela was the victim. It completely offended my sense of universal justice that she could conceivably be victimized a second time by the school system, and none of it her fault.

Tom pushed himself away from his perch on the edge of the worktable as though to leave.

"One more thing, Tom. You remember the lodge that Locke was a member of?"

"Yeah, I remember you told me that you found the place through Lou's dealings with him as a lodge brother."

"Did you know that Harding was a member of that same lodge as well?"

A frown crossed his forehead. "How did you find this out?"

"Lou mentioned it when I was explaining to him that Harding was the owner of the apartment complex and that he had refused to offer me a lease. Not that I was about to sign it at that point anyway." I just had to be sure I got that out there. Sheesh. A girl has her pride.

"Hm. Harding said he barely knew Locke, outside of an absentee employer-employee fringe relationship. Now, I suppose that could be true—that even as members of the same organization, they weren't on each other's radar. But you're right. It is something that needs to be clarified."

And that's all that I asked. I knew there was no real reason to have latched on to that particular point . . . so, why did my inner senses all stand up and take notice at the repeated mention of "the lodge" over the last couple of days? That's what I needed to understand.

The devil is in the details . . .

The voice again, chiming in with Grandma C's intonations inside my head. At least it was nice to know that, whatever "it" was, it agreed with me. This time.

After showing Tom out, Marcus came back to computer command central and leaned against the door frame, smiling at me. "Why is it that the more you mention this lodge thing being bandied about, the more the hairs start to lift on the back of my neck and the more sense it seems to make that there is something weird going on, somehow? I'm beginning to think that whatever you're picking up on, it's catching," he said with a rueful shaking of his head that made his dark curls fall down around his eyes.

"Sorry?" I offered, smiling back at him. "Anyway, it's not like you haven't worked your magick on me, making me see things I never even thought to look for before."

"Ha. Yeah, we're mutually guilty of that, I guess."

He came purposely forward and, putting his hands on the armrests on each side of me, he leaned in to engage me in one of his ultraspectacular lip-locks. Completely distracting me. At least until my cell phone rang. The call screen identified the caller as Tom.

"I should probably get this?"

Marcus nodded.

"Maggie," Tom's voice said in my ear the moment I flipped the phone open, "listen. Don't freak out, but . . . I just thought I saw someone hanging around Quinn's house."

My eyebrows shot up, and I turned to face the window, where the blinds were down but not closed. All I could see was the soft light from the lamps and the colorful glare of the computer monitor, with dark shapes for me and Marcus, and an ominous wall of blackness beyond. "Here? Now?"

"Yeah. Dark, shadowy. Moved from the landscaping toward the backyard. I had pulled in to the driveway to turn around when I saw it. Got my spotlight out, but whatever it was, or whoever, was gone."

I shivered. "All right. Thanks for letting me know."

"You have Quinn keep an eye out, huh? And he needs to install some security lights. Jesus, it's black as pitch back here."

"What's up?" Marcus asked as I hung up the phone.

Setting Minnie down on the desk with a grumble of protest, I rose on one foot from my chair and reached for the rod that twisted the blinds to a closed position, securing my need for safety before answering. "Tom said he thought he saw someone hanging around the house and yard while he was turning his car around. He checked it out with the spotlight, but whoever it was was gone by then."

"Here? Now?"

I uttered a shaky laugh, rubbing my hands up and down my arms to dispel the goose bumps that had arisen there. "I think I hear an echo. Yes, to both questions."

A fierce, determined expression arose on his face. "I'm going to get a flashlight and go out myself."

"Do you have to? I mean, Tom did just check things out."

"I know the place a hundred times better than he does." He dropped a swift kiss on my brow. "I won't be long. Promise."

While he was out there, I distracted myself by going around and checking all windows to be sure the locks were secured, and all the curtains and blinds to be sure they were drawn. Passing through the living room, I saw the cameras that Marcus had never completely retired—the very ones he had employed a month or so earlier, when he had (correctly?) suspected Tom of being guilty of drive-by stalkery—when a sudden thought struck me. Why not? I switched the power on, wishing we had had the foresight to have them running all along. Oh well. Forewarned is forearmed. If anyone came around later tonight, while we were sleeping—assuming any sleep was to be had on my part—they would be caught. Candid Camera 2.0. A part of me all of a sudden wished that Marcus wasn't opposed to gun ownership. Maybe he had a nice, old-fashioned baseball bat lying around.

"No one," he said when he came back through the kitchen door. "I even checked the loft over the garage."

"'Kay," I said, swallowing hard to keep my nervousness at bay.

But not concealed. "Hey, hey," he said, taking me into his arms and holding me against him. I tucked my head beneath his chin and breathed him in. "You're not worried, are you?"

"No . . ." I lied.

"It was probably just a dog or something, sweetness. I

honestly didn't see anything back there, and there was nothing to indicate anyone had been hanging around, either."

I nodded, willing for the moment to let myself be lulled
by the sense of security he offered. And yet, when the lights
were out, I couldn't help but wonder . . .

Chapter 17

I did sleep that night, nestled in the warm crook of Marcus's strong arms. I also spent quite a lot of time staring at the ceiling, listening to the sounds of the living world around me and hoping none of the sounds were portents of a break-in. I wasn't sure. A couple of times, I could have sworn I heard a slight tapping, so slight that it blended into the other noises that were common in older homes: creaking, groaning, the whishing of air through oversized ancient duct-work. I convinced myself that it was just my imagination run amok, that I was just making myself nervous . . . even though Minnie also lifted her fuzzy black head at that very moment to listen intently for several long minutes before finally lying back down to return to sleep.

I was being silly. It was just a coincidence.

Marcus, with his uncanny ability to sleep through anything, didn't even flinch.

When morning finally came, I breathed a sigh of relief.

And I felt pretty silly for worrying. It was so easy to feel foolish for my fear with dawn glowing on the horizon. I left
Marcus sleeping and crutched myself into the kitchen to
make him something special for breakfast. Special because he
did so much for me and asked so little, and I wanted him to
know how much I appreciated him. With bacon sputtering
on the stove and a hot cup of tea cooling on the counter, I
went out on the back porch to the birds singing their melodic chorus to the dawn. The porch swing was a little iffy for
me to back into with crutches, so I stood there on the edge,
watching the light growing and expanding all around me.

It was just as I was intending to go back inside to check
on the bacon and start the eggs and toast that I made a final
circuit of the back porch, checking out the mounds of mums
whose buds were cresting out on the far end. That was when
I saw it.

I stumbled back a step before I found my footing,
then turned myself on my crutches with the kind of speed
and agility that resisted crutch-assisted efforts. "Marcus?" I
called as I hit the threshold and kept on going. "Marcus! Are
you awake?"

"I am now," I heard him groan from up the hall as I made
my way down it.

"You have to get up," I told him.

My face must have conveyed my urgency, because he sat
up then and there. On any other day I would have stopped
to admire the way the sheets fell away from his chest and
pooled around his abdomen and hips, not to mention the five
o'clock shadow that, combined with his tousled black hair,
gave him a swarthy look that hovered somewhere between
bed head and bed god. He pushed the hair off his face and
swung his legs over the edge. "What is it? What's wrong?"

"Just get some pants on and come look."

The bacon was just crossing the line from cooked to scorched, so I flipped the burner off as I crutched past to wait for Marcus in the doorway to the porch. He was right on my heels, though, with nothing more than a pair of unfastened jeans giving him even a modicum of modesty. I led him out onto the porch and jabbed a finger repeatedly in the pertinent direction. "There."

He looked to see what I was pointing at. In the passing of a moment, his expression changed from blind searching to curious uncertainty to full-out incredulity as he saw the footprints in the freshly turned dirt of the flower bed. The flower bed that stood *right beneath the window to Marcus's computer command central.*

"Shit. Tom was right. He did see someone out here last night."

I nodded anxiously. "But were those marks made before Tom saw them and chased them away with his searchlight . . . or after?" Yeah. I just lived to torment myself like that.

He stepped down onto the grass and carefully knelt, making sure to avoid the impressions. "Lug-sole boots or shoes of some sort. A man would be most likely to wear a style like that. Someone not too big. Those feet aren't too much larger than yours."

I certainly hoped that was supposed to mean it was a smallish man or a man with smallish feet, and *not* that I was the female equivalent of Bozo the Clown. Minus the freaky red 'do. "Should I call Tom?" I asked him.

I could tell he didn't like the idea of running to Tom for protection every time something happened, but I could tell he also realized how much this assault on my sense of security bothered me. He nodded. "Call him."

It took Tom a little longer than I'd hoped to get to Marcus's house for what amounted to the third time in as many days . . . and yeah, trust me, I was weirded out by that, too. But, regardless of that, I had enough time to finish breakfast, wash dishes, bathe, do my hair and makeup, and get dressed before he finally showed up around eight thirty.

"Sorry it took me this long," he said. "You said it wasn't an emergency, and I had already scheduled an early morning meeting with the bank manager. What did you want me to see?"

Marcus led the way out through the kitchen onto the back porch. Tom followed Marcus, and I picked things up from the rear, staying as close as my crutches would allow.

The expression on Tom's face was unreadable as he knelt down to examine the print markings, much as Marcus had done two hours before him. "You found these here this morning?"

"I did," I told him. "I got up early and came outside to enjoy the sunrise."

"Did either of you hear anything last night? After I left?"

"Not me," Marcus said.

"But he sleeps soundly," I offered, and then winced at the unwitting cruelty of my interruption when I saw a look of pain flash behind Tom's eyes, before he managed to mask it away behind a pretense of neutrality. "I mean . . . I thought I heard something. But it's so hard to tell with older homes. And I was really trying not to make myself more nervous than I already was."

In spite of his personal feelings, good, bad, or otherwise, Tom's professional, no-nonsense tone never wavered. "I can't tell, looking at this, when the tracks were made. Before I scared them off, or did the person I saw return later? We may never know. And we may never know the reason they were here, if someone knew what they were looking for . . . or if it was someone with an eye on your expensive equipment. I think that's probably the likely scenario. Do you have insurance against theft? If not, I would think about it, if I were you. Take the proper precautions. Lock your doors, your windows, keep your curtains drawn. Invest in a home security system."

Did he really think it was burglars? Why didn't that resonate with me? I stared down at the crisply formed prints in the dirt, frowning, trying to see in my mind's eye what had happened and who had made them, but for whatever reason, I could not. *Hey, Grandma C? I could really use some help here. Any chance that you could lend me the wisdom and whatever else is needed in order to make sense of this?*

I continued to mull this over as Marcus went inside to take a phone call and I watched Tom take some photos of the prints, using a tape measure for size perspective. Tom finally rose and dusted the dried grass bits and crumbs of dirt from his knees. "Interesting turn of events, huh?" he offered offhandedly.

Life. Is it ever not interesting? And isn't that the point? To be intrigued, compelled, and fully engaged in the ever-changing moment? Whatever the experience, life is a gift, to be lived to its full measure. Staying in the moment. Although, that could be difficult in those particular moments that brought fear and anxiety.

"How was your appointment this morning?" I asked, needing a change of subject.

The look he threw me was disconcerted. "How did you know I was just thinking about that?"

I shrugged and attempted a smile. "Just lucky, I guess?"

"Whatever." He shook his head to clear his thoughts. "The manager was very accommodating. He gave me the names and addresses for all the accounts that had transferred or wired money directly from their accounts into Locke's bank account."

That was exciting news. "And?" I prompted.

He sighed, shaking his head. "Just my luck. There are some important people here, Maggie. I gotta tell you, I am not thrilled about this. These are not the kinds of people you want to piss off if you intend to continue to have a career in city government. Some of them are real movers and shakers of Stony Mill. DA Ledbetter is going to want to tread lightly. Sheriff Reed, too. They're both up for reelection next year." And then his eyes took on a shrewd light, and his expression morphed into something sly and cunning. "I, on the other hand, know that it's my business to get to the bottom of this. Whether Ledbetter decides to pursue or not, that's his business."

"Do any of them have children who are middle school age?"

"Funny you should ask," he said. "I did get ahold of the middle school principal at home late last night. He was curious as to how I had received word of the situation with his suspended teacher . . . but that's because he is protecting the school's interests, I think, and wanted to know whether Miss Miller was going to fight the process through legal avenues. Don't worry—I told him that information was privileged. But, when he heard that it could possibly be related to a criminal murder investigation, he was more than happy to cooperate, to the fullest extent." If a voice could contain a smirk, his would have.

"And what did he say?"

"He said they'd traced the pics of Miss Miller back through forward after forward, kid to kid. A couple of the kids had received it through email because they didn't have texting, and it showed the whole string of forwards. It seems originally to have come from one particular boy. An eighth-grader named Austin Poindexter."

Poindexter? The Poindexters were well-known in Stony Mill. They owned a string of hardware stores around the area. They could definitely be classified as town movers and shakers.

"And is Austin Poindexter's father on that list of bank accounts?" I asked him, because I could feel a connection there, something to explore.

Tom gave me a manly blink, times three. If he were a woman, his eyelashes would have fluttered. "I can neither confirm nor deny . . ."

I grinned in spite of myself at his roundabout and casual way of nonconfirmation. "There is no need." Another thought occurred to me. "You know . . . social organizations like lodges often include many prominent citizens among their registry."

"The lodge thing again?" He looked at me askance. Skeptically. "You and your feelings."

And it was because they were feelings that he was so willing to dismiss the notion out of hand. It wouldn't be the first time his personal prejudices muddied his vision. "Why not? Look, I can't explain why I get these feelings. All I know is that I keep getting nudges about the lodge. And secret brotherhoods? It wouldn't be the first time unsavory little details had been kept from coming to light by people bonding together over their secrets."

"I thought you said Quinn's uncle was a lodge member."

I had, and it was the one thing that really bothered me. Because he *had* just the other day asked Marcus to speed up his own hard drive, much like Locke had hired Marcus to do. And he *had* mentioned videos and pics. But Uncle Lou wasn't like that. He couldn't be. And in his favor, he did seem unaware of the whole pics-for-sale thing. When he spoke of Angela Miller being suspended, he seemed surprised by the nature of the pictures and uncertain as to how the whole thing could have come about. For now, Uncle Lou had the benefit of the doubt as far as I was concerned. Because I knew Marcus and the type of man he was, and I knew how much he respected his uncle. Out of respect for Marcus, it was the least I could do.

To Tom, I shrugged. "He is. But I doubt you'll find that every member would be in the know about everything that happened within the organization."

"Hm. Probably true."

"Look, we know Uncle Lou is a member. But he's been the one person throughout all of this that has given information without withholding a thing. In other words, I'm certain he's not hiding anything. Why not run the names past him? Maybe you'll be able to find out what you need to know without alerting anyone within the organization that aspects are being investigated."

He nodded. "I'll do that." He took Lou's number from me.

After Tom left, I went inside and found Marcus in the computer center. The window beside him was open. "Hey," I said, coming up behind him and putting my hand on the crook of his shoulder.

On the desk in front of him was one of his old computers—he had added the hard drive from Locke's apartment to the computer's existing drive and was just setting it aside so that he could get to work. "Hey."

There was a heavy tone in his voice, a quietness not usually there. "What's wrong?"

"You two were . . . awfully cozy."

I gaped at him and uttered a soft cry of surprise. "Marcus Quinn. Are you . . . are you jealous?"

He brushed my question aside. "Of course not."

"You are! Don't deny it, I can see it on your face."

"Well . . . maybe for a minute. Or less."

I shook my head, smiling softly. "There's no need to be, you know. Tom is a good guy, but he and I . . . we never meshed, really. You know?" I stroked my hand down the back of his head, then leaned down and looped my arms around his chest, laying my cheek along the side of his warm, strong neck. "I never felt with him the way that I do when I'm with you."

"Oh." He turned his head toward his shoulder and nudged his way into a surprisingly sweet kiss. "Good."

I'll say.

Reassurances and everything else out of the way, there was nothing more to do but . . . "I suppose it's time for me to head in to the store now." Amazing how much could happen in a single morning, and I could still make it into work to bring home the bacon. It had to be better than this morning's burnt offering at least.

"Check." He bounced up out of his chair with all the restored assurance of a man who had just been told that he had nothing to fear from another man. Even an old boyfriend. "Do you want Minnie today, or can she stay with me? I kind of like her here. Maybe I'll have to keep her forever," he teased.

"Only if you keep me, too," I teased right back.

"Hm. I might have to do that," he teased again. Only suddenly he didn't sound teasing at all.

My heart leapt into my throat, and I was forced to catch my breath. I didn't say anything. I didn't want to think about it or influence it or jinx it in any way. We would cross that bridge if we came to it.

Or did I mean "when"?

*   *   *

The morning whizzed past for both Liss and me as we finished the preparations for the weekend's coming Sidewalk Days, deciding what was safe to be put out on tables, what would be marked down, how we could best showcase some of the wares we had to offer. This would not be an event meant to play to our witchy clientele. This was for the mundanes, the regular, everyday folk who had no idea that when they searched for their favorite scents, lotions, and antiques, they were rubbing elbows with witchy folk who came from Indiana and all four surrounding states to sample our more witch-centric wares in person. Our air-conditioning had gone out sometime during the night—electrical in the old building was not quite up to modern needs—so it was hot, and we were both sweating and tired.

Around eleven as we were finally nearing the end of our preparations, my cell phone buzzed in my pocket. *New Message from Tara*, the front screen said. Hm. Texting while in school, against school rules? Shamey, shamey.

Yo, Mags. I'm supposed to pass something on to you for your cop friend, Officer Stuffy. From Abbie Cornwall. She wants him to know about the cameras. Big mirror in bedroom—she broke accidentally while moving in. Locke

The message ended due to too many characters. I waited, not quite patiently, for her thumbs to tap out a second message. Finally another message popped into my Inbox, continuing on from the previous text.

flipped out, sent someone in to fix it. Afterward, she found small, battery operated, remote control camera. Had rolled under her bed. Fallen from behind original mirror? She thinks. Wants Officer Stuffy to know in case is important.

A camera behind the mirror?

And if Abbie hadn't broken it, would anyone ever have known?

Not until Locke was dead. And maybe not even then.

A third text came in.

More cameras possible, Abbie thinks. All apartments? No sense to be in just 1. Mgr was creepy. Always watching. Didn't say b4 cuz afraid would be in bigger trouble.

Bigger trouble. Bigger trouble? Good heavens, sometimes teenagers simply did not use their heads.

My mind was running at a mile a minute, turning over and over all of the things we'd learned about Locke and his strange little eccentricities since he had earned such an ignominious end.

The words of an old Tennyson poem flitted in a whimsical path across my thoughts: *Out flew the web and floated wide; the mirror crack'd from side to side; "The curse is come upon me," cried the Lady of Shalott.*

Ah, dear Lord Alfred. His prescience astounded me. It was as if he had seen Stony Mill in his mind's eye long ago. What web were we all ensnared in? What curse? And was it one that we were subjected to? Or one of our own making?

I texted Tara back, telling her to thank Abbie for me, and to let her know that I'd pass on the info.

Bet your booty I would.

A camera behind the mirror.

That would certainly explain the different perspectives I had noticed in the pics on the thumb drive. The way some seemed to be taken from outside of the room, through the window, and others seemed to have been taken from within the bedrooms themselves.

Did all of the apartments in the complex have these cameras built in? My guess would be a resounding yes. Wow. Wow, wow.

"What's up, ducks?" Liss had evidently seen my raised eyebrows and had attuned to them accordingly.

I explained what Tara had texted to me as I tapped out a text message to Tom, asking him to call me when he got a chance.

Liss was shaking her head in astonishment. "The things that happen these days. I suppose I should be thanking my lucky stars Geoffrey insisted on building the Gables," she said, referring to her late husband and their manorlike home on Victoria Park Road, "even though I still find it ostentatious and far too much for an old bird like me. Although, since I am an old bird, I suppose it would all be a very moot point. No cameras awaiting me in my cupboards. And on a day like today, I suppose I should be grateful for that," she said, lifting her hair from the nape of her neck and fanning herself with a thin brochure she had at hand. "Good goddess, it is hot out today."

I laughed. "I hate to tell you this, Liss, but perverts come in all shapes and sizes. Some like their prey very young, and some, not so."

"Ooh, do you think so?" She almost looked intrigued, which I found even funnier. "Never mind, if you're intent on laughing at me. I am a poor, unaccompanied widow, you know."

"Who could have her take of any number of gentlemen, need I remind you," I pointed out. "Young or old. Er. Older. Not old. My mistake."

The corner of her mouth curved in a pretty smirk. "Well, perhaps I just haven't found my One yet."

Or perhaps her One was the husband she had lost. But that didn't mean she couldn't still have some fun. Sow some wild oats. Or even some tame ones. Her husband was dead. She was not.

Another text buzzed in my pocket. This one was from Marcus.

Hey, sweetness. Running over to campus to pick up all my books and materials will need for Monday, and have meeting with counselor. Be back on time to pick u up. Wait til u see what I found on hard drive. Love.

Love.

I know, I know. It was awfully early for that. But it still made my heart go pitter-pat.

Buzz. A second from Marcus.

"Gracious, you are in demand today," Liss teased.

Forgot to say . . . Ran out and am pretty sure forgot to shut Minnie into her room. Don't think I left any windows open, but . . . Worried about her with the screens. :(

I frowned and bit my lip. Minnie had done a number on one of the bedroom screens one Saturday afternoon when Marcus had taken me out to pick up a DVD rental. We hadn't been gone long, but long enough for Minnie to attempt her great escape into the great green yonder to join her favorite feathery compadres, thanks to the razor-sharp talons she spent a good deal of time making sure were in top form. One shredding zip of the screen, a curious poke through of her round-jowled head, and "escape artist" was her middle name.

Thank goodness she had been too distracted by the twittering birds around the feeder to go far.

"What's the matter?"

I looked up. "Marcus texted to say he was worried he'd forgotten to close the windows."

"Oh?" Liss glanced out the windows, puzzled. "Well, that shouldn't be too much of a problem. The sky is clear as a proverbial bell."

"Normally it wouldn't be a problem," I agreed with her. "Except we also left Minnie there with him today, and he also forgot to close her into her room. Remember the last time we did that?"

She covered her mouth. "Bird feathers. Everywhere!"

"Precisely." Oh, Minnie hadn't caught any of the little winged darlings. She had, however, given them a run for their money. Feathers, feathers, everywhere. The little furry-faced rascal.

Liss looked at me.

I looked at Liss.

"Are you thinking what I'm thinking?" she asked me.

I was hoping I was.

"Well, it *is* hot in here today. And we can't just leave the mischievous little darling to her own devices, now can we? And we *could* stop for a quick ice-cream treat for lunch on the way . . ." That was Liss for you. Always game for the truly important missions in life.

It didn't take the two of us long to come to a mutual decision. Liss put the "Be Back Soon" sign up on the front door and locked it, and then we scurried out the back to Liss's black Lexus. It was blisteringly hot inside its smooth leather interior. We were going to need *lots* of ice cream after this.

The Old Burger Dairy was on the way, so we stopped there first. Drive thru, of course. The trouble was, it seemed most of Stony Mill had that same idea at the exact same time. We decided cups of ice cream would probably be the best option if we didn't want to be wearing as much ice cream as we managed to inhale. I opted for Double Strawberry Fudge Ripple; for Liss, it was Vanilla Custard Raspberry Swirl. Who needed sandwiches and fries when there was ice cream to be had on a hot late summer day? We were happily licking it off our spoons before Liss could put her Lexus in gear again. With that out of the way, we zoomed off toward our destination

My cell phone rang just then. Tom.

"Hello there," I said into the mouthpiece.

"Hey. Got your text asking me to call. What's up?"

"I was given a message to give to you. Information to give to you. From someone you've already questioned. She was afraid to talk to you again, but now that she's thought about it, she wanted you to know."

"Who are we talking about here?"

"Abbie Cornwall."

"The teenage girl who used to live there."

"And who was expelled from the apartment, along with her mother, for defying the terms of the lease agreement, at Locke's discretion. Yeah. Abbie."

"What about her?"

"No, no, it's not about her. She wants you to know about the camera. Tom, while she was living in the apartment, she found a tiny camera. She accidentally broke the mirror in her mother's bedroom, and after the glass fitter had left, she found a camera that must have fallen out of the space behind the mirror and rolled under the bed. And Tom, I think Abbie's the one who was telling the other tenants about her suspicions that Locke was spying on them. I think she thought if there was a camera in one apartment, it was likely there were more. She didn't say anything to that effect, but . . . that's what I think. It makes sense." I gave Liss a sidelong glance, realizing what I had just mentioned in front of her. Maybe she hadn't noticed.

"Wait, whoa, Maggie, back up there. There was a rumor going around that Locke was taking pictures of them?"

I had forgotten. Tom wasn't there when I heard that. "Well, yeah. I was chatting with one of the tenants yesterday, and she let out that she had overheard you talking about the, um, the *things*," I said, with slightly belated deference to confidentiality, "with Marcus. She seemed rather pissed, actually. Anyway, I'm wondering now if that's the reason Angela Miller wanted out of the lease so badly."

"Hm. Possible."

Liss pulled her Lexus up to the curb, uttering a long-suffering sigh as she cut the engine and it sputtered and conked no less than six times before it finally shut off. She looked over at me and mouthed, *Sorry, ducks.*

"I would guess that Abbie might still have the camera, if you wanted to see it. At least that would exonerate Angela beyond a shadow of a doubt with the school board, since it means the pictures weren't shot with her knowledge," I said as I clamped my cell phone between my chin and shoulder and Liss and I slowly made our way through the front gate and up the broad steps to the bungalow's front porch. "Assuming you see fit to release that information in time. Oh, hey. Did you talk to Lou?" I had to stand on one foot and lean my crutches against the siding in order to free up a hand to unlock the door.

"Yeah. I guess I gotta hand it to you. You were right, Maggie. About the lodge connection and Locke and his side . . . business, I guess you'd call it. Austin Poindexter's father is a lodge member. And per Lou Tabor, every last name on that list would also be found on the registry to the club . . . except for one."

Minnie came rushing out and swirling around my feet as soon as I pushed the door inward. Liss picked her up and carried her back inside, cooing to her, checking windows as she went.

"And which one was that?" I resituated my phone and picked up my crutches, trailing behind the two of them. Walking from the bright, sunny outside to the curtain-darkened room inside made me blink as I attempted to regain my vision and equilibrium.

"Alex Cooper," he said.

Alex Cooper. Alex Cooper? "Tom . . ." I was starting to get that eerie feeling again. The baby-fine hairs on my arms were suddenly standing on end. "This may be just coincidence, but . . . the tenant I was talking to yesterday . . . the one who first told me about the rumor that Locke was taking pictures of tenants . . . that was Alex*andra* Cooper."

"The name on the account was most definitely Alex," Tom said, but I could hear the hesitation in his voice.

It occurred to me suddenly that there had been no pictures of Alexandra Cooper amongst the scandalous photos on the hard drive. At the time, I hadn't even realized. But now that I did, I couldn't help wondering why she had been the lucky one to have been left out. She and Abbie Cornwall. With all of my senses tumbling over one another in a jumbled, urgent chaos, I made my way back toward the computer room at the rear of the house as quickly as I could manage, with Liss and Minnie hot on my heels.

Why had Alexandra been the lucky one? Abbie, I could see. If Locke had managed to obtain pictures of her, maybe he'd destroyed them once he realized she was underage. He'd been in trouble for that once before—maybe he'd decided it was too much to risk a second go-round with the law. Maybe, just maybe, that was the whole point of the no-children-under-the-age-of-eighteen rule in the first place? But Alexandra . . . why would she have been any different from the other tenants? He had given her a generous deal to sign the lease. Obviously he must have found her attractive. Why no pictures?

Maybe they just weren't kept on the thumb drive, I reasoned. I needed to see the hard drive itself.

"I don't suppose she has a brother by that name? Or a father, or an uncle? What was the address on the account?"

"The address . . . let's see, I've got them right here. Somewhere." I heard the sound of pages flipping. "The address is . . . Wait. The address is the apartment complex itself. Apartment 1C."

"That's her apartment," I said, biting my lip.

"That does not make sense."

The computer room was as bright as it was outside. The shades were pulled high, not closed the way we usually left them. Marcus really must have been in a hurry. At least the window was down. I immediately crutched my way to the desk where Marcus had added Locke's disk drive to an existing PC . . . but, even as nontechie as I was, I could see that the slot on the computer in which he had installed it was empty, open space. I frowned, looking around, lifting papers, looking in drawers.

"It's gone." On the other end, Tom didn't say anything. My voice had been faint, maybe he hadn't heard me. "Tom, the hard drive. I don't see it anywhere."

"What do you mean, it's gone?"

"It's not in the computer Marcus installed it into. It's not on the desk. It's not in the drawers. I just don't see it. Liss, do you see it?"

She had been lifting, sifting, shuffling as well on all the surfaces I couldn't reach, but to no avail. She shook her head. "I'll call Marcus," she told me. "Perhaps he moved it elsewhere for safekeeping."

"What's going on, Maggie?" Tom said in my ear, drawing my attention back.

"Liss is calling Marcus. Hang on."

But Marcus hadn't moved it. He had left it installed, and was as shocked to hear it was gone as I had been to discover it missing. "No, luv. You stay, get your things done. I'll let you know if anything turns up," I heard Liss tell him. To me, she said, "Marcus says, no worries. Things could be worse."

He was right. Probably. I was just having some difficulty at that moment grasping how, when what could be a crucial piece of evidence in a murder investigation was missing.

"Maggie. Look." Liss had moved over to the window. Because the shades were pulled high, I could see the backyard clearly—the big oak tree in the center spreading shade all around with its sheltering arms, the old livery barn-now-garage off to the right, the tumble of wild roses along the fence in the back. It was so bright and pretty, with the breezes rustling through leaves and swaying branches, the filtered sunlight dappling the ground. A world apart from the strangeness.

"No," Liss said, gently nudging me. "There." She pointed toward the ground. Or, more important, to what was lying on the ground. The first thought my scrambling brain came up with was Minnie, that Minnie had been up to her tricks . . . but Minnie was here. Inside, behind the closed window.

"Tom . . . ?"

"I'm on my way."

"Tom, the screen to the window. It's on the ground. And

the window isn't latched." I had made sure to latch it last night. I know I had. Was it a window Marcus had opened while he was working this morning?

"Just stay on the line. Christ. Have you checked the house?"

I shook my head, not even caring or thinking that he couldn't see me. "No. There was no indication that someone might have been in here."

"I want you to close yourself in the computer room until I get there. Does it have a lock on the door?"

Too late. "Liss is already checking the house," I told him, just seconds after she had slipped away into the hall. "I don't think anyone is here, honestly. Why would they be? They have what they came for. I doubt they'd stick around."

Because that was it, really, wasn't it? Whoever it was who was watching us in the computer room last night, they had known where to find it. The footprints beneath the window. They had been watching us, and now they had what they wanted. Had they been watching today for a time when we had both left the house? It seemed almost certain to me. I was at work, as usual. As soon as Marcus left, they made their move. Pretty gutsy, in broad daylight, but then the yards between properties were fenced and somewhat overgrown with tall bushes and vines. And since most people were at work, maybe it wasn't such bad thinking after all. Because most people around here don't have security systems and security cameras to worry about, they just locked their doors and their windows . . . if they thought about it at all.

Security . . .

My eyes opened wide as the precaution I'd taken as a vague afterthought last night suddenly returned to my thoughts. In my mind's eye I saw myself as I had walked around the house, checking window lock after window lock, curtain after curtain and, as I moved past Marcus's cameras,

I saw myself switching them to "On" on a whim. Just in case. Because you never knew.

"Cameras!"I blurted out loud.

"What?"

"Hang on!"

I clicked the button for speaker phone, and clamping the phone in between my lips, I made my way toward the camera on the side of the house where, if anyone were to get to the backyard, they'd have to pass at some point.

"Maggie, what is going on? Do you have me on speaker?"

"Mm-hmm." I unhooked the camera from its tripod and flipped open the side-panel display screen. "Han' on a se'ond."

"It's all clear in here, ducks." Liss came up behind me to see what I was up to. She watched as I started rewinding back through the recording of the last sixteen hours.

Outside we heard a car pull into the drive. Too fast. The tires squawked in protest.

"I'm here," Tom said into the phone. "Let me in."

Liss scurried to get to the door, while I kept rewinding, ever so slowly. Back, back, back . . .

"What are you doing?"

Tom was at my shoulder, but I wouldn't take my eyes from the screen. "I turned this on last night, after you left. I just remembered. I was hoping . . . maybe . . . that I had caught whoever it was on camera."

"Well, look at you. When did you get so smart?" Tom asked.

I made a face. "I will pretend I didn't hear that."

Tom and Liss hovered over me, one at each of my shoulders, watching the screen as intently as I was.

And there it was. Just prior to the noon siren, not ten minutes after Marcus had texted me that he would be leaving for the afternoon, looking like a normal, everyday woman about town.

Yes, *woman*.

Dressed in yoga pants and a zip-front workout jacket, with a baseball cap pulled down low, she might have been anyone out for an early afternoon jog. Except she walked past the window coming from the direction of Marcus's backyard as though she owned the place. I didn't see the hard drive in her hand, but she could easily have slipped it inside the jacket for safekeeping. The camera lens angle was wide enough that we could see her jogging nonchalantly away from the house and down the sidewalk. I was betting she'd had a car parked somewhere nearby.

Tom was shaking his head. "Alexandra Cooper."

I nodded, feeling a little dazed. "Alexandra Cooper."

Chapter 18

I was having some trouble processing the image we were all seeing on the screen. What would Alexandra Cooper want with the hard drive recovered from Rob Locke's private room at the New Heritage apartment complex? What could be so important that she would first take it upon herself to linger in secrecy, watching us, waiting for the opportune moment to make her move, and then to strike, by invading Marcus's house and home office in order to steal a key piece of evidence in a murder investigation?

What the hell was she thinking?

Next to me Tom reached for the radio clipped to his shoulder. "Dispatch, Fielding."

Through the radio came a squelchy sound that cut out to the words, "Go ahead, Tom."

"Dispatch, request a car be sent out to New Heritage apartments, number—" He looked at me, eyebrows raised in question.

"1C," I told him.

"Apartment number 1C, that is number one Charlie, to pick up suspect Alexandra Cooper from her home and take her into custody. I'll be heading over to the high school, in the event that the suspect has headed into her place of employment.

"Roger that, Tom."

"Dispatch, this is in connection to the Locke murder investigation. Officers should use all precautions."

"Understood, Tom. Clear."

Tom turned to me. "Maggie, I—"

"I know, Tom," I cut in swiftly. "Go. We'll be fine here."

He nodded, striding toward the front door. Liss and I trailed behind him, as though by remaining in his presence as long as possible we could lend him the protection of our mutual energies added to his own.

He swung the heavy wooden door inward and began to open the screen door, pausing to turn back toward me. "I'll—"

Whatever he had been about to say was cut off by a flash of silken blackness that swept past his feet.

"What the—" he said at the exact time I cried out, "Minnie!"

My escape artist of a cat had taken advantage of Tom's diverted attention to make a bid for liberty, happiness, and the pursuit of fine, feathered friends.

A pained look crossed Tom's face, followed by one of sheer impatience. "Sonofabeehive," he muttered, obviously torn between the call of duty and the instant urge to run after my rascally, wayward feline.

I shook my head. "Go. We'll get her."

"Sorry," was all he could say before he took off for his car, starting it and throwing it into reverse in a singularly coordinated movement. "Hope you catch her," he said just before he peeled out of the driveway, leaving Liss and me in suspended motion on the bungalow's deep-seated front porch.

Just for a moment. And then we, too, launched ourselves into motion.

"You check the front and the neighbors's yards," I recommended, "and I'll head toward the back and the garage." Truthfully I suspected that was where she was heading. The window she loved best, after all, faced the backyard and a trio of bird feeders. I was hoping that was foremost in her fuzzy little brain when she decided to make a blazing run for glory.

I kept my eyes peeled as I crutched-hopped my way up the driveway, peering beneath bushes, behind perennials, and in the twisting branches of the aged crabapple trees that separated Marcus's driveway from the neighbor's property. No Minnie. Undaunted, I kept going until I stood beneath the giant oak tree in the center of the backyard. The going was slower back here on the uneven ground, but even more worrying, the grassy area beneath the feeders was devoid of any sign of a glossy black furball with jewel-color eyes avidly watching the flurry of wings above.

I was starting to get worried. Where could the little rascal have gone?

Turning in a slow circle to survey the yard in overview, I decided the best place to check next would have to be the old livery barn, aka the Man Cave. It was a place I didn't frequent often, since it was most definitely male-centric. But it certainly would offer a mischievous kitten with plenty of hidey-holes in its dark interior, and with the door standing ajar just a mite, it seemed a no-brainer.

"Minnie," I called as I approached the gap between the big double doors. "Here, kitty, kitty, kitty . . ."

Shifting myself sideways to get out of the way, I started

to pull the door on the right to swing it all the way open. Its hinges complained, giving a rusty squawk, but it hit the wall with a soft *thwump*. Dust motes rose all around me in the filtered sunlight coming through the leafy bowers of the giant oak.

I thought I heard movement inside, but the lack of windows ensured that the inner sanctum remained sacrosanct.

There. I heard it again.

"Come here, girl," I called, shifting myself forward so that I could reach for the door on the left. "Here, kitty . . ."

As I closed my fingers around the handle and began to pull, the door's center of gravity seemed to shift. And because it did, it seemed to be swinging toward me faster than I could step out of the way.

Correction: "Seemed to be" wasn't quite what I would call this. It moved toward me as swift and hard as if it had been shoved by some unseen force on the other side.

And that was because it had been.

I realized that just as the door smacked into my right crutch, knocking it into me and my overgrown, sparkly, bedazzled cast. The impact was just enough to throw me off balance and knock me for a loop in one awesomely grandiose, butt-crunching sprawl that raised even more dust into the air and sent my crutches flying. My legs flew out from beneath me as my tailbone hit the dirt, sending exquisitely sharp pain zinging through me. I sat there a moment, stunned, while the dust settled around me . . . until I became aware of the figure that was standing over me, just as quiet. Just as stunned?

Talk about déjà vu . . .

Only not . . .

I blinked into the glinting sunlight. "Ms. Cooper?"

It was. Alexandra Cooper, in the flesh.

For a moment time seemed to stand still as we stared at each other. My mind was whirring. She'd already broken into Marcus's home and stolen the key piece of evidence in a murder investigation. The question was why? And a close second would be, how far was she willing to go to protect whatever secret she was keeping? Because something big must have driven this usually very collected high school teacher to go to such lengths.

Her attention flickered away from me. To the left. To the right. Her tongue poked out to wet her lips. My heartbeat rose to a roaring level in my ears when her gaze transferred back to me, because what I saw in her eyes didn't look quite human.

The roaring got worse when I watched her hand stretch, ever so slowly, for something that was leaning against the wall just inside the door. Whatever it was, I knew it couldn't be good.

That thought was enough to jar me out of my momentary disconnect. In the same instant I saw her pull an old garden rake into view, my own scrambling fingers had found my nearest crutch.

I don't know if I anticipated her swing or if my intuition just switched into high gear of its own accord as a self-defense mechanism, but as I lifted my crutch and pulled it around toward me, it caught the force of her strike full on. The aluminum vibrated with the shock of the blow, sending pulsations ricocheting up my arms so strongly that the crutch fell from my suddenly numb fingers. My eyes locked with hers. Another defense mechanism, as though I could hold her in place, motionless, harmless, if I could just keep up with that strange, intense contact. I knew I needed the crutch for protection now more than ever, but I was afraid to tear my gaze away, afraid that she would strike again in that lost moment.

Such cold eyes, filled with an empty, intense void.

My groping fingers closed around the crutch just as she abruptly lifted the rake high overhead for a second blow. *Too late*, the fear inside me whispered as I watched the beginning arc of the rake's iron teeth. *Too late . . .*

I closed my eyes, not wanting to watch it come near. And so, I'm sure you can understand why when I heard the bone-crunching *thud* and didn't feel it, I was completely confused.

My eyes flew open to the completely befuddling image of Cooper laying inert on the ground and Liss standing over her, the rake now in *her* hands with the flat of the iron tines pressed against Cooper's throat.

"Maggie, dear, why don't you call Officer Fielding while I keep an eye on things here, hm?"

Yeah. I think I could do that.

It was all over before we knew it.

The details came out so quickly. While Liss was saving the day in pure John Wayne fashion, the officers Tom had sent over to the New Heritage apartment complex were discovering a few things of their own in Ms. Cooper's apartment. Things like an envelope full of glossy photos of herself. And then there was the laptop on her dining room table, which coincidentally enough still happened to be opened to an Internet search on how to permanently destroy the data on a hard drive. The girl was set. Or she would have been if the cameras hadn't caught her in the act.

The only problem was, the girl . . . wasn't.

A girl, I mean.

Oh, I know. I had no idea. I'm not sure how any of us were supposed to have known, or even could have known.

Even worse, no one found out until Tom took her down to the police station to question her.

Him.

Whichever.

It kind of all came out from there, though. She wouldn't answer their questions at first, but sometimes nature has a way of ensuring justice will be served. Or maybe it was just the caffeine in the coffee. It's really hard to keep up the pretense of living as a woman when you aren't allowed to use the ladies' room without a witness and you still have all your male parts. And with Alexandra, it was all just that. A pretense. A life lived as a lie because of the lie that was her life. A life that insisted that she had been born male, when she had felt female from her earliest memories of existence.

We didn't have all of the pieces when we found Alexandra's image on the video camera. We only knew that she had, for reasons known only to her, overheard Tom making arrangements with Marcus to access the hard drive, and she must have stalked us back to the bungalow from there. Stalked us, staked us out, and when the coast was clear and we were both out of her way, she made her move.

His move.

Is there a guide to political correctness these days? Because this day-to-day change stuff is crazy-making. Who keeps track of these things?

It was self-preservation, you see. Because she had no idea what was on that drive. She had no idea it even existed. She had thought that, by destroying the computer in Locke's office, she would be wiping out the very existence of any and all remaining evidence he might have had that he had been holding over her head.

Locke knew about her, you see.

Oh, not when he first offered her the lease. He had no idea who she was. But she knew him. They had gone to the same high school, lived in the same neighborhood in nearby Fort Wayne. She had heard of his history for the distribution of child pornography and had heard that he had "turned over a new leaf," at least according to his family. Not that that meant anything. But he didn't recognize her—mostly because she had gone to great lengths to perfect her appearance and gestures and body language in order to live life as a woman rather than as the male she had been born, to forge a new life for herself, filled with people who didn't know her. People who would accept her for who she really was. People for whom the old adage "What you see is what you get" is accepted as universal law.

Small-town folk.

Stony Mill kind of peeps.

Here no one questioned that she might not actually be everything she said she was. She grew out her hair into a thick mane of which any woman would be proud, changed her name from Alexander to Alexandra, assiduously removed body hair on a daily basis, and was never seen without sturdy foundation garments and a face full of makeup so carefully and skillfully applied that no one could tell where the makeup ended and the skin began. And she became . . . female. For all intents and purposes. Like an actor deeply immersed in his craft, she lived as a female every day of her life, without fail. Everything was perfect.

Until Locke started up his old tricks again.

At least it wasn't with underage girls this time. He did have that going for him. Or maybe he'd just decided it was too big a risk. Locke was the one who insisted there be no children under the age of eighteen in the complex. But then, he knew he had had "security" cameras installed with the renovations. No one seems to know when the idea struck him, but strike him it did. He handpicked his tenants carefully, enticed them with special rent deals subsidized (knowingly or unknowingly—that is still up for debate at this telling) by Harding Enterprises through ownership of the property itself. And with his ties to an organization the men in his family had belonged to for years, he found a ready supply of customers for his . . . entrepreneurial vision.

The women he rented apartments to were none the wiser.

Not until Abbie and her mother broke the rules. And not until Abbie broke the mirror.

Abbie was the one who first seemed to notice something amiss. Whether it was intuition that made her veer away from the mildly creepy manager or whether it was the sounds in their apartment and the personal items that moved around with no explanation, the suspicion was raised in her mind. Breaking the mirror, finding the camera . . . that was just the nail in the coffin.

But by that time, Alexandra Cooper had moved into the apartment upstairs and had recognized Abbie, her unappreciative student from the high school. A chance mention to Locke—was it intentional, as Abbie seemed to think, or was it completely innocent as Alexandra Cooper had suggested?—had landed Abbie and her mother out on the streets, their lease revoked. Maybe it didn't really matter in the end. Maybe what really mattered was that Abbie was safe from Locke's secret vice. There were no pictures of Abbie Cornwall found on Locke's thumb drive or his hard drive.

But Alexandra's problems were only beginning.

Because Alexandra's secret that she worked so carefully to conceal was all too soon discovered. And Locke was not a man who could be trusted with anything.

For him, what had started with simple candid-camera nude shots through the windows had morphed into filming young women with their partners du jour through remote control cameras secreted in their bedrooms behind "built-in" mirrors. But Alexandra . . . it soon became all too obvious that Alexandra was different. Very different.

She was not what she appeared to be.

And what she appeared in no way to be was really the story, as far as Locke was concerned.

An entrepreneur 'til the bitter end—literally—Locke decided a schoolteacher like "Alexandra" might be willing to pay him to keep her secret. At least as much as his male customers did for access to the special "art" he was more than happy to provide.

That's where several brothers from his lodge came into play. There were plenty of them with money to burn. They didn't know where he got his artwork from. They didn't care. If it even occurred to them to ask, they wouldn't have. They were buying a service. Who knows what young Austin Poindexter thought when he found erotic photos of one of his teachers on his father's home computer. He was an eighth-grade boy. Thinking is not one of their fortes. All he knew was that he had come across something that was going to make him top dog in school among the other boys his age. That was his goal in sharing the pics that nearly got Angela Miller fired, and it had worked . . . until the principal started asking questions.

All Alexandra—Alex—wanted was to preserve the first time in her—his—life when she'd ever been happy. When she'd ever felt free to be herself. Without judgment. Without fear of reprisals or exposure. She had begun to equate Stony Mill in her mind with her home, her safe place. For her, it was worth fighting to save.

She paid him for a while. She was even relieved when he kept the payments "affordable." But that changed, eventually. Locke got greedy. Most blackmailers do, eventually. And when he threatened to send her pictures to her principal, the school board, and even expose her to the Stony Mill Gazette, she knew she had to do something drastic, or the perfect little home she had created for herself would be burned to the ground in the flames of righteous horror and recrimination. She'd be labeled a pervert. A sexual deviant. She'd never be allowed to teach again.

Locke had sealed his own fate. Alexandra Cooper had made sure of that.

Don't we all? With each and every decision we make throughout a given day, however small, however far-reaching, we bring something into our life. If Locke had realized the enormous consequences of his actions, would he have chosen differently? Maybe so. Maybe so.

Alexandra Cooper, on the other hand, had never felt she was given a choice. And because she felt betrayed by her own body, perhaps she never truly had been. Her only choice was to try to be the person she felt she was within the deepest, innermost parts of herself, and her misguided decision was made to protect that choice at whatever cost. And through protecting her own fate, she assisted Locke with his.

I didn't know what was going to happen to her when she was sent to prison for her crime. To me it seemed unthinkably cruel to send her to a prison full of the worst kind of males in existence, to suffer whatever indignities may come to a "man" like her. It seemed a fate even worse than a death sentence. But justice must be served, and crimes must not go unpunished. Especially the high crime of murder.

Angela Miller was exonerated by the quiet word that Tom chose to have in private with the middle school principal.

Although he couldn't go into specifics due to the sensitivity of the evidence, he was able to reassure him that she was a victim of a crime and not the perpetrator of some sordid deed. At the same time, the student body rallied behind her, with a combined strength that surprised all. They had arranged a silent sit-in to demonstrate their support of her, and then steadfastly followed through. Students showed up bright and early on a Saturday, and filled the halls, in complete and utter silence; it was the quietest the school had ever been with that many people in the building, and the effort was noticed. Enough that, had Tom not stepped up, it would have given the principal pause. A glimmer of light in a dark situation. A sign of hope, that there was still humanity and dignity all around us, if we but opened our eyes and *see*.

Lou decided he'd had enough of the lodge brotherhood. There were too many questions, too much less-than-savory behind-the-scenes activity that had come up through recent revelations. Not everyone in the organization was in the know—case in point—but it was all too much for Lou. As he told Marcus, "It was the thought that anyone might think that I was in some way involved, too. The town is going through some tough times right now, and it's pitting people against each other, making them suspect family, friends. I suppose it's only natural . . . but it is sad. I don't need or want to play into that." It made me sad, too, because I myself hadn't known quite what to think about his membership in the group when the details started filtering out. At least at first. But Lou's character shone through in the end, thank goodness. I would hate it if the experience had tarnished his reputation in any way, and in a town like this, you never know.

And so it was with great relief that Marcus and I settled into our last utterly free weekend together without the cloud of the town's latest scandal to mar the sunny skies. So much had happened in the last week, it was enough to take your breath away. But the weekend was a time to recoup, to regroup, to recover, and to gird our loins before forging a plan for the coming months.

"It's going to be busy," Marcus warned me as we lay, lazily entwined, on a woven hammock in the backyard beneath the spread of the old oak. We had just gotten back from lunch with his Uncle Lou and Aunt Molly and were enjoying what was left of the afternoon before Marcus needed to get ready for his evening gig. "Classes. Homework. Jobs on the side."

"I know," I said, pressing my lips to the strong, corded muscles in his neck.

"You'll have your work, too."

"Mm-hmm."

"And the N.I.G.H.T.S. We've not been as active through the summer, with people constantly on the run, but that will change as the wheel turns and we move into fall. The thinning of the veil means lots more activity, and that always brings opportunities to explore, investigate, and understand."

"And I'll have my cast off, so I'll be able to participate." Glory be, hallelujah, soon, soon, soon.

He slid his hand down my thigh, curling a moment behind my raised knee and then resting it on the hard, nubby surface of the bedazzled cast. He chuckled. "I would say I'm going to miss it . . . but it will be nice to have a night that doesn't include hard knocks. My shins may never be the same."

The vixen in me dictated that a comment like that deserved retribution of the swiftest kind—like rolling him to his back and having my way with him. All in the name of demanding spoils and booty from the defeated. Most definitely the booty. But the success of such activities in a hammock were questionable. It might even be dangerous.

I mollified myself with a kiss and a sigh.

"We'll make it through, though."

"With a little luck," I added, laughing.

"Who needs luck when you have a witch in the house?" he countered.

"Or even two." Except that brought up the subject of my living arrangements again. Once Marcus was attending classes and my cast came off, there really was no reason for me and Minnie not to return to my apartment on Willow Street. Even though Steff wouldn't be there for much longer. Maybe I could still search for an improved living situation. One that didn't include living in a slightly eerie basement apartment without even the solace of my best friend living two floors above.

I tried not to think about that, but the loss of Steff would be a big one. I wasn't sure I was ready for it.

Marcus had felt the shift in my energy. "You know, we never finished talking about that."

"About what?"

"About you moving your things in here. You are staying, aren't you?"

My breath had gotten stuck somewhere between my ribs and my throat. "Well, I don't know," I said a little shyly. "I mean, I don't think you really asked. I mean . . . did you?"

His fingers were playing with my hair, twisting strands of it into spirals and then brushing the ends along my jaw and neck. "I'm asking now."

"Seriously?"

"Seriously. I've gotten kind of used to having Minnie around. It would break my heart to have to give her up—

ow!" he said, laughing, as I reached up and tugged hard on his ear.

"I think you deserved that," I said, giggling myself, as the ebullience of the thought of staying here . . . of staying with *him* . . . filled me.

"Hm. Probably. So . . . what do you say? Do you think I deserve you?"

Danger be damned. Shifting cautiously in order to not flip us over onto the ground, I eased myself over the length of his body. His arms came around me, one beneath my hair, the other smoothing repeatedly down the small of my back, and he was smiling up at me with a look in his brilliant eyes that took my breath away entirely. "Oh, I most definitely think you deserve me."

"You don't think this is too soon?"

"Hm. Probably. But I think I can risk it if you can."

It was amazing, all the things a man can make a woman feel with a single, luscious kiss. Desire, yes. Heat, most definitely. But what about all the other things, like the wonder of being so alive that the power of it fills you to bursting, or the delicious thrill of being taken, countered by the equally delicious realization of your own power over him. But underneath all of this was the warm, wonderful sense of belonging, and of being safe.

And isn't that what home is all about?

Guess Liss's spell really worked.

As if there was ever any doubt.